ISTORIA BOOKS
presents

The Old Ashburn Place

Winner of the Dodd Mead Pictorial Review Prize
for Best First Novel of 1935

a novel by Margaret Flint

D0880104

This book is a work of fiction. Characters and places are either made up or, if real, used fictitiously. Any resemblance between fictional characters and real people is entirely coincidental and not intentional.

Get on the Istoria Books mailing list!
Subscribers learn of special limited-time-only discounts. Sign up at the website where you can also view other Istoria Books titles:
www.IstoriaBooks.com

The Old Ashburn Place
by Margaret Flint

ISBN-13: 978-0615679129
ISBN-10: 0615679129

Published by Istoria Books 2012
Cover image: "And Everything Nice" by Bryce Cameron Liston
Introduction and Author Biography copyright 2011 by Sara Mitchell Barnacle

Letter from the Publisher

Dear Readers,

Margaret Flint was my grandmother. This volume is a collaborative effort by her grandchildren to get her prize-winning first novel into a 21st century format.

I grew up knowing Grandma had been a novelist — Mom kept a full set of the Flint novels on the bookcase in the study — but it wasn't until we started this project that I came to appreciate the scope of Grandma's skills as a writer. I hear in her prose the voices of relatives and see the Maine landscape I visited every summer as a child.

The story is set a hundred years ago, in the first decade of the 20th century. Grandma was born in 1891 and published the book in 1935, so she was very much looking back to the Maine she remembered from her youth. That immediacy rings throughout the novel. While all the characters are fictional, they were clearly people she knew.

This publication is a family project involving three generations of Flint descendants. In particular I want to thank my cousin Sara Barnacle for her introduction and author bio, and my sister Leslie Lebl for her proofreading and general moral support as we struggled through the process. I also want to thank Timothy Helck, grandson of illustrator Peter Helck, for his help in tracking down records and preparing a bio of the artist.

And now, sit back and enjoy *The Old Ashburn Place.*

Matthew T. Sternberg, President
Istoria Publications, LLC

Margaret Flint's fictional setting for most of her novels is "Parkston, Maine." This was not a fantasy land, like J. R. R. Tolkien's "Middle Earth," but a carefully observed and faithfully reproduced region of actual rural Maine. For her first novel – *The Old Ashburn Place*, written while she still sojourned in the Deep South – this was a remembered setting comprised of scenes from earlier visits to West Baldwin, Maine, to the holdings, neighborhood, and stories of her ancestral family on her father's side. The eight novels that followed in quick succession were written after the $10,000 cash prize won by that first novel in 1935 had allowed her, now suddenly widowed in 1936, to bring her family back to Maine in 1937.

The Dodd, Mead – Pictorial Review First Novel of the Year Contest award set in motion a series of publicity appearances and author talks in New York City, Boston, and around the country.

"Family privacy," she wrote years later, "was impossible. I was further interviewed and photographed, and I learned the hard way never to face the camera without first going into a huddle with the mirror and the make-up kit." The press caught her by surprise once, leading her to tell an interviewer that her hair had been stringy, and "I looked as if I had just murdered my husband."

With that flurry past, Flint eagerly immersed herself and family in her longed for "promised land" in the hills of western Maine, the setting for several subsequent novels and other writings. She never returned to the South, except to delve into her memories to write her second novel, *Valley of Decision.*

Her characters were drawn from the rural and village life unfolding around her. Margaret Flint, as "Mrs. Jacobs," was active in West Baldwin's civic life as well as its social life which centered on Grange meetings, bean suppers, and community dances. She was often seen quietly taking notes on a colorful turn of events or on the quirks of speech of a local wag.

She mixed and reconstituted her notes into new characters, so that none of them would be truly identifiable with their models. However, a biographer reported that Margaret's sister Edith Flint Coe had insisted that Charles Ashburn was in fact an actual person, and both sisters had vied for his attentions, especially at dances. A local woman is also quoted as saying, "I could hardly wait until Margaret's next novel was published to see who in town would be in the story." (Jack Barnes, in "A New Look at Margaret Flint," *Bittersweet Magazine*, Dec. 1980, p. 8)

Edith Coe also described the site for the Ashburn farm as being at the very end of a road at the top of a mountain in the area referred to in real life as in the novels as "back o' the mountain." And in fact, some have felt that Marian Parks, the unrequitable love of Charles's life, was in fact the author herself.

Flint was especially noted for accuracy in using and portraying the local dialect, with its echoes of Elizabethan grace.

"Margaret Flint not only has succeeded in depicting rural Maine as it was during the early twentieth century when it was possible for closely knit families to earn a living and find happiness on small farms," wrote Jack Barnes, "but she also has preserved for posterity a rapidly vanishing dialect as our hamlets become more and more cosmopolitan. She has done for the dialect of the hills and valleys of western Maine what Mary Ellen Chase has done for the dialect of the eastern Maine coast." (Chase's most famous works include *Mary Peters*, *Silas Crockett*, *Windswept*, and *Edge of Darkness*.)

There were other authors writing about rural Maine at that time, notably Gladys Hasty Carroll, most remembered now for her novel *As the Earth Turns*. (For a comparison and contrast between Carroll and Flint, see *"Beautiful, Entire, and Clean"; The Maine Farm Novels of Margaret Flint and Gladys Hasty Carroll*, by Beverly Seaton. *Colby Library Quarterly*, Vol 17, no. 1, March, 1991, p.39-45.)

Margaret Flint often claimed to have no imagination. A magazine article quotes her as telling an audience at one of her book talks: "I have to take what I see and put it into a story." (Jack Barnes, in "A New Look a Margaret Flint," *Bittersweet Magazine*, Dec. 1980, p 4). Given her deep involvement in rearing her six children, remodeling the old inn into a family homestead, canning the fruits and vegetables from her beloved garden, and keeping her house impeccably clean and orderly, she had no patience with people who would say, "I should like to write, if I only had the time." (ibid. p. 8)

A central aspect of the Flint novels that set them apart was their grittiness, in that the characters broke the Ten Commandments with about the same frequency as their real-life counterparts. She wrote frankly about aspects of human psychology and sexuality that made some blush at the audacity of "that Mrs. Jacobs." Her emphasis, though, was on the psychic toll these misadventures cost, rather than on the clinical details of adultery or homosexual attraction. Some readers have called her ahead of her times, and this openness – though fairly tame by today's standards – may have cost her some acclaim and readership in her day by comparison with the milder, more romanticized fiction many other regional writers were publishing.

The Old Ashburn Place was set pre-World War I, allowing its readers of later eras to see into a future that her characters could only guess at. Rural Maine in the late thirties was still climbing out from under the Depression, but the Depression had been only another twist of the screw. Maine's heyday had been the brief era of clipper ships, lumber barons, and the American China trade. Flint ancestors had supplied, from their groves of giant pines, masts for the British King's navy. In fact, a few of those trees that were marked but not cut still stand within the original family land grant, the markings now buried within two centuries of bark growth.

For a time, canning shops and shoe factories succeeded the early Maine industries, but by the forties, decline was gaining as factory owners began moving their operations to warmer climes. Maine soil, much of which is out-classed by the rich farmlands of the Midwest, was no longer central to economic growth. So farm folks were often poor, but a Maine mystique based on the natural beauty of the state and its former economic and cultural glories still prevailed and even intensified. Flint novels always feature characters who appreciate and even feed on that beauty, and they are the ones who stay on and succeed, if modestly.

The substance of Flint novels has been summed up well by an anonymous biographer for Jiffynotes.com:

> "The land serves as the background for the values of Flint's characters, but her major focus is on individuals coming to terms with what life has brought them. Her novels do not offer the reader escape into pastoral retreats. She takes the country life as it is, and writes about people living it."

(http://www.jiffynotes.com/a_study_guides/book_no tes/aww_02/aw...)

Sara Mitchell Barnacle is one of the author's grandchildren.

Author's Note

While I have tried, in this book, to give an accurate portrayal of the rural New England scene, I have not taken any characters, descriptions or incidents directly from anything in my own personal knowledge or experience. A few actual place-names have been used, to be sure, but the essential setting of the story is imaginary. *The Author.*

Prelude

Charles Ashburn looked up from his straight young rows of corn and leaned on his hoe handle, raised his straw hat a moment to let the summer breeze riffle through what was left of his hair, and gazed absently off across the valley.

It was sightly. Hills, and valley, and winding, crystal river — sky of deep, transparent blue and clouds of billowing white — air so clear that it seemed to shine like plate glass — here was beauty, clean-cut and vigorous, yet gracious withal; a beauty lavish in its spaciousness and vivid coloring, yet restrained in its neatness of outline, its purposeful upthrust of hills, its wind-swept cleanliness of naked rock, its tucked-in fields and dark green wood lots.

Charles Ashburn, hoeing the young corn on the southwest slope of Saddleback, was far from beautiful. Not tall, nor especially broad, he yet had the look of a powerful man. At the age of twenty, he had seemed all of thirty-five; now, at fifty, he was just about the same. Time had thinned out his pale, soft hair and whitened the stubble of his beard; years of toil under the summer suns, and the dazzling whiteness of Maine winters, had long since burned and creased his naturally fine white skin into the semblance of weather-beaten age. He was, as his native idiom puts it, homely as a stump fence, and yet there had always been something attractive about him.

Probably it was his rugged self-respect, his quiet dignity of bearing, saved from pompousness by the keen, alert restlessness of his eyes. He had the Ashburn eyes, deep, small and colorless except for the black glint of the pupils; but peculiar to Charlie was a certain quick, sidewise glance, guarded and aloof, yet without a trace of furtiveness — a glance that could take in more in one second than most men see in an hour.

Now, as he stood leaning on his hoe handle, taking one of those habitual moments of rest that kept him from ever getting really tired, his quick ear caught the sound of an automobile on the road at the foot of the mountain, and he straightened up. A heavy roadster was turning in at the old Parks place across the valley. Charlie's heart jumped, and he drew a quick, deep breath. It was Marian.

For more than twenty years, he had watched Marian Parks Witham come and go. Five or six times a year she came, and each time he relived the various happenings that had brought him to what we was — a lonely, hard-working old fossil whose life had been given over to gaining happiness for everyone but himself.

Marian's car had climbed the perpendicular road, braced ladder-wise against the sky, and had gained the shelf on the side of Pigeon Mountain where the old Parks place nestled as contentedly as a setting hen. Charlie could see the car at the horse block, could see, diminished but clearly outlined in the distance, the trim little woman who got out first and unlocked the side door of the house, then the two other figures that followed. Marian had brought her girls with her this time. That would mean more cars coming later on, bright lights late at night, lean, tanned young people in white duck pants, irrespective of sex, or in those bathing suits which, as Marian remarked last summer, were "nothing much before, and a little less than half of that behind."

Charlie laughed shortly. Marian was always getting off something like that. She was as keen-witted as he and, with her education and her experience in the broad world outside the hills, she had always been several jumps ahead of Charlie. That had been the trouble. She had come to him too late, had come after years of hard work and poverty on this rocky little mountain farm had hammered out of him all the youth and elasticity he would have needed to get her and keep her.

Marian and the girls had disappeared inside the house. Charlie wondered if the Parks children were coming too, the little tykes who were blood relation to himself, the children of Graham Parks and Hilda Ashburn. He sometimes thought he loved them more than he loved youngsters who had been born and raised on the Ashburn place, born of his brother Morris' second marriage. Morris' older children had grown up and gone away long ago — gone — independent of their Uncle Charlie!

"Gosh!" he thought, leaning there on this hoe handle, "gosh, I'm gettin' old. Old. And what have I got? Other people's kids — a farm only half my own — other men's wives — aw hell –"

He flung down the hoe and stood a moment, tense with rebellion. Then he relaxed, turned about dejectedly and made his way to the stone wall that loomed higher than the infant corn, lowered himself somewhat stiffly and lay stretched on his back in the tender grasses under an apple tree. The weeds would be right there when he got good and ready to grub them out. For the present, he wanted to think.

Chapter One

It was in the early 1800's that the Ashburns had settled in Parkston, Maine. The original homestead had been a log cabin, the walls of which still stood, covered with the clapboards and plaster of the later structure; thick walls, so deep that the generations of children had sat cross-legged on the window sills and played with their playthings, or stared out at the driving rains and snows.

The house, as it had been developed by alterations and additions throughout the years, was typical of the Maine countryside — low-posted, with two dormer windows on the front, facing east, a broad doorway with fanlights at the sides and above, and a central chimney to serve the main part of the dwelling. On either side of the front door were two small, twelve-paned windows, and there were two more below and one above on each gabled end. You could see at a glance that the Ashburn place had good rooms upstairs, under that broad and gently sloping roof. There was an L running back at right angles to the house, and as high as the house part way, then dropping off to a low, narrow, covered passage which connected the milk room and woodshed with the barn. You could walk from the parlor clear to the cattle tie-up without going outdoors, which was a comfort in bad weather.

The house and L were painted white, but the barn had never known paint. It was shingled, and so far as anyone could reckon, for fifty years it had been acquiring its soft, glossy finish of weathered gray. One tall elm towered high over the house; the lower, bushier maples and two silver-tongued poplars shaded the steep and rocky lane. Around the granite slab that was the front doorstone grew the thicket of lilacs whose heavy purple cones of bloom made the air sweet in the very early summer.

The land sloped abruptly down, in front of the house, into the valley where the roadway twisted along, and a stone wall bordered the lane — a stone wall with big, tender ferns growing close to it, and sometimes the exquisite pale pink, five-petaled roses; at other seasons, the strong yellow goldenrod, and the magenta hardhack. Back of the barn, the mountain side rose steeply, but not far, for the Ashburn Place was nearly on the top.

Charlie's first recollections were of his mother, tall, gaunt, tragic-eyed, working, working always with toddling children at her heels; and of his father, coming and going as if driven by a force he dared not defy, yet willing in his obedience.

This Hilda Ashburn had been well educated. She had told them that many times, and she had drilled into them all the respect for learning, the conviction of its necessity, had left with them her determination and her ambition, and, as a cement and stabilizer, her deep, abiding family loyalty.

Not long after her death, Charlie, rummaging in the attic for some old deeds and letters he needed, had come across his mother's diary. Written finely in a neat and well-bound book, it was like a photograph of her. And, like her life, it stopped short in the middle, though its final entry was made years before her death.

In the dim light of the attic window, at odd moments stolen from labor in the fields and barns, slowly and laboriously Charlie had read it all. Then later, after his brother Morris had brought home a wife and shoved Charlie into a room of his own, he had taken the diary from the attic and hidden it in the bureau drawer under his clean shirts. It became almost his bible, for in it he read and reread the ideals, the plans and ambitions, the sufferings and joys that had been his mother's life.

Hilda Bowers had come, a girl no longer young, to teach the school "back of the mountain." She had boarded with the Simmses, down the road a piece from the Ashburn place, and she had been rather lonely there. Johnny Simms was mentioned in the diary, but even then he was courting the Alviry whom he later married. Evidently there had been little in that home or in the community to interest Hilda socially. Morris Ashburn was mentioned, at first somewhat derisively, then tolerantly, and at last with warmer and more personal interest.

"He is peculiar," wrote Hilda in her book, "yet far from dull. How maddening — that the only man whom I might marry now should be so old and down at the heel!"

Then came evidence of a rapidly progressing courtship. Her vision inspired by her own loneliness and the boyish and abject way in which the old fellow made love to her, she came to see, in the shabby and middle-aged hermit that was Morris Ashburn the Third, the makings of a man. She came to see in the tumble-down old Ashburn place the makings of a home. The fierce maternalism in her which spinsterhood had in no wise dried up responded to this double appeal. She knew she was not attractive, and she seized upon this "old maid's last chance," and flung all her energy, all her passion, all her keen and practical intelligence, into making a success of the marriage.

The Ashburn place took on new lease of life. Morris the Third waked up and regained a measure of the sturdy, red-blooded manhood of his tribe, which in him had begun to run rather thin. In his forceful and passionate Hilda he found the vitality and common-sense balance he long had needed.

Entries in the diary told of the mortgage whereby cash was raised for fertilizers and tools. Morris the Third worked, under his wife's guidance and (remembering her, Charlie suspected) under the lash of her tongue; and gradually the old Ashburn place regained something of its traditional trimness and efficiency.

And then, with startling promptness, Morris the Fourth arrived. Thereafter, Morris the Third was known, the township over, as Pop; and the name was apt enough, for in quick succession were born three others, Charles, Herbert and Alfred.

Record of turbulent years was there in the diary — record of hard work and economy and indomitable courage. Hilda was driven, but not beaten yet. A few more years, and the mortgage would be paid off. Then they would begin to build toward education for the boys — education, college, even, that would make them great and famous men. Of that, Hilda had no doubt. Charlie could have cried over this repeated declaration of faith; she had so little to go on!

And the last entry in the diary was one, not of defeat perhaps, but unmistakably of frustration.

"There is another baby coming. I had thought four of them enough! I can get through with it, but there will be no more time for writing in my book. I would have liked to have at least one baby in peace and comfort, taking things easy and being really happy over it — but that will never be for me. I shall have to work, and work hard, whether I feel like it or not, just as I have always done. I am not sorry — I would do it all over again — but—

"The agony of labor is nothing to these months of nausea –"

And that was the end of Hilda Ashburn's diary. The fifth child arrived well within Charlie's memory, a little girl whom they named Gladys.

In the following years, the mortgage had been cleared, and further improvements had gradually been achieved — buildings had been kept painted, machinery housed and free from rust; there were six cows and sometimes more, and they had cream on their table, and small fruits and vegetables from the big garden on the south slope near the barn. In the winter, the cellar was full, with apples, potatoes, and turnips, with barrels of salt pork and crocks of pickles, canned garden stuff and jellies. Hilda had realized in large measure her ideal of country living — Charlie was sure of that.

Well could he remember the code they lived by, the morale that made the family a coherent entity. They must all go to school; they must be clean in mind and body; they must work hard and not fuss about it; they must pull together all the time, in all things; and they must boil the dish towels every day.

Funny, Charlie often thought, how that last point had been so important to his mother. The old towel bars, which Pop had fixed for her just outside the kitchen door, in the sunny corner of the L, were there to this day; and

Morris' second wife, now stout and middle-aged, hung the towels and milk strainers there each morning, sweet and white as Hilda Ashburn would have wished.

Things had been bad after Hilda Ashburn's death. Gladys had been ten years old then, when little Hilda was born, and the mother, too old and tired for the ordeal, had yielded up her earthly cares, and had lain in her casket looking quiet and peaceful and young.

With her going, the heart of the whole tribe seemed to stop for a time, yet they lived on somehow. Dark, nightmare days, with the house full of chattering neighbors, some saying the baby could not live, others declaring that it could; the hideousness of the funeral, the grim, stark desolation of the house as the confusion subsided and everyday affairs went cruelly on — all this had been indelibly stamped into the memory of each one of them.

Gladys, so long regarded as the baby, took over the care of the house, with the help of Alfred and Herbert and Pop. Pop had always been handy with the children, and now he devoted himself to the wee mite who he wished had never been conceived. For weeks, there was a struggle with her food; the doctor advised a formula, and then he changed it; neighbor women came in and fussed around; nothing seemed to be just right; but at last Pop himself hit upon a combination of milk and baby food from the drug store, and little Hilda began to gain.

Not so Gladys, who seemed to shrink and grow old before their eyes as she cooked and swept and washed. It would have been easier if she had not kept on in school, of course, but the mother's teachings had been thorough — school was essential, and the housework must be managed as best it could. It was bad enough for Charlie and Morris to leave high school and give full time to the farm; it had to be, with Pop tied down as nursemaid — the younger ones must get enough education to make up for that. The family average must somehow be raised and kept within sight of Hilda Ashburn's goal.

They got along. Morris and Charlie found that by going right straight ahead with things, as if they were in their thirties instead of in their teens, they did about as well as anyone. They were both strong and full grown, and they had always worked on the place. They had merely to grow up and take on responsibility, and they did it. Herb helped them some with chores, but Alf fitted into the housework better. He seemed handy about it, and poor little Gladys surely needed him.

Alviry Simms came occasionally to clean the house and help with extra work, but they could not afford to have her often. She taught Gladys many things, and kept an eye on her.

Little Hilda throve, and at last she was safely through the danger periods of infancy, a small, wiry, gypsy-like child with the keen, knowing Ashburn eyes.

"Hilda's got a head on her," Pop often said.

And as she needed his ministrations less and less, Pop sat back and began to take it easy. That second youth which his wife had given him could not survive her passing. Doggedly, devotedly, he labored over the child of his old age, but when she finally graduated from bottles and diapers, he gave up and frankly became an old man, sitting in the kitchen rocking chair.

Tall, lean, stringy, with yellowed and drooping whiskers, he sat there viewing his little world from out of deep, keen eyes that saw everything while they seemed to stare vacantly at nothing. He seldom spoke but, when he did, it was to say much in a very few words. About all he did was to bring in the wood and keep the fires going, yet the children loved him with a respect bordering on reverence. Their mother had taught them that, and long after the moss had begun to cling to her headstone, her influence remained a big and vital thing, Morris and Charlie might indeed be, practically, on their own as farmers, but Pop remained the head of the place. His chieftainship was never expressed, much less insisted upon, by him, but it was never challenged. The boys planned their work themselves, made their own decisions. But before they went ahead, their plans were presented to Pop. He usually approved, occasionally added a suggestion, and once in a blue moon he grunted a disapproval, but he never made any fuss. He just sat there in the rocking chair and looked on with much interest and little comment.

The two boys learned, in a hard and grueling school, what it is to get a living for a family off a few steep, rocky acres of cleared land and a medium sized piece of timber. Under their mother's regime, the apple orchard — one of the largest in town — had been kept up. They knew enough to spray and prune, to grade and pack for market according to bulletins they got from Washington and Orono. They knew, for their mother had drummed it into them, that the difference between a smart, up-and-coming farmer and a down-trodden and shiftless one is education. They knew that hard work is not drudgery if a man gets somewhere by it; it is hard work ending nowhere that takes the heart out of him.

They often talked of their mother. "Seems-so," said Pop, one day, "seems-so, somehow, your mother was always grateful to me. Damned if I know why. She had a hard time here, but there 'twas — she was grateful!"

Charlie was beginning to understand this, but he said nothing. It was all there in the diary. Morris Ashburn the

Third had given to his wife the dignity and protection of his name; he had given her a definite domain over which to rule; he had given her physical and spiritual completeness; and he had given her motherhood. She had been grateful.

So Morris and Charlie grew to an early manhood, capable, responsible, steady; well liked, too, for they were quick on the trigger in conversation, and could hold their own among the men who gathered to settle the affairs of township, state, and nation around the hot, pot-bellied stove in winter, or the hitching rack in summer, at the store at Gag Corner.

Herb and Alf were about as much alike as a hawk and a hand saw. They were usually together, but they were totally different. Alfred, small and slight, was easily the best-looking of the Ashburns. He was a brilliant student, and on top of that he was handy. He could repair a broken chair, paint the kitchen walls, or run the rusty old sewing machine and mend torn sheets and pillow-cases, make towels out of grain sacks and chair cushions out of burlap bags. This work amused him, and the Ashburns never told. They were a hilarious lot and ragged each other unmercifully, but not for the world would they have let it be known outside that Alfred could sew and cook and wash just like a woman.

Herb never could understand Alf's tastes, but he admired them none the less. Herb was big, gaunt and restless, and as he grew up he cared less and less for school, more for working in the fields and woods. He usually had chances to earn, for a strong, capable boy was always in demand in haying season, or plowing or planting time. Some of his earnings he spent for himself, but nearly all he turned over to Gladys for family use. All he wanted was a little change to jingle in his pocket and a decent suit to wear to "times."

The boys all wore their clothes well. From the Ashburn side, they had a natural grace of bearing, and a self-respecting neatness and restraint impelled them to wear blue serge and dark ties and socks. Their stiff linen collars were collected in a bag behind the kitchen door until there were enough of them to send to the Portland laundry. Other boys might wipe their collars off with a damp rag and wear them till they cracked, but not an Ashburn! Their mother had taught them better than that, and Gladys saw to it that they toed the mark. She inspected their necks and ears, and scolded if they neglected their chins too long. It was Alf who loved to chase her with a lathered brush, cornering her in the pantry, or pushing her into the wood-box as he smeared her face, while Pop looked on chuckling almost inaudibly. Pop seldom participated in the family "amplifying," but he loved it.

Gladys was rather pathetic. She grew up tall and very thin, with great, restless, hungry eyes, dark like her mother's. She had a quiet manner, and a nervous flush that came and went easily. She worked indefatigably. She had to. Doggedly she kept on in school, missing many days and making poor averages; but she would not give up. She was methodical, and reduced things to a stark simplicity, but what she started, she finished. Some of the niceties on which her mother had insisted, such as sash curtains and tablecloths, were discarded in the strenuous years of little Hilda's infancy; but, though they might live mostly on bread and butter and beans, what they had was good and plentiful. The boys might have only three shirts apiece — two for work and one for "times"— but those shirts were washed and mended and ready to wear. Even the baby, active and mischievous as she was, in her coarse little gingham aprons had a neat and put-together look, with the dirt on her never more than a day old. Gladys was known as a smart, likely girl, and the women in the neighborhood, especially Alviry Simms, looked out for her, and bragged of her capability.

It was in canning time, and at spring and fall cleaning, that the poised stability of the Ashburn tribe was most seriously threatened. For it was then that it seemed necessary to call in Alviry Simms to help. Alviry was a trial and no mistake. If they could have made out without her they would all have been heartily glad of it; yet when the rush season came, and Gladys grew bent and pale under the strain, it was a relief to have Alviry sail in and take charge of things for a week or so, though it did drive them all nearly frantic.

Alviry was widowed now, and living at the place where Hilda Bowers had boarded so many years ago; and she had a weak-eyed, vapidly pretty daughter of twenty-odd named Nell. Everyone knew that Alviry had plans. She would marry Pop any time she could get him; or she would marry Nell to either Morris or Charlie. Even more cheerfully would she have welcomed a double wedding of the Simmses into the Ashburn tribe. The whole scheme was too obvious for comfort, yet there was nobody in the whole township who could work so fast and efficiently, or for so low a wage, as this designing widow. There was no one else who would come, in season or out of season, and stay contentedly as long as she was wanted, or longer, never complaining, never shirking, never demanding. It was a wonder, Charlie often thought, that Pop was able to withstand her.

Alviry was a pretty woman, dark, small, vivacious, wearing her years gracefully; and she was a model housekeeper. Charlie and Morris were agreed that Pop might do worse, except for two considerations. These were the undying love and loyalty of the whole tribe for the departed Hilda Ashburn; and the widow's embarrassing encumbrance, Nell.

"My gosh," was Morris' comment, "Pop can marry the widder if he wants to, but deliver me from havin' to take on that washed-out piece o' calico that goes with her!"

"Now, Morris," soothed Charlie, "she ain't so bad. Just think how kind an' gentle she is. Don't bite nor scratch, nor have no bad habits. Kind o' pretty, too. Neat little shape—"

"Take her yourself if ye like her!"

"Aw, she wouldn't look at me!"

"She will when I ain't around, and you know it."

Charlie pushed back his hat and scratched his head ruefully. (He was getting slightly bald already.) "Oh, gosh yes. 'Twouldn't make much diff'rance to Nell, nor her mother either. Kind o' pitiful, somehow — two women so doggone set on gittin' married, and not a chance anywhere. But we don't want any woman around here in Mother's place."

But in spite of all this, the widow persisted in regarding the Ashburns as a rosy chance, and she continued to come. Through her ministrations, the old house was kept up decently enough, even though Gladys did keep on in school. It was Alviry who made the serviceable little aprons for Hilda; Alviry who taught Gladys to churn and can and make jelly; and it was Alviry who talked with Gladys, with perhaps more kindness than wisdom, as she stretched up into womanhood.

"Can't do without Alviry," said Pop drily, "but danged if we could do with her — all the time!"

And so they got along, working side by side, playing too; and if they lacked much that their ambitious mother would have wished them to have, still they had much that was solid and good, fundamentally clean and decent.

Charlie, looking backward, had a feeling of warm satisfaction at the memory of this strenuous, often difficult, yet withal simple and progressive period of the family life.

Chapter Two

Gladys must have been about fifteen when Alviry came for the last time to attend to the spring cleaning at the Ashburn place.

It was in May, and the mud was fairly well dried; horses had almost finished shedding their winter coats; the mayflowers were gone by, and the bewildering enchantment of apple blossoms had settled in opalescent drifts on the mountain sides; stiff little feathers had appeared in the baby down of the newest chickens; plowing was making ready for the planting time. By these signs women knew that it was spring cleaning season, and on a Monday morning Alviry Simms duly arrived to remind Gladys, and to take charge.

Gladys had been up since four o'clock, as usual, getting the wash ready so that Pop could finish hanging it out after she had gone to school. She was tired, and her back ached, and she was worried over the algebra which always seemed too much for her. It was a relief to see Alviry come in, so fresh and energetic; sweet to feel that she could with a clear conscience leave in the widow's capable hands the reins of the household for a week or so.

Alviry hung up her sweater behind the kitchen door and poured herself a cup of coffee.

"Now you git along, Gladys," she said briskly. "I'll have your Pop lug out the baskets and I'll have them clo'se hung out before ye can say scat. Here, Alf, you pick up them dishes before ye go to school. Hilda, baby, let Alviry wash yer face. There. Got your lunches?"

"No, I'll fix 'em," said Gladys listlessly.

"Go 'long and git ready, deary," said Alviry. "What ye got for 'em? Any beans left?"

"I guess so. Look in the pot there on the stove. There's pie in the butt'ry."

Gladys dragged herself upstairs to her room, and Alviry fussed about, fixing the lunches. She split cold biscuits and spread them lavishly with butter, baked beans, and piccalilli. She cut quarter sections of dried-apple pie and set them in saucers resting on top of the biscuits in the pails. This seeming rather meager, she got two doughnuts apiece from the earthen jar in the buttery and tucked those in on the side.

"Pity there ain't any decent apples left," she said, as she fitted the covers on the tin pails and set them in a row on the dresser, near a stack of school books.

Alf had cleared the table, and now he stood before the kitchen mirror, combing his hair.

"How's it goin' these days, Alf?" asked Alviry as she filled the teakettle.

"Oh, I'm all right. But say, Alviry, doesn't it strike you Gladys is looking kind of peaked?"

"Yes. She's thin. Looks real silarupy to me. Does she complain?"

"Gosh, no. She doesn't know how. She just keeps going and looks fagged out all the time."

"Tain't right for a girl to work so hard, and I've

always told your Pop so."

Alf winced, and turned his back as he got into his coat. Of course Alviry would have to say that! And then go to work and show them all how perfectly she might take the burden off Gladys!

Herb had the team at the door, and he put his head in.

"Come on, Gladys – Alf – Hilda – Git goin'!" he yelled. He had none of Alf's quiet precision of speech.

Alviry buttoned Hilda's sweater and pulled her little woolen cap well down on her head. Hilda had been going to school since she was three, so that Gladys could take care of her. It was against the law, but no one had ever protested. And now that Gladys went with Alf and Herb to the Cornish high school, they dropped Hilda off at the little schoolhouse back of the mountain, leaving her to walk home in good weather, or wait for them when it was bad. She was such a little mite, with her reader and speller and dinner pail!

The team drove off and Alviry returned to the dishwashing. Pop came in with an arm load of wood.

"Mornin', Alviry. How be ye?" he inquired politely.

"Oh, middlin'. Looks like cleanin' time, don't it?"

"Yep. Guess it must be." Pop sat down with a sigh.

"Now, Morris Ashburn, you git right out o' that chair and lug out them baskets o' clo'se. I got to do these dishes and then git right at the upstairs soon's I git 'em hung up."

"Wash and wipe the dishes – Hang 'em on the bushes!" sang young Morris, coming in with two pails of milk which he set in the sink.

"Git out o' here, good-for-nothin'," snapped Alviry good-humoredly. "Can't you milk a cow without gittin' the pail smeared with manure that way? Ain't there enough bother round here without havin' to clean manure off the outside the pails?"

"Aw, dry up, Alviry." Morris grinned at her and took down his pipe from the shelf, filling it from a can that stood there.

"Where you workin' today, Morris?"

"In the orchard, sprayin'."

"Think all this new-fangled sprayin' does any good?"

"Maybe not. But them that does it gits the best crops."

"Well, maybe so. Say, Morris, what do you think about Gladys? Don't she looked peaked to you?"

"Gladys? Oh, I dunno. Maybe she is sort o' thin."

"I tell ye what I think. I think she's workin' too hard, and she's been doin't ever since your mother died. 'Tain't right. She's gittin' old 'thout ever havin' a chance to be young."

"Gosh, yes. But what can anybody do about it?"

"Well – "Alviry's small, bright eyes snapped and she stood, dishrag in hand, obviously preparing to say a good many things.

Morris grinned again.

"Keep at it, Alviry," he jeered, as he left the house. "Keep at it. Ye may land him yet!"

Alviry sputtered. That was the trouble with these Ashburns. They were too quick on the trigger. Saw right through everybody. She slammed clean plates and cups into the cupboard, strained the milk and washed and scalded the pails, washed the towels and the strainer and hung them, snow white, on the bars outside the kitchen door. No wonder Gladys was thin, having to do all this every day before she could get off to school! Pop, there in the rocking chair, was some help to her, maybe, but not much! Alviry sniffed.

She got the wash on the line and then went upstairs. The Ashburns didn't have much – that was one thing that made cleaning easier than it might have been. Just plain, bare rooms, with none of the clutter of accumulated clothes and papers and rubbish that most folks had to dig out twice a year. Alviry was quick as a flash, and she had finished Gladys' and Hilda's room before it was time to get dinner for Pop and the boys. And her mind had been working as fast as her hands. Right now, when the younger folks were all at school, was the time to have it out with Pop and Morris and Charlie about Gladys.

She was setting the dinner on when they came in – she had boiled potatoes, and fried salt pork, and the last of the string beans she and Gladys had canned the previous summer; there was enough left of the dried-apple pies, also. It was a house-cleaning day dinner, but she had wisely made sure that there was plenty of it.

Morris and Charlie came in first. You would hardly have known them for brothers, except for the steel-gray, deep-set Ashburn eyes. Morris was tall and lean, with straight, jet-black hair thrown back carelessly from a forehead that was white from the protection of the old felt hat he always wore. The rest of his thin, big-featured face was burned by the sun and darkened by the thick black stubble of his beard. Charlie was shorter, and rather heavy, and had he been a student or a white-collar man, he would have been a decided blond. He was burned brick-red, however, and his silky yellow hair was thin on top. Both boys were homely enough to stop a doughnut frying, but they were lovable, somehow. It was a good, pleasant sort of ugliness, Alviry had always thought.

Pop, blinking from the sun, came wandering in.

"Hello, Pop," said Charlie. "Been workin' hard?"

"'Bout's usual," replied the old man, as they all sat

down to the dinner. "Been holdin' up the south side o' the barn. Nice an' warm there today."

"Yep. Good chance to catch up on your whittlin'."

Alviry knew that this was said in fun. No disrespect was intended. Pop's laziness was accepted, even condoned, as much a part of him as his thin, high-bridged nose, his straggling moustache, his tall, stooped frame, or the Adam's apple that was the barometer of his emotions, when he had any.

The men ate earnestly, wiping their plates clean at last with half biscuits which they ate as more sophisticated diners would eat an after-dinner mint. The boys topped off with glasses of rich milk, but Pop wanted another cup of tea. Alviry poured it, bitter and black, from the enameled teapot on the stove. Pop stirred in milk and sugar, tipped the heavy, floridly painted moustache cup over his nose, and drank audibly. Alviry watched him. It was nearly time to speak of Gladys.

Pop set down the cup, drew the damp ends of his moustache into his mouth and let them out again. His meal was finished.

"Morris," began Alviry, "I ain't a bit satisfied with Gladys. Are you?"

"Oh, she suits me all right." Pop was noncommittal.

"I ain't findin' fault with her. Not that. But she's too thin, and she ain't got the git-up-and-git she ought to have at her age. I tell ye, the girl's workin' too hard, and she always has been. 'Tain't right."

"Well, Alviry, it never seemed just right to me that she should lose her mother, but what can ye do about it? Things just come along. Ye got to take 'em as they come."

"Up to a certain point, ye got to. I grant ye that. But something can be done about Gladys."

Morris and Charlie exchanged a long look, and Morris filled his pipe thoughtfully. Charlie seldom smoked. His worst vice was chewing a toothpick, and now he bit viciously into one.

"The main trouble with doin' anything about Gladys," said Pop, "is gittin' her to agree to it."

"Have ye ever really tried?"

Pop shrugged. "Maybe not. What ye got on your mind?"

"I think, Morris and I'll bet ye the boys agree, that I'd better stay right on here till school closes, anyhow. I'll git the cleanin' done, and then just stay on so she won't have to do a thing but just tend to her school work for a spell. Land knows you need a housekeeper here."

Pop sat tipped back in his chair, whittling at a plug of tobacco.

"Needin' one and payin' one is two different propositions," he said.

Young Morris sat slouched forward, eyes half shut. If he felt any uncertainty on the brink of a decision, no one would have known it.

"I'll see to the cash," he announced.

Charlie threw him that quick sidewise glance of his. "How so?" he asked.

"We got the plowin' and sprayin' most done. You can manage without me for a spell. Maybe Pop could help ye in a pinch."

"What you aimin' to do?"

"Work for old man Dennis. Heard him ask Herb at the store last week. Herb said he couldn't till school closed."

"What's Dennis up to?"

"Buildin' a barn. Wants stones hauled for a foundation. Usin' his own team."

"Humph. All right."

Morris and Charlie left the table. Alviry began to gather up the dishes.

"Well, Morris?" she questioned.

"All right, Alviry. Maybe you're right. Try it a spell, anyhow, long's Morris can bring in the cash."

"I know I'm right; you'll see. Now you fill up that woodbox so I can git the ironin' done this afternoon."

Pop escaped to the woodshed. It seemed to him he was never quite safe in the kitchen with Alviry there.

They had less trouble than they had anticipated in getting Gladys to countenance the change; indeed, her unexpected willingness to spend the money indicated her need of rest. Morris earned more than enough to pay the widow, and he kept on at the Dennis place after the foundation of the barn was done.

Pop actually worked that spring — not too hard, but enough to keep him away from the house in the daytime. For Alviry's suit was hot. She worked, as Pop said, like the devil in a whirlwind, and on many days she brought her daughter Nell with her to help. The old Ashburn place took on a shine and polish such as it had not known for many years. Curtains were hung in the windows. "Damned rags," Pop called them, "shuttin' out the light." The floors were first wet, then sticky, then slippery, with scrubbing, paint and shellac. There were new calico covers on the chair and sofa cushions. The indefatigable widow passed nothing by in her efforts to make the Ashburns want her, and realize how much they needed her.

"If ye want to do it, Pop," Charlie told the old man, "never mind about the rest of us. We can stand her."

"Maybe you can, but I can't. Too damned fussy."

"Kind o' nice for Gladys and Hilda."

"I know. But we can hire her again if we need her. Cheaper'n marryin' her, in the long run."

Charlie laughed.

But the house was nice, and comfortable, and Gladys gained five pounds. With Alf's help, she passed her algebra. She even made herself a new dress, working on it nights and Saturdays. The widow was well worth what they paid her. But always in the house was this alien presence — Alviry, fussy, chattering, inquisitive, and, worst of all, so tiresome! Kindly and honest and clean, but good lord, how tiresome!

And so, the day after school closed late in June, Gladys told her she would be needed no more. There were protests, even tears, but Gladys had always had a mind of her own.

"You've done fine for us, Alviry," she said warmly. "Goodness knows no money would ever pay for the pains you've taken with everything. I'm just as grateful as I can be — we all are. But what would I do with myself all summer without my work? And if Morris doesn't stay home and help Charlie some, they might have to hire another man. That wouldn't be good sense, now would it?"

"They wouldn't neither, not with Herb and Alf at home."

"Well, anyhow, I like to do the work myself, Alviry. I really like to. I'll send for you every time I need help, I promise that."

So Alviry ceased to come, and the Ashburn tribe settled back into its self-sufficiency again. Pop pulled down the curtains in the downstairs bedroom where he slept, and the kitchen rocking chair was seldom unoccupied as it had often been during Alviry's regime.

"By golly, it's good to call your soul your own once

more!" he said. "We can breathe easy till cannin' time, I spose."

They did not realize yet that Alviry would never be called back to help Gladys with the work.

Chapter Three

So long as Alviry came daily to clean up the Ashburn place, Morris continued to work for Dennis, and, according to custom, he took his noon meals there. This would have been all well enough, had it not been for the oldest Dennis girl, young and softly pretty, who helped her mother with the cooking and serving and was so very considerate of Morris Ashburn's comfort and tastes.

Morris was obliged to admit to himself that he had started the affair. That seductive piece of woman-flesh, touching his hands as she passed him a clean roller towel, leaning over him as she filled his coffee cup, gazing at him with large, dark eyes that were hesitant and shy until he gave back an answering look – really, what could a healthy young chap like Morris do but start something?

True enough, he met with no opposition whatsoever, from either the girl or her parents. Indeed, he slid into the affair as if on a toboggan enthusiastically pushed from behind, and, before he had time to realize it, he was officially "keepin' comp'ny" with Elsie Dennis. After he quit working for the father, he returned on Sundays to visit with the family, and to sit far into the night with Elsie in the darkened parlor; and he took her to all the dances and "times" as well.

"My goodness, Morris," exclaimed Gladys, one day shortly after she had resumed her rule over the Ashburn household, "what are you doing with so many shirts and collars? Does Elsie make you dress up every time you go there?"

"What's the fun o' sparkin' if ye don't make a good complete job of it?" replied Morris.

"Humph. Spose ye'll have to be gittin' a hoss an' buggy o' your own next," suggested Pop.

"Not by a jugful," retorted Morris. "I can stand the shirts and collars, but if that girl can't put up with the old hoss and team, she can git some other feller to take her out."

"She'll have to ease off on ye at hayin' time," said Charlie drily, "we got to rake with that hoss; he'll be too tired to go sparkin' nights. So'll you."

Charlie didn't think much of Morris' going "girlin'," and he thought less of it as the weeks went by. But it was natural enough. Morris was twenty-one and fond of girls, and Elsie was a cute little trick. Charlie himself paid little attention to girls. He liked to dance, and took a girl home now and then and kissed her good-night, but that was all. He had never had a "steady" and didn't want one. Maybe Morris was different. Maybe he had a right to go girlin' if he wanted to; but it did seem rather risky, with all the family the two boys had to take care of right now!

The affair came rather suddenly to a head, one night in the late summer. Morris had taken Elsie to a dance, but Charlie, rather sleepy after a long day's work, had gone to bed early, grateful that he was still a free man. It was a little after midnight when Morris came stumbling into the large south bedroom which they had always shared. He lighted the lamp, and as he lunged toward the bed, Charlie saw that he was rather the worse for wear. Not drunk, but overwrought about something.

"Wake up," Morris said harshly. "I'm in one hell of a fix."

"Aw, can't it keep till mornin'?" yawned Charlie. He was seldom greatly concerned about Morris' fixes, for they usually got adjusted soon enough.

"I got to tell ye now," Morris insisted. "Git awake, can't ye? I'm damned if I know what I ought to do."

"Well, let's have it." Charlie sat up and yawned again. Morris stood there, shamefaced and bewildered but determined.

"I got to marry Elsie," he blurted. "I got to marry her right off."

"Huh? Why, you can't. You ain't got anything to marry on."

"I know all that, but I got to, just the same."

"Since when? How long you been makin' a fool o' yourself? Good God, Mother'll turn over in her grave – "

"No, she won't. I mean, that's what I want to keep her from doin'. I mean I got to marry Elsie before it gits that far. Don't ye see?"

"Well, if it ain't got that far yet, why marry her? Why don't ye just quit her? It wouldn't break your heart any."

Morris sat down on the bed and sighed heavily.

"That's just what I'd like to do," he said, "but 'twouldn't be right. It's gone too far for me to just quit her, somehow. But dog take it, sometimes I wish I didn't care whether 'twas right or not!"

"I spose ye got to play fair," Charlie admitted. "But you ain't so crazy about her, are ye, Morris."

It was a statement of fact rather than a question. These two were more than brothers. Young as they were, they had been through deep waters together.

"Oh, I like her well enough. I spose I must have been crazy about her by spells, or I wouldn't be in this fix. But I ain't ready to marry. I don't want to."

"You might-a thought o' that sooner," grumbled Charlie. This marrying would upset the whole family; in all their planning they had never reckoned on such a thing.

Morris rubbed his hands together, thinking, groping inexpertly in the realm of the terrifying future, the perplexing past.

"It's this damned business of ridin' around nights, and settin' in a dark parlor," he remarked at last. "It'll git ye, every time."

"Looks like it gits a lot o' couples married in a rush, that's a fact."

Long they sat there, the lamp throwing inky shadows on the low gabled ceiling, the sounds of summer night coming in from the trees and fields – crickets, and the monotonous, repeated cry of a whippoorwill, the strident, untimely crowing of a cock. The problem was a big one, and they must work it out together. The idea of consulting their father did not enter their heads. As usual, a completed plan would be presented to him for his official sanction.

Finally Morris spoke again.

"Well, what in tunket am I goin' to do? Tell me that."

Charlie shrugged hopelessly. "You told me you're goin' to git married. God sakes, ain't that enough?

"Yeah. But what we goin' to live on? Where are we goin' to go?"

"Kind of up to you, ain't it? I can take care of things here, now Herb's big enough to do man's work. He won't mind leavin' school. 'Twouldn't be right to ask Alf to quit, though."

"No. We got to educate Alf. Herb's different. Say, Charlie, if Elsie lived here, 'twould make things a darn sight easier for Gladys. No need to have Alviry at all. It would ease off on Pop, too, not havin' to dodge the widow any more."

"Say, that's so. Hadn't thought o' that side of it. We'd be everlastingly rid of Alviry, for a fact – and Nell too."

"Charlie, if I marry Elsie, I can't git roped into marryin' Nell or anyone else. That's somethin'!" They both laughed over that and then sobered down again.

"The main trouble is, Morris, we got too much family already for the acreage. No cash to buy more land. We're stuck. Now you talk about bringin' a wife home –"

"That makes it sort of up to me to bring in some cash," agreed Morris. "Well, I did it this spring – I can do it again."

"Yep. You'll have to."

"Seems queer – an Ashburn workin' out. Of course, Herb always has, but he's just a kid."

"Well, workin' out is no disgrace, if ye do a good job o' work. Better'n debt."

"Spose you're right."

They talked until gray dawn reminded them of impending chores; then Charlie rose.

"Git some sleep, Morris," he said. "I'll git Alf up to help me."

A week later, Elsie moved into a house already full. Charlie gave up his place in the south bedroom, where he had spent every night of his life that he could remember, and now the door was mysteriously shut at night upon the bridal couple. The youngsters regarded Elsie with awe at first. As a neighbor, they had always known her. As Morris' wife she was a new creature.

She was a pretty little thing, soft and young. Her brown eyes were large and rather prominent, and matched her fluffy hair in color; the deep dimples in her cheeks drew one's attention from the sensuous fullness of her mouth and her deceptively receding chin. That chin was not weak – it was stubborn; not aggressive, but immovable.

Morris was not unhappy.

In September, Gladys, Hilda and Alf began again their daily drive to school, while Herb stayed at home to help Charlie, and Morris hired out. Morris got on well. He was a quick, spasmodically eager worker, tall and lithe and handy about everything. He was keen, too. Had education ever come his way, he would have made excellent use of it; since it didn't, he accepted his lot light-heartedly, never realizing what he had missed. He accepted his status as a benedict with the same casual insouciance.

It was Gladys to whom the coming of Elsie meant the most. With grateful relief, the too-mature little girl handed over her cares to Elsie, more freely and contentedly than she had ever yielded them to Alviry's temporary rule. She devoted herself to her school work, and began to take on flesh and color and comeliness.

"Gladys seems to be kind o' catchin' up with herself," Pop remarked.

"Yep," Morris replied. "It makes me kind o' glad I brought Elsie here after all."

Elsie intrigued Pop. It was he, sitting there in the padded rocking chair in the corner of the kitchen, sucking away at his rank old pipe, rising occasionally to bring in an arm load of wood – it was Pop who really saw things with those keen, half-shut, half-smiling, tolerant eyes.

"Wouldn't trust Elsie no further'n I can spit," he told Charlie one day.

"Why not? Gosh, I'd have said she was honest, anyhow."

"Well, I dunno. Maybe I shouldn't have said that. I ain't had any cause to mistrust her. And I like her. She's capable. Good cook. Good butter hand. Keeps the dish towels clean."

"Oh, well, Pop, you ain't got to trust her. I guess Morris is satisfied, and she ain't got much chance to git into mischief on top o' this mountain."

Charlie was rather lonely and sober these days. The room in the shed loft into which he had moved was pleasant enough, especially after Alf had finished it off for him, and Gladys and Elsie had fussed around and made it comfortable; but he missed his old companionship with Morris. It was far from being all over, but it was changed. On the other hand, he found he had more time to think than he used to have, and he grew to welcome the stillness of the shed chamber, overcame the feeling of being left out as he climbed the back stairs to get to it.

When apple picking season was over, Morris began to talk of taking the big team to the woods for the winter. Cash was needed, and Charlie and Herb would have little need of the horses; they might as well be earning something instead of eating their heads off. Pop unexpectedly had an opinion here.

"You ought to be the one to go, Charlie," he objected. "You're the single man."

"That's just it – I don't need the cash and Morris

does."

"What odds does it make who earns it? It all goes back to the place anyhow. And a man ought to stay with his wife."

"Aw, Pop," protested Charlie, "Elsie's all right. She won't mind. I can't leave the hens anyhow, and Morris is a better hand with the horses than I am. Besides, he likes the woods and I don't."

Pop gave in with a shrug, and Morris went.

Elsie missed him at first, and her large eyes were sometimes blurred with tears. But she was always busy, and, though the Ashburn hilarity was entirely new to this rather stolid daughter of the Dennises, she came to understand it in a measure. She never had a come-back for their banter, but at least she learned to recognize it as an incomprehensible yet inevitable part of the family life. She was fond of Pop and waited upon him dutifully, but she depended on Charlie. He was the man of the house and, now that Gladys had so willingly given up the position, Elsie was its mistress.

So, gradually, as the snow deepened and the cold intensified, she settled down into the family. And it became a matter of habit that she and Charlie should sit there in the kitchen after everyone else had gone to bed, their chairs close to the glowing stove, talking or not, as they happened to please; Charlie with the Portland daily paper on this lap, Elsie with her mending basket.

"Gladys brought home her report card today," Elsie would say.

"That so? How'd she make out?"

"Pretty good. She gits on better in English than she does in geometry. Alf says he can help her some with that, like he did last year with the algebra."

"Yep. He's smart all right. Say, I got a whole case of

eggs today. They've been sort of holdin' out on me lately, but this is more like somethin'."

"Thirty dozen is doin' good for winter," Elsie would agree.

Often Elsie would bring out a left-over half of a pie and a pitcher of milk, and they would eat before banking the fire for the night. Charlie was contented enough; yet sometimes, when he went shivering to the shed chamber, he caught himself thinking of that more comfortable room where Elsie now lay alone, soft and warm and young. It was not in him to covet his brother's wife, but sometimes he thought that he, not Morris, should have been the married man.

Little Hilda was sick that winter. The illness did not last long, and the wiry little creature made quick recovery, but they were all well scared one night, when the doctor came and said it might be pneumonia. Elsie did well. She made Gladys keep away, and worked, stolidly, untiringly, obediently, until the danger was past, sleeping fitfully on the kitchen sofa, while Pop kept watch, but never absent. Charlie came in one day to find her there asleep, huddled childishly on her side, one arm hanging limply over the edge of the sofa; and he felt of the rough little hand. As he had feared, it was cold. He went to Pop's room, where Hilda was now safely sleeping, and brought a comfort and covered Elsie and tucked her in. She stirred a little but did not wake. Charlie stood looking down at her wondering what it would be like to have a girl like that for his own. Of course she was sort of dumb, but easy to get along with. She was pale and untidy as she lay there; she had been through a hard stretch, poor kid. He was about to touch one of her little brown curls with his big red hand when Pop came in from the woodshed.

"Git about your business, Charlie," said the old man with unusual sharpness. "I'll look out for 'em."

Hilda was soon well and back in school, but even after Elsie was rested up, the evenings by the kitchen stove were not the same. Pop had become restless, he said, and took to sitting up later.

The winter was not long. Occasionally, Charlie and Herb took Elsie and Gladys to a dance or to a church supper; sometimes there were evening programs at the school and always there were the Grange meetings. Elsie's parents frequently came for Sunday dinner.

The hens wintered well, and the year's supply of wood was hauled with Mr. Dennis' team, and sawed and stacked. Then all of a sudden the sap was running, and it was spring, and Morris came home.

He was weather-beaten and hard as a rock, and the horses were thin; but the winter had been a good one. He had brought home his pay, instead of drinking it up in true lumber-jack fashion.

They were standing outside the kitchen door, basking in the spring sunshine while their dinner settled, Morris, Charlie and Pop. Elsie had run out to the clothes line, and Morris was watching her.

"Yep," he said, "I managed to bring home every cent, and a damn good thing, too. Elsie's goin' to have a kid in June."

"Humph – tell us some news," grunted Pop.

"News? Well, ain't I? I never knew till today, and she said she never told a soul."

"Some things I don't need to be told." Pop sucked at his pipe.

Morris laughed. "Have to start early in the mornin' to fool you, huh?"

"Pity you didn't start for the woods earlier," put in

Charlie. This would complicate matters. The house was already full; the farm, he had long since realized, was too small to support another family.

Elsie, coming back with an armful of clothes, smiled at them all impartially, rather vaguely.

"I told 'em, Elsie," said Morris, and escaped toward the barn. That was just like him – to create a situation and then duck out!

Elsie stood there, her arms full of clothes, her hair blown by the wind, her cheeks reddening self-consciously, and Charlie noticed for the first time the fuller curves of her soft young neck, the heavier outlines of her figure. He had heard tell that it usually didn't show much for six months. Pop patted her shoulder.

"Ye fooled Charlie, but ye couldn't fool an old feller like me," he said; and she threw him a look of sheer confidence and affection.

"You're pretty young," he continued, "but after all, that's what you're made for."

"Yes, I guess so," she replied. Then she passed them by and went into the house, dumped the clothes on the ironing board, and with quick steps began clearing away the dinner. The day's work went on. Elsie was game about it.

At first, Charlie had supposed that the ordeal would be difficult for them all. He had thought of the possibilities of disaster, remembering wild tales whispered about this and that young mother whom they knew. Morris told the doctor to stop by some day when he was in the neighborhood, and he came along in May, staying a while and asking Elsie some questions. When he left, he called Pop aside.

"She's all right," he said. "She'll be perfectly all right; but tell Morris this – whatever you do, try to keep her away from the damned women."

Pop nodded wisely. "By gory," he admitted, "the tales the women pick out to tell would scare the daylights out of any man. Often wondered how my wife ever stood 'em."

"Most women have courage enough to put their husbands to shame," replied the doctor.

Morris did warn Elsie, and more than once Charlie stayed around the house when Alviry or other neighbors happened in. He knew that, so long as he or Pop was there, the tales would remain untold. But the few which Elsie did hear disturbed her not at all.

"Land sakes," she said, "if I was to listen to all I hear, I'd lie down and die right now and save myself a lot o' trouble."

Morris gave her ten dollars one day, and told her to buy what she needed, so she studied the catalog nights and then sent off her order. After that, she had Alviry come to wash and iron, and devoted herself to sewing. Her mother came often to sit with her and to help her. Charlie watched proceedings a little wistfully. Elsie was rather pretty now – quiet and busy and apparently happy, just a bit pathetic sometimes when night came, and she was tired. Morris got work off and on which kept him away, and often it was late when he got home. Charlie was sorry about that, for Elsie really needed companionship and sympathy. She did not complain at all, but her large, placid eyes took on a look of dumb distress and appeal, and Morris should have been there more often than he was, to answer it. Charlie was sure, had she been his wife, he would have taken her in his arms to comfort and encourage her.

But she was not his wife. She belonged to Morris, and that was that.

The baby was born in midsummer, on a hot and humid day, in the midst of a thunder storm. Alviry and the doctor were there in good season, and Alviry carefully shut out every breath of air from the upstairs bedroom, where Elsie lay. Mrs. Dennis, when she came, approved of that. The doctor muttered to himself but knew it was no use to oppose them.

Pop sat in the kitchen, quite unmoved by the hub-bub, but Morris and Charlie hung around uneasily.

"Can't we be doin' something?" asked Morris.

"Hell, no," replied the doctor testily. "You've done enough. Get out o' here, both of you."

They got out.

"Might's well git somethin' accomplished," Charlie suggested, so they hoed in the garden. That was near the house, and the work made things easier, until the thunder shower drove them to the cover of the barn. There, they just sat. They might have thought of more chores to do, but they couldn't get up any interest in them.

"Well," said Morris, "this fracas makes me feel real down-right married."

"Guess Elsie feels more so," commented Charlie. It seemed to him Morris was getting off easy.

"Oh, well, women take it all in a day's work," Morris assured himself. "Piece o' work I wouldn't want to tackle–"

A flash, and a terrific clap of thunder silenced Charlie.

"That must-a struck pretty close!" exclaimed Morris.

Another frightful shock made them look about uneasily. It was no joke when a barn full of hay got struck by lightening.

The next roll of thunder was not so near, and they sat back again to wait. Perhaps ten minutes passed, and then

Mrs. Dennis came tiptoeing through the woodshed to find them.

"You can come now," she said. "It's a boy!" She was much excited.

The raw, red little creature which the grandmother so proudly exhibited there by the kitchen fire was nothing to wake up and holler about, Charlie thought. He could remember his first sight of Hilda, but surely she hadn't looked so queer!

"Spose he's all right?" he inquired.

"Land sakes, o' course he's all right. A grand big baby!" replied Mrs. Dennis emphatically, as she began unwrapping the bundle and rubbing the little head and face with vaseline.

Charlie glanced at Pop and was reassured by the old man's evident satisfaction. Morris watched, speechless. He shoved back his broad old hat, which he so seldom removed, and scratched his head solemnly. Then he sat down on the sofa.

"Don't ye even want to know about Elsie?" asked Mrs. Dennis tartly.

"Elsie? Oh, sure – she all right?" Morris was absorbed in his thoughts, and in watching this first dressing of his son and heir.

"She seems to be, but you can never tell so soon. If she gits by the third day all right, she'll be just fine."

"The third day?"

"Yes. You can't really rest easy until that's over," Mrs. Dennis informed him. It struck Charlie that she was enjoying the uncertainty – that the women seemed to get a lot of fun out of the whole performance. It interested them, and no wonder! It was their job.

By and by Alviry came downstairs and told Morris he could see Elsie. Charlie watched him as he slowly straightened up from his place on the sofa and took off the hat. Morris – married. Morris – a father. Morris – looking scared and uncertain, climbing the stairs to go to the south bedroom and speak to his wife.

How much did Morris care about Elsie? Charlie had wondered many a time, and he wondered now. It seemed to him that a man ought to feel tender toward the wife who had bravely and safely borne his child; that it ought to mean something rather special. And here Morris was more puzzled and embarrassed than anything else. He had not even asked after Elsie's welfare until reminded of it!

The baby was crying, with a wheezy, quavering sound that grew louder until it seemed all out of proportion to the tiny body.

"Won't he bust somethin'?" asked Charlie.

"Oh, no. He's all right. Him des' don' wike dis gweasin' an' dwessin', do him?" cooed the Grandma. Charlie fled. He never had been able to stand baby talk.

Elsie stayed in bed the orthodox ten days, passing the fateful third without mishap, and then came downstairs. Alviry bustled about the place another week, and after that the family routine went on, with the added interest of Morris Ashburn the Fifth, who, in the eyes of his young aunts, was a paragon of sweetness and beauty. The girls cared for him mostly. Elsie went back to her cooking and cleaning and churning, and the washings which were bigger than ever.

Elsie was a good housekeeper.

Chapter Four

The years went by, swiftly, draggingly. It all depended, Charlie thought, on the way a fellow happened to be feeling. Sometimes, more often than not, in fact, he felt good. The quick-moving, busy monotony of the days, enlivened by the thrill of progress and achievement, the delight of changing seasons, was in the main very satisfactory. Life was on a sound basis of hard, exacting toil which brought visible and tangible comfort to those for whom he labored. His body was the tough and useful tool of his indomitable will and ambition. Emotion scarcely touched him in those days. He had no time for it.

Yet he was not a hard man. He loved his people; he loved Morris' children; he loved his poultry and his fields; he loved his home. It was all well worth working for.

But while there was work in plenty, there was also play. The Ashburns were a hilarious lot, for all their seriousness, and they all loved to dance.

Parkston, like all neighboring communities, had its Grange Hall, where public dances were often held; and it had as well a hall, owned by one Henry Church, designed originally as a roller-skating rink, but later used for dancing. People came from anywhere within a radius of fifteen miles to dance at Henry's — it was the biggest and smoothest floor they could find.

And it was at Henry's one night that Gladys Ashburn met her John.

They had, as usual, begun planning for the evening's frolic in the middle of the afternoon. It was Saturday, and the supper of beans and brown bread would require little last-minute preparation. They were all eager for a bit of fun. Spring housecleaning, young chickens, plowing and planting had been keeping everybody on the dead leap for weeks. It would do them all good to kick up their heels.

Then, too, along with the spring rush of work, Gladys had made herself a new dress. It was a green and white striped cotton, with stiff little white frills at the neck and at the elbows. The fresh color of it and the immaculate crispness of the frills reminded Gladys of the out-of-doors, and the bright sunlight on fresh young leaves.

"I've just got to go somewhere and wear my dress," she had told Elsie; and Elsie had been acquiescent enough.

They had heated extra water on the stove, and had given Young Morris his bath before supper. The baths always took considerable scheming. After supper, Morris and Charlie would have their turn. It was May, but still pretty chilly after sundown, so they would have the tall, three-paneled screen, with its tightly stretched denim cover, set up around the kitchen stove, and a washtub on an old braided rug behind it. You could tell just who was having a bath if you happened to be sufficiently familiar with the Ashburn wardrobe to recognize the shirt draped over this screen. Or if you knew who it was trying so hard to sing!

The screen was already in place when Charlie came in with the night milking. His turn would be next; then, while he and Morris were shaving by the bracket lamp over the sink, Elsie and Gladys would modestly take their pitchers of hot water to their own rooms. After they had started for the dance, Hilda, and then Pop, would bathe by the stove. Pop would be sure that there was wood enough. It sure took a stack of it to heat all that water, but it must be done.

Charlie lifted the pails of milk up onto the table.

"What's up?" he asked, glancing sidewise at the screen.

"I'll be done in a minute. Girls want to go to Henry's," came Morris' voice from the shelter.

"Thought it must be you. Ain't another pair o' pants in town so worn out in the seat."

"Now hear who's talkin'!"

"What ye been doin' all day, anyhow, Morris?"

"Helpin' Pop."

"I thought as much." Charlie looked around for the milk strainer, and Elsie, always watchful, was there to hand it to him. She was washing the supper dishes while Gladys and Hilda dried them. Pop had filled the wood box and sat at ease.

Charlie fitted the strainer in its nickel frame over the top of a cream can, and poured the milk from the fullest pail in a warm, white, foaming stream.

"We're a little short lately," he remarked, "but that black heifer's doin' well. She ought to freshen next week. 'Bout time."

"She'd better. Got to have plenty o' cream to spare when wild strawberries come," said Pop.

"Who's got time to pick wild strawberries?" inquired

Elsie, somewhat acidly.

Charlie answered: "Oh, Morris'll pick 'em. He likes to. Makes him feel he's worth his keep without wearin' him all out."

By way of reply, a cake of soap sailed over the top of the screen. Gladys and Hilda both yelled at once; Elsie and Charlie made a dive for the flying missile, but both of them missed it. The soap landed with a splash in the second pail of milk.

"Morris Ashburn, you great lummox!" cried Elsie, coming with her dishrag to wipe up the spattered milk; but the rest of them laughed uproariously. Pop, chuckling in the corner, said he guessed a little soap wouldn't do the pigs a bit o' harm.

In her stolid way, Elsie was furious.

"Pigs!" she muttered. "A good six quarts o' new milk goin' to the pigs! I never in all my born days saw such crazy goin's on as there is in this house. You'd think milk was as easy come by as water, the way you go throwin' soap into it."

"Go tell all that to the black heifer," Morris suggested amiably as he came, partly dressed, from behind the screen. "Maybe if ye fuss at her a spell, she'll freshen right off."

Charlie took off his overalls and jumper and hung them in the woodshed; then he sat down on the sofa, near Pop's corner, to wait while Morris emptied the washtub and picked up his litter of towels and soiled clothes.

"Well, Charlie," Pop remarked, "here ye go steppin' off to Henry's, and no steady girl yet."

"Want I should have one?" Charlie was not much interested in a reply. Pop just wanted to pass the time o' day, and it didn't cost anything to be sociable.

"Yep. Ye need a wife. Time ye was lookin' around."

"Girls ain't scarce. Guess there'll be one handy when I git ready to keep comp'ny."

"Not so sure. They have a way o' takin' up with the fellers that's on the job. Time you git around to it, there won't be one left that's worth your trouble."

"Oh, I guess I'll make out all right," Charlie replied easily.

He had taken girls out some, but it wasn't best to take the same one twice running. It set folks to talking, and then a fellow was likely to get caught up with, the way Morris had been. Charlie was too wary for that.

At a little after eight o'clock they were ready and set out in the two-seated wagon, Morris and Charlie in front, Gladys and Elsie on the back seat. It was a pretty night, and there were many teams on the road, for the mellow, faintly scented air, the thrilling sweetness of vociferously awakening night life in the fields and ponds, the large and placid moon serenely riding the sky, all combined to entice a goodly crowd to Henry's dance.

It was nearly nine o'clock when Tom Giles, the fiddler, appeared. Tom had been playing for dances for forty years, and his repertory consisted of about ten tunes. But how he could play those ten! There was clapping of hands when he came in. The young folks had been waiting for him, but they were used to that. He always allowed them plenty of time to finish their chores at home, to take their hot baths, dress, and drive to the hall. Nine o'clock was soon enough for the music to begin.

He took his place on the platform, tucked his fiddle under his chin, and with a quick, appraising look downward he made sure that the cuspidor was placed at exactly the right angle so that he could hit it as he played. Willie Sanborn, the pianist, with a pink shirt and a green tie and a double row of bright gold teeth, struck a note for

Tom to tune by. The drummer, a gaunt and silent fellow from out of town, sat waiting. There were a few shrieks from the fiddle like the wailings of a stuck pig, and then impressive silence. Tom spat ceremoniously; then the real music began.

Gladys had the first waltz with Charlie, then the march and circle, and then another waltz. A girl always gave those numbers to her escort, and besides, she liked to dance with Charlie. He was smooth and light on his feet, remarkably so for a heavy man, but he had not quite the life and spring to him that Morris had. She seldom danced with anyone but her brothers, partly because she did not care to, and partly because the boys her own age were shy of her.

As the lines formed for the first contra-dance, a Boston Fancy, Gladys noticed a stranger standing in the doorway — a thickset, ruddy, fair-haired man, who was staring at her. She threw back her straight young shoulders and turned to the man next to her for the balance and swing. A few measures later she met Charlie in the figure and she asked, in a low hurried tone, "Who's that man by the door — looking this way?"

The dance went on — balance and swing, chassé to the right — and Gladys met Charlie again.

"It's John Freeman, from East Parkston," he told her as he passed.

Gladys threw herself into the rhythm of the dance with an odd sense of excitement. She was tall — as tall as Charlie — and very slender, though erect and full-breasted. Her dark hair curled slightly, and her firm cheeks reddened with the heat and exercise; her dark eyes warmed with a light and intensity new to them.

Balancing with Morris, she threw back her head and laughed suddenly.

"Give me the next round dance?" she asked him.

"Sure. What's up?"

"I like to dance with you. You're so tall."

"Promenade all!" called Tom Giles, and the dance was over. Gladys stood by an open window, the cool night air soft against her face. Charlie leaned on the window sill, idly, passively enjoying what was merely another dance to him.

"Who is this John Freeman?" asked Gladys.

"Oh, nice enough feller. Owns a feed and grain business over at East Parkston. Got a lot o' money they say."

"He's no spring chicken."

"Gosh, no. Must be thirty-five or so. Wife died — oh, last year sometime, I guess. No kids. Better set your cap for him!"

"Pshaw — go on!" Gladys shrugged her shoulders and laughed, but she kept her eye on the man just the same. He wasn't so much to look at, but his interest in her was rather exciting. He watched her.

The music began and Morris came around for his dance. In spite of his homely face, he was rather handsome as a partner, lithe and graceful; and Gladys, at seventeen, knew more than just a thing or two.

"John Freeman wants to meet ye," Morris told her.

"You know him?"

"Sure. I've met up with him a lot o' times. Good feller. Sober. Shall I bring him around?"

"I don't care if you do. Nearly as old as Pop, isn't he?"

"Oh, not quite, I guess. Not by about thirty years. He feels pretty kittenish tonight, I take it. Must have quit grievin' for his wife."

"He's a widower?"

"Yep. Got money. Good business, and all that."

Gladys was thoughtful.

Freeman proved to be a passably good dancer, and he talked easily. He seemed cool enough, but there was something in his eyes, in his manner, that made Gladys feel as if she had been shot through with an electric current. She wondered if everyone that saw them knew it; if this tremulous eagerness could be making her conspicuous. People were certainly staring; women whispered to each other; a girl whom Gladys did not know glared at her malevolently. Probably a wagonload from East Parkston had come over, Freeman among them.

"May I have some more dances?" he asked, as the music stopped.

"Guess so, if you want them."

"How many?"

"I don't know — ask me!" said Gladys, laughing at him.

He asked her — except for another number apiece to Morris and Charlie, she gave him all the rest. He wished to take her home, but she refused this.

"I came with my brothers," she said.

"Well, they won't mind. I have my own team. Please!"

"Not this time! No need of your driving two miles extra just to take me home."

He had his own team — evidently he had not come with a crowd.

"If not this time, how about the next?" Freeman asked.

"That's up to you!" said Gladys, and walked away with Charlie.

Outside, the men were unhitching their horses from

the trees and fence-posts and the hitching rack. Some carefully helped their girls to the buggy seat — others loaded up stag parties, with liquor jugs in the wagon bed. All the drinking was done either in the men's room at the hall or on the way home. No decent girl would ever dance with a man who was "likkered up," and the floor manager always kept the drinkers off the floor. Morris stopped for a swig from one of the jugs.

"Come along with us, Morris!" urged one of the party.

"Nope. Nothin' doin'. Got to see my wife home," he replied.

"Yes, you'd better see your wife home," said Elsie firmly, as he joined the family.

Charlie picked up the reins and touched the sleepy old horse with the whip.

"Well," he said gruffly, "what in time's goin' on now? Freeman doin' a job o' cradle-snatchin'?"

"My lord," said Elsie, diverted from her indignation against Morris. "My lord, if some o' those women weren't talkin'! He's been a widower for more'n a year now, and they seem to think he'd be a great catch for somebody."

"Humph!" said Gladys.

"Yes, ma'am," continued Elsie, "you can 'humph' all you want to, but you had 'em talkin' tonight. That big girl in the polka-dot dress — they say she's been after Freeman for some time now and he won't look at her. They say she followed him over here tonight. Got another feller to bring her."

Gladys laughed aloud. "A lot of good that will do her!"

Freeman appeared at the next dance at Henry's. Gladys had gone with Alf this time, but Alf was ready enough to be relieved of his escort duty and devote himself elsewhere.

Gladys knew, this second time she encountered Freeman, that the man was really in love with her; she knew it, and was both flattered and frightened.

She liked him. He was decent and steady, and he had a responsive twinkle in his eye for the Ashburn brand of humor. She had a good time dancing with him. But she would, perversely, have stood him off again about seeing her home had not Alf spoiled her game.

"Sure, Freeman, take her home," he said, barging along just as she was about to refuse. "Take her home for me. I've got a woman of my own to attend to."

So she rode home behind Freeman's high-stepping gray mare, in his springy rubber-tired buggy, her dress protected by a clean linen lap robe that was cool and smooth to her hands. Freeman did not touch her — did not even try to kiss her. Gladys wondered if he were too old to care for that! He smoked a cigar, and after she had gone upstairs to her room, and gotten into her clean white nightgown, the bland aroma of good tobacco still clung to her hair. So she did not brush and braid, as usual, but spread her hair on the pillow and laid her face against it. She really did not want to sleep, but she did sleep, and soon it was morning.

The family talked. They discussed Freeman, and they teased Gladys unmercifully. He called on Sunday afternoon, and he took her to a dance in Convene on Wednesday night. Elsie helped her to make two new summer dresses.

"Land sakes," said Elsie, "you got to dress to keep pace with John Freeman. He sure is after you!"

"Oh, hush!" Gladys had learned to blush at the mention of him, at the sight of his gray mare stepping down the main road and turning in at the foot of the lane. Some of the teasing really embarrassed her. John Freeman was regarded as her steady company, coming regularly twice a week, and sometimes in between, taking her to all the dances and "times," never seeming to regard the six miles that lay between West and East Parkston as any smallest inconvenience. But she had always supposed that having steady company meant love-making, and Freeman did none of it. He stared at her sometimes in a funny way, and he often told her she was beautiful, but he never touched her except in dancing, or lifting her in and out of the buggy. She wondered if it was because he was so old, and had been married. She was a nice girl, so of course she had never wanted any man to touch her; but she began to wonder if Freeman would ever do it, and what it would be like.

The summer was a happy one for her and before she knew it September had come; time for daily trips to school was only two weeks ahead. It would be Alf's last year, and already they were saving up for him to go to college. Somehow that must be managed; the family all agreed to that. And Elsie was having another baby. It seemed that expensive complications were piling up on the Ashburn tribe.

"You like to go to school?" Freeman inquired, the first Sunday in September.

"Yes, I guess so. Anyhow, I'm supposed to go. My mother wanted us all to get schooling. But I'm not very quick with my studies, and I'm getting pretty old, it seems to me."

"You're seventeen?"

"Going on eighteen. And I'll be nearly twenty before I graduate, the way I'm going now."

"Yes, you're terrible old," agreed Freeman. "We'll

have to do something about that. 'Twon't do to have a gray-headed woman in the high school."

The next Sunday, he came rather early, and asked Pop to ride around the mountain with him to look at a piece of timber he was thinking of buying. They were not gone long, and when they got back, Freeman stayed to supper and went home at dusk.

"Now what's ailin' him?" marveled Elsie. "Seems to me he was mighty serious about buyin' a piece o' timber."

"Yep. Serious business," agreed Pop. "Clear out o' here, all of ye. I want to talk to Gladys."

And there in the dusky corner of the big kitchen, in the smoky pink glow of the Sabbath sunset, Gladys sat for the last time on her father's lap; and she cried because the bond between her and the lazy, good-humored, understanding old man was loosening; another man was intruding on her inmost life.

"Yep," said Pop, "he asked me for ye. Said you was still a minor and he couldn't ask ye without my consent. Wanted me to tell ye first. Say, that's funny, come to think of it. Seem-so he's afraid of ye, in a way."

"He don't need to be. It's me that's afraid of him, Pop."

"Well, you don't need to be either. But if you don't like him, and don't want to marry him, just say so right out and I'll tell him to clear out and stay out."

"Do you want to do that, Pop?"

"Well, I dunno. I guess it's human nature for a man to want to shoot anyone that looks twice at his daughter. But Freeman's as well as ye can do, and o' course ye'll tie up to somebody, some day. I couldn't go around shootin' 'em all."

"Pop, Elsie's always talking about John's house, and

team, and business, and all that. I spose I ought to feel lucky that he wants me, maybe?"

"Now see here, Gal, if you like Freeman well enough to marry him, go ahead. But don't you marry nobody for what you can git out of it. Hear me. Now you think good, and if you don't want him, you don't have to take him just because he's well fixed."

Gladys sat still for some time, her tall young body huddled against the old man's breast.

Finally she said, "Pop, let him get up spunk enough to ask me, and then maybe I can tell how much I like him," and she laughed and ran upstairs to her room.

So the next day Freeman came and asked her, and she answered him, "Maybe." She was deliberately experimenting. But after he had held her in his arms, and kissed her, and pleaded with her, she changed her "maybe" to a "yes." She was still a little bit afraid, but she liked him more than ever. She really did.

"There's no sense in your going to school any more," he urged. "You're not crazy about it, and you might just as well marry me right now as keep me waiting around a year or so. I've got the house all ready, and you can change things around and fix up any way you like."

"Fix things any way I like? You mean — spend money on it?"

"Sure. You can spend money if you want to." Freeman did not smile at her — indeed he was nearer to tears.

"Gee, I never did that in my life. But what would your other wife think to see me changing things?"

Freeman answered soberly.

"She was a frail little thing, Gladys. A good bit older than I was and always sick. I took care of her. For eight years I took good care of her. But it was no use. She died.

Once, we might have had a child, but it — never did live."

"That was — too bad—" faltered Gladys. He had never mentioned his wife before, and she hardly knew what to say. But she had no need of words, for Freeman had her in his arms again, and he was doing the talking.

"You're young, and strong — full of life. You're what I want — what I've always wanted—"

It seemed that John Freeman was not too old, after all, to care for love-making!

The wedding was a quiet affair. Gladys had had little time for friendships, and Freeman's neighbors were unknown to her as yet. Then, too, Elsie was too far along to manage a real party. So the preacher came to the Ashburn place, and with the immediate family, in their best clothes, as witnesses, the knot was tied, and Gladys drove away behind the gray mare, her little trunk up-ended in the back of the buggy.

The house seemed empty without her, yet everyone was satisfied. Gladys had done well for herself.

Chapter Five

All along, during those years, Charlie Ashburn was conscious of changes within himself, changes in his thoughts, his ways of looking at things. There was a light, a sort of dream or vision, dim at first but gradually taking more definite form, which was like a guide and companion to him. He hoped that some day it would all show up plainly; but now it was vague, a shadowy, beckoning concept of completeness, of self-contained efficiency, of ultimate fulfillment. His untutored mind was unable to define it or give it name, and for the most part he was too busy to fret himself about doing so. But all that he did was in some way related to and directed toward his dream.

Elsie's second baby was a girl, Little Elsie. Pop objected to the children's names — Young Morris and Little Elsie. He said it was too durn confusin' havin' the same names around under foot all the time. But he, as well as the rest of the tribe, adored the children.

Morris was often away. He could turn a hand to anything, and his cheery boyishness made him popular. In hayfield or orchard, building a barn or laying up a stone wall, work went faster if Morris Ashburn was on the job. Home meant little to Morris except bed and board when he had nowhere else to go. His children loved him — who could help it? — and Elsie accepted him and his casual devotion rather indifferently. It was to Charlie that she and the children turned for real companionship and sympathy. Charlie was safe, dependable, always right there, while Morris was a brilliant and delightful guest who came and went.

Alf entered the State University and got on well. He had always been an able and persevering student, steadily driving toward his goal. He wanted to be a civil engineer. Just where the ambition had come from, no one knew, but his teachers had encouraged him in it, and he had always shown the engineer's aptitude for mathematics.

Herb got a job on the railroad, beginning as a fireman and then being promoted to brakeman. He bought some sheep and pastured them on the mountain. He meant some day to have a place of his own and settle down; meanwhile he was earning cold cash and saving up.

Pop had never retracted his statement that he wouldn't trust Elsie no further'n he could spit, but he seemed to like her just the same. She was good to him, and she was a neat housekeeper. Her children looked healthy and clean; the milk strainers were always sweet and the dish towels like snow; the lanterns were always trimmed and filled; the buttons sewed on; the stockings darned. She and Charlie got on well, which was a good thing. Elsie's lot was far from an easy one, but she played the game fairly. Pop was interested in her.

"She goes it as if somethin' was drivin' her," he confided to Charlie, "and it can't be Morris. He don't give a whoop what she does so long as she don't bother him."

"Why, she's just a good housekeeper, Pop. That's her job." Charlie was far from being thick-headed, but he had no time for digging into other people's minds like Pop did.

It was not long after Gladys went to East Parkston that little Hilda was sent there too. Gladys wanted her. Freeman's house was not far from the school, and the long daily drive would be eliminated. The Ashburn household was shrunken, and though Alviry came back for a few weeks at the time of Little Elsie's birth, thereafter Elsie could manage things herself. Pop, Charlie, and the children, with Morris occasionally, were the regular family. Gladys, John and Hilda often came to spend Sunday with them, and so did Elsie's parents. Herb came home when he could, though his run made it impossible for him to live at home. Alf, of course, was seldom there. It took time and money to get from Orono.

Gradually Charlie had built up a flock of Rhode Island Red poultry that was making him fairly good money. He studied into it some, read books and bulletins and magazine articles, and tried out new schemes whenever he could see any sense in them. The Boston market wanted brown eggs of uniform size; and Rhode Island Reds lay brown eggs. So he stuck to that breed, and by selection and feeding he developed a strain that laid well — beautiful, creamy-tan eggs, with shells not too thick, yet thick enough — and he candled them before shipping, so he knew that each one was perfect. At last came the time when he sent off a case of them each day, and that was enough; all he could handle, all the acreage would support efficiently. Charlie felt good.

It was on a winter day, a Sunday, not so long after Little Elsie's first birthday, that Charlie, quite by accident, found the dream, which had companioned him so long, fitted out with words.

It was the right sort of a day for such a thing to happen, clear, bright, and snowy, with sudden gusts of wind which filled the crisp air with flying sparklers. Morris was at home, and Elsie's parents were coming for dinner, so Pop had made a fire in the parlor stove, and brought some fancy Baldwins up from the cellar. He had cracked some butternuts, as he usually did on festal days, and had hinted to Charlie that the cider in the furthest barrel was gittin' jest about right. To this hint, Charlie had said an emphatic "No, by god," and the old man had relinquished the idea for the present. Of late, an unspoken agreement had been kept — the cider was not to be touched when Morris was at home. Charlie cared little for it, and Pop could carry quite a cargo without feeling it, but Morris was different. He was young, and a family man, and he liked the stuff too well to fool with it.

Elsie got swiftly through with her morning work and dressed the children in clean clothes. Then she put the chickens in to roast. At about noon, her parents, old Mr. and Mrs. Dennis, arrived. Charlie went out and took care of their team, while Mr. Dennis settled himself in the corner of the kitchen sofa — in later years, Charlie was offered big money for that long, shabby old sofa, with its gracefully curved ends and back — and proffered cigars which Pop and Morris solemnly put in their pockets to be smoked after dinner. Elsie and her mother and the children retired to the bright, warm parlor. Pop stoked both stoves and then returned to his rocking chair in the kitchen.

Charlie came in from the barn, removed his mackinaw and boots, and washed his hands and face at the kitchen sink, combed his thin, pale hair by the wavering little mirror on the wall, and put on a soft, clean sweater and a pair of low-cut moccasins. He felt good — clean and peaceful like Sunday.

"Set down, Charlie, and take it easy," invited Morris, moving over on the sofa. Mr. Dennis gave him a cigar, but he did not sit down. The low voices from the parlor attracted him.

"Guess I'll go chew the rag with the women a spell," he said.

Charlie liked the parlor, in a way. It was not so homelike as the kitchen, of course, but there was a holiday feeling about it, a suggestion of orderly well-being, and of possible festivity which certainly could not be accounted for by its rather somber furnishings. The parlor was on the northeast corner of the house, too, and never really got the sun; but that made it cool in summer, and in winter the hot little stove, crackling with good dry wood, made it cheery. The starched lace curtains at the windows were looped back over bands of brass, and through the small square panes, shining with cleanliness, Charlie could see the orchard and off across the hills. It was sightly.

Elsie was sitting at one side of the stove and her mother at the other, both rocking slightly in their low chairs, their feet, in their Sunday shoes, demurely touching the brilliant patterns of the fantastic, deep-piled hooked rug on the painted floor.

The children were there, too, and Charlie settled into the creaking, velvet-covered morris chair that was his favorite, and took Little Elsie on his lap.

The mild gossip of the two women droned on. Susan Eldridge was better of her neuritis; Alice Black had had her baby, a boy; it was said that Dick Billings was going to foreclose on the Schrader family — the mean old skinflint!

"What do you hear from Alf?" Mrs. Dennis asked.

"Why, he's doin' fine, as usual. He may have to stay out and work next year. We don't know. That would make it kind of slow goin' for him, but he says he don't care so long's he graduates before he's too old to take any interest in life."

"Well, he's smart. Let me see, how old is he now?"

"How old is Alf, Charlie? I never can remember."

"Let's see now." Charlie was drowsy but ready to oblige, "I'm twenty-four; that makes Alf twenty — he's twenty-two, almost."

"He ought to graduate by the time he's twenty-five, anyhow," said Elsie.

"How does Herb make out?"

"Pretty good," said Elsie. "He lost a few of his sheep — a dog must have got 'em — but he rounded up thirty-odd of 'em in the barn for the winter."

The talk drifted to Gladys and Hilda; then on neighborhood matters. Little Elsie snuggled in Charlie's arms; Young Morris was absorbed in a mail-order catalog, whose pictures would serve to entertain him for hours on end. Except for the low voices here, and the deeper drone from the kitchen, the house was hushed with Sabbath leisure. Charlie was glad there was no outside company today, for then there would have been loud talk and laughter, and a thread of excitement. If Herb, even, had been at home, there would have been hilarity, and the stamping of feet; but the Dennises were quiet to the point of dullness, and it seemed good to be so still.

Finally Elsie rose.

"I guess it's time to see about dinner," she said. "I put the vegetables to cook just before you came in."

"I'll help," said her mother.

"Well — Charlie, are you aimin' to set there a spell? Or shall I take the kids with me?"

"I'll mind 'em a spell," replied Charlie.

Alone in the parlor but for the drowsy baby on his lap and the absorbed little boy by the stove with his catalog, Charlie yawned, and his head nodded. More to keep awake than for entertainment, he shifted Little Elsie expertly to one side and took a book from the modest pile of them on the center table. It chanced to be the Longfellow that he picked up. He had read some of it when he was a child in school, and occasionally, in idle moments such as this one, he had leafed it through. Some of it made sense, but much was entirely beyond his scope. He knew who Longfellow was – the poet born in Maine, from a family which had originated right near Parkston. Their homestead, the Wadsworth place, was not five miles away, near the Falls. Charlie turned the pages of the book, reading inattentively here and there.

Suddenly he caught something. Plain, everyday words; plain, everyday idea. It was good. It made sense. Methodically, he studied it.

"Our todays and yesterdays
Are the blocks with which we build."

Every Maine farmer lays up blocks of stone. He gathers them from his fields, as his fathers did before him, and uses them as boundaries for his land, as foundations for his barns. He repairs walls laid up generations ago, now crumbling in the frosts of many winters. Charlie knew about building with blocks of stone.

And then he read—

"Let us do our work as well,
Both the unseen and the seen;
Make a house where gods may dwell,
Beautiful, entire, and clean."

That was it! There was his dream, set forth for him in words he could never have found for himself. "Both the unseen and the seen — beautiful, entire, and clean." That must have been what his mother was driving at all those years. That must have been the inspiration of her admonitions, her ambitions, her labors. Maybe she had even known these words — the book had been hers.

Well, so far as things seen were concerned, all was clean and good. There was much to be done before they could know the ease and family independence they all desired, but things were well under way. Maybe it was the unseen that gave him sometimes a feeling of restlessness. His world was all right so far as it went, but there was a lack, an incompleteness, that had nothing to do with the future — a lack that ought to be remedied right now.

Charlie got on well with Elsie. She was his brother's wife, his own sister and partner in matters of house and farm. She was not the type of woman to attract him greatly. Slow and sedate himself, he was intrigued by vivacity, a quality which Elsie, like most of the girls he had always known, was rather decidedly without. Often she had roused him, given him spells of uneasiness, but he had never been seriously tempted by her; never had desired her.

No. He did not want Elsie nor anyone like her, but he would like to be married. He wished that the child cuddled against him were his own. He could marry if he wanted to – he would be a fool not to know that any one of three or four girls in the neighborhood would jump at the chance — but that would be too easy. He would wait until he found just the right one, and then he would marry sensibly, decently, not under any hasty compulsion. But, he now thought somewhat wistfully, it seemed a long way ahead.

Dinner was ready. Charlie looked about for a bookmark, but there was nothing within reach, so he took the ceremonial cigar from his pocket and stripped off the band, straightened it out, and laid it between the pages. Sometime he might want to read that poem over again. He rose, handling the baby deftly so that her dryest parts were beneath his hands, and went out to dinner.

It was at about this time that they had the house wired. Enough subscribers from that vicinity had been signed up to get a line run from the power plant, and everybody was getting the house wired. Morris took a decided interest in this work, and when a new man came to the neighboring town of Brownvale and set up shop as an electrician, Morris got a steady job with him.

"I spose," Morris said to Charlie, with a conspicuous lack of enthusiasm, "I spose I might's well get me a house and move the family to Brownvale. 'Twould ease up on things here. Hilda could come home and keep house for ye."

"Well," replied Charlie reasonably, "so long as Pop lives, the place is his. You got just as much right here as I have. I can't buy ye out o' what neither one of us owns."

"No, and I can't say I'd want to give up all claim, somehow. But I'd a damn sight rather work for wages than farm."

"We got to settle things somehow. No knowin' how long ye may stick to this job. Maybe all your life. We'd get along if Hilda came home, but it'd be hard on her, drivin' back and forth to school."

Morris looked worried. "Guess it's the best way, though. I ought to have my family all together — have a place o' my own."

"Seems-so." Charlie was dubious. Morris really didn't want Elsie with him. He didn't care much about her.

They said nothing about this to Pop — he was lord over all, of course, but his prime ministers seldom troubled him with details. Elsie, however, was consulted, and she unexpectedly settled the matter in a few words.

"I don't want to leave here," she said flatly.

"But you'd have a darn sight easier time in Brownvale," protested Morris half-heartedly. "We'd get a nice little house, and have a garden, and some chickens. Just you and me and the kids. Man and wife ought to live together."

Elsie's deceptively receding chin took on the hard lines of stubbornness. She seldom said much, but about once in so often she would surprise them this way with a rather becoming streak of decisiveness, which gave accent and expression to a face that needed such — a face neither plain nor pretty, a face which, unless animated by some unusual feeling, would never be noticed anywhere.

"The kids like it here," she said. "They'd miss their Grandpop, and they'd be lost without Charlie. You board over there somewhere, Morris, and come home when you can. You'd be here most as often as you are now, I should think."

So it was arranged and, as Elsie had surmised, Morris came home almost as regularly as he had always done. The steady income helped considerably; Elsie and the children were undisturbed, and Hilda and Alf kept on with their schooling.

One of the biggest jobs Morris worked on was the wiring of the old Parks place across the valley.

Dr. Parks and his family had been coming there each summer for several years, but they had never mixed with the neighbors much. City folks, summer people, seldom did, though the fact that the Parks family had originally settled Parkston gave the descendants the right to be considered as natives had they cared to avail themselves of it. Of course, rolling in money as they were, they wanted lights in their house, and the job was begun when they came in July.

Morris had something to say when he came home after the first day across the valley.

"That girl, Marian Parks," he remarked, "say — she's gettin' to be quite a hummer! Growin' up to be handsome."

Alf, who was at home for the summer, looked up quickly.

"She's in my chemistry class," he said.

"Say," cried Elsie, "I never thought of it before, but you must see her right along, Alf. Do you know her well?"

"Who, me? Lord, no. I don't travel in her class. She wouldn't look twice at any but a frat man."

Charlie turned with that sharp, sidewise glance of his. It had always seemed to him that an Ashburn was as good as anybody.

"What do ye mean?" he asked.

"Oh, nothing. I haven't the time nor money to hit the pace she and Graham do, that's all."

"Graham — that's the boy. They're both in college, are they?"

"Yes. In my class — though as I said I don't travel in theirs." Alf laughed as if to dismiss the whole matter, but

Charlie was not satisfied.

"Are you takin' a back seat over there at the college, Alf?" he questioned.

"Oh, no. I'm all right. I've had bids to two good frats, but it takes money to belong."

"How much?" Morris cut in.

Alf named the sum. "'Twould be about that much more than it costs me now," he explained.

Morris and Charlie looked at each other, and Morris nodded.

"You join," ordered Charlie.

So the next fall, Alf was pledged Phi Gam, and the family chipped in on his initiation fees.

"Phi Gam," repeated Elsie, to whom his letter had been addressed. "Well, I don't know what that is, but he says it's as good a frat as any, and better than some. He says it's full as good as the one Graham Parks belongs to."

That seemed satisfactory. They were all proud of Alf. It was not that he was putting on the ways of the more sophisticated world, or that he probably would be able to make more money than those who stayed in the hills; all that was gratifying, of course, but their pride was in his ability to go ahead and accomplish the thing to which he had dedicated his ambitions and efforts. Alf was getting where he had headed for; he was naturally and without ostentation pulling himself up in the world. And by helping him, freely and ungrudgingly, they were part and parcel of his success. Through him, the whole tribe was living up, in a measure, to the standards set by Hilda Bowers Ashburn, whose spirit was still the dominant influence in their home.

Alf's letters were always saved up until Herb came home, that he might read them too, and Herb always brought such brief notes as he received himself. Herb had not the least desire to do as Alf was doing, but his sympathy and interest were unfailing.

Herb was a born trader. That fall, he bought a field with an old barn on it, that was being sold for taxes, and let Charlie have the use of it. The added acreage was welcome. Things were shaping up; the Ashburns were prospering.

Chapter Six

Summer always made Charles Ashburn feel frisky. Maybe that was because everything looked that way. All the colors — the new leaves, the flowers, the baby corn poking up through the brown soil, the straight, fast-growing rows of young vegetables in the garden — everything was new and sweet and full of courage. It did a fellow good just to look around and breathe deep of that smell of earth and pine and grasses. It was easier to get drunk on that fragrance than on hard cider — and much pleasanter!

May and June were mostly planting time. There was little to eat that was especially tempting, for the winter stores were depleted. The few remaining potatoes were withered and covered with sickly sprouts that looked like the fingers of ghosts pointing up through the dusk of the cellar. There had been a few parsnips, left in the ground through the winter and coming out sweet and succulent with the melting frost; but these were not popular with the men-folks. They would eat parsnips and carrots only in sheer desperation. The apples were all gone, and the always difficult dried-apple pies called forth all Elsie's skill to make them appetizing. Dandelion greens were good, of course, but it took all day to dig and clean a "mess" of them. They were really a luxury, unless Young Morris and Hilda were at hand to help with them. The rhubarb plants growing on the north side of the L, thrusting up their fleshy, rose-tinted stalks through the thick bedding of manure which both fed and warmed them, afforded one real stand-by. Gladys pulled some for herself every time she came home, and made quite a game of hunting out new ways to utilize it. Elsie had little time for experiments. Plain sauce and pies seemed enough to her.

By the Fourth of July, the new peas were ready — any forehanded farmer had new peas for dinner on the Fourth, tender new peas, pearly-green, utterly beautiful, rolling out of their symmetrical, dewy shells into an enameled basin in Hilda's lap.

Hilda was at home for the summer, and she never minded these tasks that were always left to younger girls. She loved the pretty growing things, loved to sit in the shade of the big maple tree with her work, and hear the birds, and the bees in the white clover blossoms. Sometimes she would take off her shoes and stockings, big girl though she was getting to be, and nestle her slender bare feet into the soft, cool grass.

There were other good things coming along — "garden sass" Pop called them — great, curly leaves of lettuce; radishes, both long ones and spherical; beet greens with small and tender roots, garnered in the process of thinning out the crop. Charlie had experimentally planted something called Swiss chard, too; the catalog had said that even the thickest stems of this would cook up tender, and the claim proved well justified.

There came also the wild strawberries, which Hilda and Young Morris spent hours in gathering. This was a chore; it meant crawling on all fours through the sun-baked fields and along the roadsides, picking the small, crimson fruits and separating them from their graceful stems; but when the tribe sat down to a supper of wild strawberries and thick, yellow cream, served with hot baking-powder biscuits, their sense of ample, luxurious living repaid them for the work. It was that summer that the Parks family came back to stay. There was plenty of talk about their doings. Dr. Parks, a round, bald, genial little man, certainly seemed to have made his pile. Folks wondered how anyone could make money doctoring; guessed sick people in cities must pay up better than they did in Parkston. Then it developed that he wasn't a doctor of medicine after all; he was one of the kind that wrote books — school books. Charlie had known that all along. Dr. Parks had been a teacher, and Alf had said that some of the school books he had written had paid him pretty well.

Elsie, returning from a weekly trip to the store, where she had traded her butter for groceries and bought what few dry goods she required, gave the latest report on the new neighbors.

"I saw the girl, Marian, and talked to her," she said. "She's real nice, too. Not a bit stuck up. She's cute lookin', but I can't say I like that blouse arrangement she had on. Had sort of a sailor blouse with the tail outside. Looks sloppy to me."

Alf laughed. "Wake up, Elsie — all the co-eds wear them that way."

"Well, if they do, I spose it's all right. She said her folks plan to stay right here except for a few weeks in the winter. They'll go to Florida then. Course, Graham and

Marian will stay on in college. No Florida for them! I guess the Doctor must be pretty well fixed."

"Seem to want to mix in, do they?" asked Pop.

"It looks that way," Elsie replied.

The Parks family did mix in, and so life changed for Charles Ashburn.

One night, early in July, Elsie announced that she wanted to go to the dance. Morris was at home, but he rebelled at going — said that he was too tired and had a crick in his back from crawling around the attic of an old house he had been wiring. Charlie was not enthusiastic, but, though it was a hot night and he was sleepy, he thought he might wake up and have a good time after the music began. He was glad to do something for Elsie, too. She was never very lively company, but he could understand her longing to get out and go places, and he felt that either he or Morris ought to look out for her some. Lord knows she worked hard enough.

The prospect at Henry's was pretty tame, he thought. Not many there, and almost no really good dancers. He took Elsie on for the conventional first numbers, and then left her with a group of her own friends on the bench that bordered the shining floor. There was a fellow he wanted to see about buying or hiring a cultivator, so he went to the men's room to catch him before he got too much interested in either the women or the cider to talk business.

He found his man, and then lingered, chatting idly, until they began urging him to take a drink. He didn't want it — he never had liked the stuff and they knew it — so he went back to the dance floor. Elsie was sitting alone in a corner. He decided to dance with her a few more times, and then, if nothing interesting turned up, he would talk her into going home early. He was making his way toward her between the scattered dancers, and the older people and the children sitting along the bench, when someone touched him on the arm, and he turned.

He turned, and suddenly he felt as if he had been struck — as if something had hit him right in the face and eyes. It didn't hurt, but he stepped backward, blinking.

It was a girl who had touched him — a small girl in a yellow dress, with the lamplight shining on her curly brown hair. He did not realize it then, but here was a picture that was to remain forever on his memory, sometimes a blessing but more often a torment, as long as he lived. The eyes were dark and very clear; the small face delicate, clean cut, and fresh in coloring; the trim figure vibrant with energy. One little pointed foot, showing below the sweeping folds of the yellow dress, was tapping the floor in time to the music.

Who in time was she? Where had he seen her before?

"Hello, Charlie Ashburn!" she said, laughing, "aren't you even going to speak to me?"

"Why, hello—" he stammered; then he got himself together as he recognized her. It was Marian Parks. He probably had never spoken to her, had never really seen her before, in all the years she had been spending her summers across the valley. Why should he ever have noticed her? She was just a kid, a little girl, not so much older than Hilda. But now, by the Lord—

"I wouldn't miss speakin' to you, Marian," he managed to say. "Glad to see ye back. How are ye?"

"Oh, fine! Where's Alf? Isn't he coming tonight?"

"No. Guess not. We've been cultivatin' all day, so he went to bed early."

"But you weren't tired?"

"No. I'm used to it. I keep tough." "I'll bet you

dance better than Alf." "Think so? Ever dance with him?"

"Oh, sometimes. I've been to parties at his house, you know." Charlie liked that. Alf was as good as anyone, there at the college.

"Well, come on," he replied. "We'll see who's best."

She was a tiny little girl. Her fluffy hair just brushed against his shoulder, and her hand was completely lost in his. She was light as a feather, and danced with perfect rhythm.

"What a wonderful floor!" she exclaimed, in surprise.

"You've never danced on it before?"

"No. But now that we're going to live here all the time, we thought we'd come and try to get acquainted."

"Who's we? Who brought ye?"

"My brother, Graham. I don't know anyone else to come with."

"Oh, sure. I see him, over there with the girl in red. Does he take ye everywhere over there at the college?"

"Well, no. Not there—" Marian laughed.

"You don't have to depend on him there, I take it."

"No."

Charlie did not feel much like talking to her. It was more fun just to look down at her. His arm around her was tense, but he knew better than to hold her too closely.

Girls as a rule didn't bother him much, and he was surprised at himself for being so stirred up over this one. She was just a child. He could remember her as a little girl in short dresses and pigtails tied with ribbon. Where had she been keeping herself the last few summers? Where had he, himself, been, that he had not known she was growing up? What had happened to him, anyhow? It seemed to him that he never in all his life had really danced before. He knew it was making talk, but he didn't care. That feeling of not giving a darn for anything was utterly new to him.

He danced with Marian the rest of the evening, and as he drove home, Elsie chattering beside him, he kept thinking of her, and feeling that little figure in the curve of his arm. He scarcely heard what Elsie was saying.

"What's the matter with you, Charlie," she insisted. "Have you gone and got a crush on that stuck-up Parks girl?"

Well, had he? Probably not. He would forget all about it by morning — sleep it off, work it out. Girls never bothered him long.

But he didn't sleep it off, and he couldn't work it out. He went to the next dance, hoping Marian would be there; she was, escorted by her brother again. Morris and Elsie went too, that night, and after the first few dances, Morris edged up to Charlie.

"Say," he insinuated, "got a monopoly?"

"Where?"

"The little Parks girl. Gosh, she's cute. I've been seein' her around the place, but I didn't know she'd dress up like that."

"Want to dance with her? I guess she's willin'! Says she wants to make friends." Morris danced with her, several times.

They lingered in the kitchen that night after they got home. They often did this — it was a mighty pleasant place to linger in, and talk, and perhaps even express their real feelings, really confide in each other.

The fire was out, of course, and all the daytime litter of dishes, utensils, and foodstuffs was cleared away, leaving the familiar nocturnal peacefulness and order that was the very essence of home. The electric light was burning, the unshaded bulb swinging from the ceiling between the sink and the stove; but still, on the shelf over the sink, the row of glittering hand lamps was arrayed beside the antique clock and Morris' tobacco tin, and the little green glass full of matches. The lamps were still necessary. The lights might go out at any time, and besides, not all of the upstairs had been wired.

The boys stood about somewhat aimlessly, got a handful of cookies apiece from the butt'ry, killed time until the women-folks cleared out and left them alone.

"Yes, sir," said Morris dreamily, and the sound of Elsie's step in the room above assured them she was out of hearing. "Yes, sir — quite a girl!"

Charlie went to the sink and pumped a dipper of water. Morris had danced too much with Marian Parks, in his opinion, and, much as he shrank from doing it, he felt he ought to speak his mind.

"Yep, quite a girl," he admitted, tipping the dipper up to drink.

"You danced with her considerable," Morris suggested.

"I wasn't the only one."

"Kind o' dangerous — what say?"

"Should think so — for a married man."

Morris shrugged his shoulders. "Fat lot o' difference, married or single. Alf may travel her gait, but you don't."

"Who said I wanted to?"

"Humph." Morris turned to the stairway, but changed his mind and came back, making a pretense of filling his pipe from the can on the shelf over the sink.

"She ain't pretty," he remarked.

"No. She don't need to be."

"Elsie used to be prettier, so far as that goes."

Charlie nodded. "Elsie's got more meat on her bones

— if ye like 'em that way," he agreed.

"Yep. Elsie's all right. Say, Charlie—"

"Yeah?"

"Say, she's slim, ain't she! I mean Marian."

"M'hm. Cute little thing." Charlie strolled to the door and stood looking out. It was cooler there. The still night had the soft, starlit darkness that was so eloquent of things unseen — of tenderness, of beauty, even of passion. The tall elm down the lane moved its feathery top, a dim shape against the sky; the crickets were shrill, and over on the mountain side somewhere a whippoorwill was voicing his complaint unceasingly. Charlie folded his arms across his chest and resolutely steadied himself.

Cute, she was — Marian Parks; a cute little thing, yet far from being a doll-face. She had real backbone, real spunk, real brains, yet she wasn't the brainy type after all. She was sweet, girlish, essentially feminine, yet it was not just sex that fascinated him. Charlie could think of much that she was, and that she was not, but to analyze her character, her personality, was as yet beyond him.

As yet — there, that explained it! No one could know Marian all at once. No one could take her in at a glance, nor be satisfied—

The summer night went misty before his eyes for just a moment, and then Charlie turned back to the kitchen.

"She's cute, all right," he repeated.

"You're right," said Morris. "It don't make any diff'rence whether she's pretty or not. It's the way she stands up so straight. Most girls don't have a back like that. Straight. Classy lookin'."

"Somethin' like Mother?" suggested Charlie.

"Oh, gosh no. Mother was big — heavy—"

"I don't mean her looks. I mean her mind."

Silence. Then, "Oh, yes, I guess you're right,"

Morris admitted.

And suddenly Charlie was angry. He didn't like the far-away look in Morris' eyes; he didn't like the vague something that was clouding between them. It couldn't be put in words; there wasn't a thing you could put your finger on. But something was up; something was disturbing them.

"Come on, Morris," he ordered roughly. "Git to bed. It's most milkin' time right now."

The days and weeks of summer went by.

Charlie had always prided himself on his common sense. He needed it, with the family looking to him for everything. It had got so he even had to keep an eye on Morris — but then hadn't he always? Gladys was a good bit of help, keeping Hilda and always being on hand, sort of. But in the main, Charlie was the head of the family, and he needed a level head.

And he was losing it! He was dreaming, walking in his sleep, it seemed, most of the time. All on account of the Parks girl – just a child—

Pop, from his rocking chair in the corner of the kitchen, spoke of it once.

"Look out, Charlie," he warned mildly. "You're the kind that falls once and falls hard. Like your mother."

"Talkin' don't help any," retorted Charlie.

"Who's talkin'?" asked Pop, innocently lighting his pipe. Charlie was ashamed of his sharpness. He knew too that the old man would never mention the subject again yet he wouldn't have blamed him if he had really made a fuss and issued a reprimand.

For Charlie felt like a fool, and probably, he reflected, he acted like one. His mind was just about half on his work and three quarters somewhere else, and for the first time in his life, he was losing weight. He felt thin, edgy, irritable, and he didn't like it. Strangest of all, he couldn't eat. He would come in from work as ravenous as a healthy man ought to be, but by the time he was washed and set down to the table, he would have got to thinking about that girl — Marian Parks, who was never really out of his mind — and his appetite would vanish.

He had seen Alf and Herb act that way over some of their passing crushes, and it had amused him considerably. It was not so funny now.

Tom Giles picked up a new tune that summer — a thing he seldom did. This one was a waltz, and Marian sang the words to it.

"Meet me tonight in Dreamland,
Under the silver moon…"

The smooth, slow measure stayed with Charlie day after day until he longed to be rid of it, yet when Saturday night came, there he was like a fool back at Henry's dance hall, his arm around Marian Parks, asking Tom to play the tune again and again.

Of course it was all just a pipe dream. He would never be such a blithering idiot as to fall in love with the girl. He set the full force of his will against that. She would go back to college in September, and after a spell he would get over this, no matter how wise Pop might look!

Then September came, and Marian told him a casual good-bye. He had overtaken her, really quite by chance, as he was driving up to the old Hoyt place one day to see about some fertilizer. She was afoot, and he had felt hesitant about asking her to ride in the stinking old wagon; but she had laughingly climbed up beside him, and she had told him that she often spent long hours in the Hoyt pasture, on the brink of the big ledge under the pine trees.

"It's so still there," she said, "and so fragrant. I can see for miles down the river valley, and sometimes a big old king-o'-the-woods goes flapping over. It is a grand place to think."

"Like to think, don't ye!" Charlie said.

He wanted like all get-out to ask if he might not climb the ledge with her, but he didn't dare. He knew she did not want him, and, after all, he had some pride. So he stopped just before he got to the Hoyt barn and lifted her down.

"I'll be gone before the next dance," she said. "We've had some good times, haven't we, Charlie?"

He tried to answer her, but the words would not come. He could only stand there with his battered old hat in his hands, and stammer like a fool.

"What ails you, Charlie?" she asked. "Haven't we had a good time? Why, I feel as if I were richer for having made a friend this summer."

"Friend! Oh, hush, Marian!" he said hoarsely. "You don't know what you're talkin' about."

She stared at him in amazement, and drew back from him.

It was always like that. The least bit of feeling on his part seemed to frighten her off. "Well," she said, a little bit formally, "I know you want to be about your work, so I'll be going." She held out her hand. "So long until Thanksgiving!"

Chapter Seven

If Charlie had ever really believed that Marian Parks' return to college would end his unrest, he was greatly mistaken. Of course, it was a little easier to stand with her away. He was able to sleep and eat normally, and to put a reasonable amount of attention on his work, but even so, the routine of autumn went along in a sort of mournful waltz time. Charlie was disgusted with himself. He had hoped to regain his common sense as the summer's foolishness faded from his memory — but it didn't fade worth a cent, and his common sense seemed to have fizzled out completely. And that wasn't his only worry.

Morris was seldom home that fall and, when he was there, things were out of kilter somehow. Elsie was uneasy, and she had got in the habit of watching Charlie. Careful of his comfort she had always been, but now she came near to being fussy — a thing he could not endure.

There was nothing he could do about it — no special complaint that he could make. If Elsie had been his wife, he could have had it out with her, but, since she wasn't, he had no right to clear the air with a row. He couldn't say to Morris' faithful hard-working wife: "Now see here, you leave me be. You make me tired with your fussing." Things like that were not done by the Ashburns.

Elsie began early with her plans for Thanksgiving and the winter. Just why she seemed more enthusiastic that year than she had ever been before, Charlie did not even try to figure out. She finished off the fall cleaning early in October, and then she made mincemeat, setting the ten-quart crock of it away in the cellar to ripen. She worked outside with Charlie, picking apples, until she complained that she saw apples every time she closed her eyes, and that her insides were tired. For all her energy, she had been variable in temper all along, and this complaint of being tired was utterly unlike her. Charlie wondered. Little Elsie was three years old now—

He asked Morris about it.

"Hell, no," said Morris. "She won't have any more. Says she knows when she's had enough. Suits me. I like kids, but too many of 'em would be altogether too much of a good thing."

"Guess you're right. We ain't got acreage enough yet, even with Herb's land, to take care of much more family. But what in time does ail Elsie, do ye spose? She acts like all possessed sometimes."

"How should I know? Gosh sakes, I got something to do besides keep track of a woman's cantankerousness."

Charlie looked at him sidewise. "Should think you might be some interested. She's your wife. You're sort o' responsible, ain't ye?"

"Maybe so," admitted Morris, with his characteristic shrug of the shoulders. There was something in his make-up that never let him really grow up. He might have been capable of taking on responsibility had he been driven to it, but he wasn't. Charlie had, through the years, been gradually assuming it all, and Morris, who was always ready enough for manual work which he got paid for, was lazy and indifferent when it came to thinking a thing through and acting on his own hook. So long as Charlie kept an eye on Elsie and the children, and bore the brunt of Elsie's ill humor as well as the comfort of her pleasanter moods, why should Morris fret himself? If he brought home the cash periodically, and spent his holidays amplifying around for their entertainment, that seemed to be all they expected of him. He did not realize that he was coming to pair off Charles and Elsie Ashburn in his mind.

Freezing weather set in early in November, and so they killed the pig. Elsie worked over the lard and sausage, and helped with the smoking of the hams, shoulders, and bacon. The fat chunks of side meat were packed in a barrel of brine in the cellar, ready to be baked with the Saturday beans for the coming year. Roasts of fresh meat were sent around to the neighbors, and what was left lay, frozen hard as a rock, in a box in the north corner of the L.

Caring for the pork was a hard job, Charlie had to admit; but Elsie had gone through with it every year, before this, without such a touse. She seemed to feel well enough, yet her temper kept slipping, and she flashed out at Charlie with no provocation at all. Even Pop was puzzled.

"Seems-so Elsie's just a little mite on edge these days," he remarked.

"Yeah," agreed Charlie, "I guess Morris ought to be home more. She don't get out enough. Ought to go around, go to dances, Grange meetin's, and all that. She's always after me to take her, but I ain't got the time."

"After you, is she? Better watch out."

"Huh?"

"You know how folks like to talk. Better not take her out too much."

"Oh, gosh, Pop, nothing to worry about that way. I ain't got time for women anyhow, much less those that belong to someone else."

"Humph," said Pop, lighting his pipe.

Elsie had invited her parents for Thanksgiving dinner, and Gladys, John, and Hilda would be there too. Herb would surely come, but Alf had written that he could not make it. It would be a big crowd to feed, as usual, and Elsie hustled through with the washing and ironing that week, so that she might bake the pies, both pumpkin and mince, and a batch of yeast bread. She got cranberries from the store and made jelly of them. John Freeman sent over a turkey, so big that the oven could barely accommodate it, and Elsie dressed and stuffed it on Wednesday. She was forehanded. She always did things systematically; her every move was purposeful; and her recent irritability seemed for a time forgotten — the holiday mood was upon her.

"There," she said, as she hung up the dish pan after the Wednesday supper, "I'm all done but fixin' the vegetables and roastin' that turkey in the mornin'. How about the dance, Charlie? "

Charlie had been waiting since September for the annual event, the Thanksgiving Eve dance at Henry's, and he did not want to take Elsie.

"Is Morris comin' tonight?" he asked.

"Yes. He called up and said he'd be along and meet us at the hall."

"All right, then."

The hall was full that night. Outside, the air was clear and cold; the ground, under a light fall of snow, was hard as metal. Within was warmth and liveliness. The stove, its maw full of pine logs, glowed red all over; the heated air was full of laughing and chatter, and the heavy scent of soap and cheap perfume, the unescapable smell of the barns.

Charlie, standing back to the stove, saw Marian when she came in, her brother with her, and he felt himself grow hot all over, then cold. She had on a long, fur-trimmed coat and a little fur cap, and her cheeks were red. She did not see him at first, but joined a group of girls in one corner, taking off her coat and cap and hanging them on a hook on the wall. She fluffed up her hair with both hands, and replied cordially to something one of the girls had said. Then she turned, saw Charlie, and waved her hand to him.

Charlie would have liked to evade, to pretend he had not seen her, and to dance with another girl first. Or even to have made his way to her gradually, stopping to speak to people on the way. But he could not. He went directly to her, feeling that he did well not to run. The little devil pulled him like a magnet.

It was half relief, half torment, to get his arm around her again. He had not forgotten her in the least, yet it seemed to him that he had not known how sweet she could be. Maybe it was her dress that made the difference — it was darker than anything she had worn in the summer, and it brought out the red in her cheeks, the dark flash of her eyes.

Morris came in, a little late, but in time to look after Elsie, dutifully taking her on for the first waltz, the march and circle, and the second waltz. Then he left her on the bench and elbowed his way through the crowd to where Charlie and Marian were standing. Charlie felt a sudden stab of uneasiness and antagonism, which was in no wise alleviated as Morris soberly shook hands with Marian, with a word of greeting, and asked her for the next dance.

There was nothing for Charlie to do but dance with Elsie. And to make things worse, he found he had to step lively to get another turn with Marian. Morris was always right in the road, and he was the better dancer of the two. The girl seemed to like him!

It was about half way through the evening that Charlie noticed Elsie was worried.

"Folks will talk," she said, "if Morris dances with that Parks girl any more."

"Let 'em," replied Charlie, "then they'll be givin' me a rest."

"Well, you're single. Talk can't hurt you."

"'Twon't hurt Morris so long's there's nothin' in it."

"Nothin' in it!" scoffed Elsie. "Morris has been crazy about her ever since last summer."

"So?"

Elsie did not answer, but pulled Charlie to his feet to dance with her.

He was thoughtful. This must be what had made Elsie so moody and unlike herself all, the fall. She was jealous. That was too bad. Morris had been rather cool for some time; he ought to get wise to himself, and walk the chalk before there was any scandal. Maybe a good talking-to would help. Charlie dreaded it, but he could do it if necessary.

He had the "Home, Sweet Home" with Marian, but he took little pleasure in it. He was sick with worry, and Marian could not help noticing it.

"Why are you so sober, Charlie?" she asked innocently. "You haven't made me laugh once tonight."

"That so? Well, maybe if you knew what I'm thinking about, you'd get the big laugh of your life."

Charlie looked down at her sidewise, with that quick, all-seeing glance of his.

"You might tell me!"

"No, ma'am. You might laugh, or you might get mad. No tellin' which."

"Oh, is it about me?"

"What else do I ever think about?"

"Why, Charlie!" She stared in amazement, and then she did laugh. "Good heavens, are you trying to make pretty speeches?"

The holiday passed well enough. The gathered Ashburn tribe was hilarious, as always. The dinner was good. Gladys, who was "expecting" at last, sat quiet in the morris chair, glowingly handsome, while the devoted Freeman hovered about to wait on her. Hilda was growing up fast, still small and gypsy-like, but rounding out prettily, sparkling and full of fun.

"Got ye a feller yet?" teased Herb, who seldom saw her now that he was on the road.

"I'm getting me one," she retorted. "I haven't really landed him yet, but I'm doing well."

"I'll warrant ye are!"

Charlie had always loved a family holiday like this, but now there was something strange in the air, something out of kilter. Probably it was the widening breach between Morris and Elsie, which her words of the night before had suddenly made apparent to him. It was not right. It was not "entire and clean." Charlie was troubled.

The men were in the kitchen, lounging replete with dinner and lighting up their cigars, when Pop spoke from his rocking chair.

"Things change," he remarked.

"Yep," said Morris.

"Things change," the old man repeated. "That's about all ye can be sure of in this world – change, all the time. Kids growing up — like Hilda. No time at all since I had to button up her pants for her." Pop chuckled.

"It's only folks that change," Charlie offered. "Nothin' else changes much. Oh, sure — we get ahead all the time. Get better machinery. Get lights — power — all that is change. But what does it amount to in the long run? Plenty of other kids comin' along all the time — needin' their pants buttoned."

"That's so." Pop puffed out a great cloud of smoke, blue and fragrant. The women were busy; Mrs. Dennis was washing dishes; Hilda was drying; Elsie was clearing up and putting things away. Gladys was in her easy chair in the parlor, amusing the children, who were full and sleepy and easily pleased. Old Man Dennis was frankly asleep in a tipped-up chair by the kitchen stove. Pop was a fixture there in that old rocking chair; Morris and Herb sat somnolent on the sofa.

Charlie got into his mackinaw ready to make his afternoon trip to the henhouses, and he stopped in the door and looked back. He sighed heavily. Everything seemed all right to the eye. Orderly, contented, serene. Was he the only one that felt queer? Probably not. Both Morris and Elsie were off their base, he supposed. He hoped Morris did not feel as bad as he himself felt — so restless and hungry and frazzled out, all on account of ninety-five pounds of girl!

The cold air outside braced him up some. Change, Pop had said. Change, all the time. You got life all fixed up for yourself, and then something you couldn't help to save you came along and raised hob all around.

Marian Parks was having dinner over there in the old house across the valley. They had company, from

Portland, she had told him. City folks, in fine clothes, with a different speech from that of the hills. Marian's own kind, sleek and soft. Charlie found himself seething with scorn for them, and then pulled himself up short. It was for that very sleekness and softness that he loved Marian Parks.

Loved her — that was what ailed him. In spite of all his effort and determination to keep clear of it, he was in love for the first time in his life, and he didn't like it a bit!

In the following weeks, he kept hoping that things would clear up some. He thought maybe Morris had just been infatuated for a while; that he and Elsie might patch things up. Maybe Charlie himself would be able to snap out of it and show some sense.

But it was no use. Christmas was soon upon them, and with it came further changes for the Ashburns.

The pending arrival of Gladys' baby was far more on the family mind than preparations for the holiday. Elsie's children had been welcomed, and duly fussed over, but after all Elsie was an Ashburn only by marriage, while Gladys was flesh of their flesh; her ordeal and her triumph would hit nearer their hearts.

The doctor had told her to watch out for the fifteenth of December, and a room had been engaged for her at the hospital — in the small house next to the Doctor's own, which he opened up for such occasions, importing a nurse from Portland. Obediently, and encouraged by a few preliminary pains, Gladys went on the fifteenth; but nothing happened, so she went back home, and the nurse returned to Portland for another week. It was funny — that ignominious return from the hospital with nothing to show for it, and the Ashburns laughed with their neighbors. John Freeman got the worst of it, really, for his taking to himself so young a wife, and his obvious and abject devotion to her had been pretty freely commented upon. Now, he countered the jibes by putting on an anxious expression and hinting at complications, so that his friends of the post office and barber shop respectfully let him alone. Gladys, though she didn't mind the teasing, declared she wouldn't stir out of the house again until she was plumb sure.

However, on the morning of the twenty-second, the evidence was unmistakable. John hustled her back to the hospital; the nurse was summoned again, and barely got there in time; the complications which John had really led the community to expect failed to materialize, and Gladys brought forth her son as a healthy, happy young female should. They named him Jack.

Chapter Eight

Charlie had brought Hilda home on that eventful twenty-second, and Alf had come for the holiday. Herb, too, showed up, having hopped the midnight freight. The house was full of life and warmth and laughter, though it did seem queer without Gladys.

At breakfast they sat long over their bacon and johnny cake and coffee, mostly all talking at once.

"By golly, Hilda, you're gettin' to be quite a gal!" said Herb.

Hilda colored and smiled with pleasure but entirely without shyness, and Alf watched her with interest. She had always been a favorite with him. Now he was delighted to see her growing pretty and feminine, seeming to progress toward an early maturity without the usual awkwardnesses and agonies of adolescence. She had fire, spirit, intelligence.

"Charlie tells me they think you can sing," he said.

"My teacher seems to think so. I don't know," the girl replied. "I'd like to well enough — I mean really learn something about music."

"We'll have to see about that," Alf returned.

The untutored Ashburn tribe had always marveled at the volume of melody which sometimes poured out of that childish throat and breast; now it seemed that they had been right in suspecting that the voice should be trained. It would take some planning, but they would manage it somehow, of course.

"We'll have ye hollerin' like a screech owl around here yet," Herb taunted her, and pulled her hair to prove he did not mean it.

Elsie stepped to the stove and got the coffee pot to fill the cups again.

"You boys'll have to shave and doll up tomorrow night," she warned. "They're givin' Uncle Dan a surprise party, you know. We're all goin'. Whole town's goin' near's I can make out."

"What is it," asked Morris, "his birthday?"

"Yes. And two of the daughters are home, so they got up this affair — or rather, I guess it has just grown. I've got to take a cake. Guess I can bake one big enough in one of the old milk pans."

Hilda looked up with quick interest.

"Set a baking powder can in the middle of the milk pan," she suggested. "I saw Gladys do that once. It keeps the cake from burning on the sides before it's done in the middle."

Alf saw a quick look of appreciation flicker in Pop's deep eyes. Maybe the girl could sing, but she could be the practical housewife too.

"You goin' to the party, Pop?" asked Charlie.

"Oh, lord no. Too much like work. Dan Chadwick can dance and fiddle in his old age if he wants to — I got done with that long ago."

"Didn't think we could drag you out," Charlie

answered. "Well, you can have the stove good an' hot to thaw us out when we get home."

"You'll need thawin'. Paper says colder weather's comin', and it ain't hot right now."

It did turn colder, but even so the night of the Christmas Eve party at the Dan Chadwick place could hardly have been improved upon. It was clear and brilliant, a full moon riding the sky and striking sparks from every snow-laden twig and branch.

Since Pop would not go, they decided to leave the children with him, so Elsie got them to bed before she changed to her best winter dress. Hilda had a new one, and there was some concern about her wearing it the first time. Elsie was pretty sure it would fit, and Gladys had approved it a week ago, when it had been finished; but you never could tell about a dress from just tryings-on. It had to be really worn before you could bank on it.

"Why can't we go, Mama?" asked Little Elsie, from her crib in the corner of the bedroom.

"You're better off at home," Elsie replied, rather indifferently. She was never unkind to her children; never so very sharp with them. She always did her duty by them carefully. But it was Hilda who went to the crib-side and explained, warmly and lovingly.

"It's so cold, Dearie," she said, "and anyhow you wouldn't want to leave Pop here all by himself, now would you? Poor Pop — he'd think nobody loved him if all of us went off!"

"Parties are sissy anyhow," yawned Young Morris from the other corner.

Charlie had put both seats in the pung and they all piled in, Morris, Elsie and Charlie in front, and Hilda and the two boys in back. Pop came out and tucked in the heavy blankets and the frowsy old buffalo robes. There was straw in the bed of the pung, covered over with a horse blanket, to keep their feet warm.

"Now you take care of the horse, Charlie," Pop warned. "Stand him in if ye get a chance, but anyhow git him out o' the wind and cover him good."

"Sure thing, Pop!"

Charlie had always liked such a party going as this — the whole family together, their destination the familiar home of a friend. But tonight he was less interested than usual. For one thing, he knew that Morris and Elsie had had a row. Elsie had been asked to invite the Parkses, and she had neglected to do it. Neglected it, Charlie knew, deliberately, hoping that they would not be there. That was mean, and yet he could hardly blame Elsie. Of course, as the nearest neighbors to the Parks place, the others had assumed that Elsie would attend to this. Her not doing so was sure to make talk, if anyone found out about it. It was just enough to set tongues wagging, and give substance to any chance suspicions— Oh, well! So, as they slipped along the hard-packed road, the bells jangling like little Christmas chimes, there was rather tense silence on the front seat of the pung. Not so in back, for Hilda was in high spirits, and the two boys were making up for lost time in their hilarity.

They had just made the turn in the road before entering the dark pine lot referred to as "the gore" when Herb sang out,

"Team tryin' to pass ye, Morris!"

Morris edged the heavy pung as far to the right as he could, and a light sleigh flashed by them, a high, clear voice calling:

"Hello, there, Charlie!"

"By Godfrey," said Morris, "Marian and Graham are goin' after all."

Elsie was glum. "Somebody else must have told 'em," she conceded.

Charlie thought it served her right. Her ill-natured little scheme had failed, and the funny part of it was that probably nobody would ever realize that there had been a scheme, unless gossip had gone farther than he supposed.

And suddenly the party took on a decidedly festive tone for him. Suddenly the moonlight was alluring; the bells sounded gay and light-hearted; the sharp knife of the cold, dry air was sweet and cleansing. Marian would be there, after all!

It was four miles to the Dan Chadwick place; four miles mostly through the woods. Several teams passed them, but yet they were early enough for Charlie to find room to stand the horses in the big, hay-scented barn. It was comparatively warm in there, with the horses and cattle tied up so close together, yet he used the horse blanket with a buffalo robe thrown over it. He was not one who could enjoy himself without being sure his animal was comfortable.

But having made sure of that, he groped his way through the long woodshed, through the creamery, through the back entry, and into the warm, bright Chadwick kitchen. He stamped the last trace of snow from his feet, stowed his cap and mittens in his overcoat pockets, and laid the coat on the pile of them already collected behind the door.

It was a good crowd. Everybody out. Nice night, and old Dan Chadwick was popular anyhow. All the lamps in the house were lighted, some set high on shelves, out of the way, others on wall brackets, and in each room a large hanging lamp was suspended from the ceiling. The Chadwicks had always been well fixed, and had things comfortable.

Charlie looked around. There were girls a-plenty there. Girls of assorted ages and sizes, dressed in their good wool dresses, or in their dark skirts and fresh white shirt-waists. The older people were collected in the parlor, for the big room used as kitchen, dining room and living room was cleared for the games. The table was pushed back against the wall and the rag rugs were piled under it. Uncle Dan was there, a tall, thin, finely proportioned old man, with a thick shock of snowy hair and a bushy white beard and blue eyes faded and almost tearful behind his glasses.

"This is great fun," he was saying. "I'm surprised most to death. I might-a known something was up, though, with Betsy makin' me take a bath right after supper. Darned if I hadn't orto have known."

The three daughters, one resident and two visiting, hovered devotedly about the old man, and saw to it that he was well provided for; and soon he was prevailed upon to get out his fiddle.

His fiddle was a good instrument, handsome to see and mellow in tone, and he had made it himself. Uncle Dan could do anything with his hands, and this in spite of the fact that both were crippled by long years in his sawmill. Thumb and forefinger were gone from his left hand, and were entirely without sensation on the right, due to severed nerves at the wrist; yet with these hands he did exquisite cabinet work, and had made, and could play, his violin.

Charlie watched him with interest. He had a cork-stopper fitted into a metal frame, which he slipped over the stump of the left forefinger, and with this stopper he pressed the strings. He had taken off his coat, in the heat of the kitchen, and his full white shirtsleeves were no whiter than his hair and beard, as he bent his head lovingly to his music.

Lines were forming for "jib-along."

Charlie, of course, got Marian as a partner, and there was Graham taking the floor with little Hilda. She looked pretty enough, Hilda — the new dress set well on her. The Ashburns were proud that she should have taken the eye of the somewhat citified young Parks.

Uncle Dan warmed up to the tune, and the couples began moving. Charlie locked elbows with Marian in the figure, and she cried out,

"Oh, this is fun!"

And it was fun. More fun, in a way, than a public dance; more neighborly and intimate and genial. After the "jib-along" there were drop-the-handkerchief, and post-office, and going-to-Jerusalem. They even formed lines again and did a Boston Fancy, something there was seldom space for in a private house. The great old kitchen rocked and echoed with the frolic.

It all had begun well enough for Charlie, but as the games went on, his happy mood was broken. Morris took Marian away from him, and kept her away. Just that in itself was bad enough, but it was also making talk — a thing the Ashburns abhorred, and usually succeeded in avoiding. Now, Elsie was no longer the only one aware of Morris' infatuation. It was written on his face; his whole figure, so lithe and graceful, was eloquent of it. And Charlie saw that Marian was enjoying the party tremendously, and he was sick with jealousy.

However, sulking would do no good, and his interference might possibly stop some of the talk; so he crossed the room to where they were standing. As he neared them, he saw that he must be actually intrusive to gain their attention.

"My God," he muttered to himself, "things have

come to a pretty pass when I want to choke Morris!"

He did not choke his brother, but he did lay a heavy hand on his shoulder.

"Elsie wants ye, in the parlor," he said.

"Huh? Oh — Elsie—" Morris pulled himself back to reality and straightened up to his full height, his tanned face rather flushed. He had probably been to the cider barrel, but it was not all that.

"All right," he said, "I'll get goin'."

Charlie was furious. He had always loved Morris; next to the memory of their mother, Morris had always been the dearest thing in his life. But all that was changing. He could have hated Morris now for neglecting his wife, for making a show of himself, for daring to look with desire on this fragile little girl who seemed to be tearing the Ashburn tribe-loyalty to shreds!

Still it was a good party. Elsie's cake cut well, and so did the many others; the ice cream was rich and smooth, and served heaped in the dishes. The coffee was hot and strong. It was after midnight when they got back home, and the fire Pop had left for them was pretty well died down.

A good party, on the whole; yet the Ashburns separated for the night in somewhat silent constraint. Morris had acted the fool; Elsie was sore; Charlie was angry and jealous; Herb and Alf were puzzled and disturbed and rather embarrassed; Hilda was too sleepy and too ecstatic over the fun she had had to do other than go right to bed.

"It's most mornin'," said Charlie. "I'll chuck the stove full right now. Fire'll still be here for breakfast."

At the church social, later in the week, things got even worse. It was after that social that Charlie and Morris came so near to a serious quarrel.

The "time" was a baked-bean supper in the church vestry. Everyone was there. Horses were hitched outside the church at every hitching post and tree, as well as in the long covered shed. The night was clear, still, and white, with the crisp, dry cold that stimulates more than it chills. The whole town was out, ready for a hot supper and a good time.

Within the vestry, long tables were set, with the Sunday school settees drawn up instead of chairs. It made a good bit of laughter, since every time one person got up or sat down, five others had to move also. But no one minded that.

Nell Simms was there, looking faded and sentimental in a bright plaid dress, and it so happened that she was beside Ben Sparks on the settee. Ben was long, lank, soiled and cynical, lousy with money, everyone said, but snug as the bark to a tree, and a hopeless bachelor. That Nell sat beside him may not have been wholly accidental. Nell was always lookin' around.

Ben settled down to his supper, scooped his knife into the generous, steaming plate of beans, and expertly conveyed the laden blade to his mouth. He didn't spill one.

"Say," he complained, "this bench is too fur from the table. Beans git all cold 'fore I can git 'em to my mouth."

"Well, Ben," shrilled Nell, at his elbow, "what shall we do about it — hitch up?"

"Hi, there," came a hilarious yelp from the end of the table. "What you up to, Nell? Askin' Ben Sparks to hitch up? Gosh!"

Nell reddened, as the joke was passed from that table to the next, and around the vestry, but she was pleased, on the whole. It was a little something, even to be teased about a man!

But all jokes were leaving Charles Ashburn cold that night. It was the same old tangle. Parks and Ashburn getting altogether too thick. Sometime there would be the devil to pay and no pitch hot.

Elsie was on the supper committee, busy with the other women in the corner of the vestry, by the stove. They were ladling out the great bowls full of beans, slicing the round loaves of brown bread, refilling the two big coffee pots that Hilda and another girl were carrying from table to table.

Hilda was hardly as big as the coffee pot she carried, but she managed it well enough, and was laughing like a witch. Graham Parks kept calling her back to where he sat, and Hilda told him tartly that so much coffee was bad for him. He vowed he could drink as many cups as she would pour.

Graham's usually cool gray eyes were warm with amusement and admiration. There was nothing to worry about; Hilda was a child, a little girl; Graham was a decent sort, but a hard-boiled young collegian. His playing with Hilda meant nothing whatsoever, but somehow all this funning reminded Charlie of a yarn his mother used to tell.

It was about her own mother as a child of eleven — Hilda's age. A new schoolmaster was expected, and he was to board around, coming first to this child-grandmother's home. The little girl had shyly hidden behind the door when she heard the young man's horse in the yard, and she had peeked through the crack of the door to see him. She had given one look, and fallen dead in love with him. Her love had never changed or wavered and, not many years later, she married him — he was this little Hilda's grandfather, and Charlie's.

It would never do — Charlie shivered.

Old Polly Maxim, who sent off news items to the Portland papers, had cornered Charlie and was pumping him about the family. How was Gladys gettin' on? and where was Herb at present? Did Alf enjoy his college? and when was he goin' back to Orono? Was it true that Gladys had been terrible sick and they had had a consultation?

"Oh, Lord, no," replied Charlie hastily. "That's all talk. She got on fine. Who told you any different?"

"Oh, I just heard," simpered Polly, and went on endlessly with her nosey questions. And while he was thus hampered, Charlie saw Morris slide into the place on the settee beside Marian Parks, saw Hilda bring him his coffee, pass him the beans and brown bread, the cabbage salad and the pickles. Morris was settled there all right. Marian flashed her eyes at him as she passed him the butter, and Morris took on the blear-eyed, lovesick expression he had worn at the Chadwick Party. Marian seemed to like it. She talked, and laughed, and raised hell generally.

Charlie had come to the vestry normally hungry, but he lost his appetite. Food would have choked him. He got his cap and mackinaw from the nail on the wall and put them on and walked home.

He was still humped over the kitchen stove when the family came home, and he did not move as one by one they eased off to bed. At last only Morris was there, leaning his elbow on the stove shelf and thoughtfully smoking his pipe. The silence between them was thick and ugly. It was Morris who finally broke it.

"What are ye peeved about?" he inquired.

"Hells bells, who says I'm peeved?"

"Humph!"

"Well, if you want to know," admitted Charlie, "I

think it's bad enough for you and Elsie to be livin' apart, without you gettin' yourself talked about with Marian Parks."

Morris raised one eyebrow self-consciously.

"Well, gosh sakes, Charlie, it's nothin' to you. Marian will never think twice about either one of us, and everybody knows it."

"Elsie don't like it."

"Then she can lump it. She gets all she wants out o' me."

"Don't talk like that, Morris. It ain't right."

"And what's that to you? Since when has it been any o' your mix what goes on between Elsie and me?"

Charlie got to his feet and turned away.

"We're both mad," he said. "Let's shut up. Talkin' don't get nowhere, and we might say too much."

There was more silence, in which Morris finished his pipe and rapped the ashes out into the stove, while Charlie stood, back-to, warming himself before going to his frigid room in the shed loft.

Finally Charlie said, as if the words were being dragged out of him: "I've made a fool o' myself over that girl, Morris. Don't you go and do the same. You've got even less right than I have."

"Aw, can your chatter!" rasped Morris.

Charlie turned on him, and they stood eye to eye, glaring.

But the savage glare melted, and they both turned away at once, sheepishly, too much the Yankee to display their love, their deep loyalty.

"Hell, let's get to bed," muttered Charlie.

"Aw, sure. We're a pair o' fools, that's all."

Chapter Nine

The life history of Charles Ashburn might have been a very different matter could the following summer have been omitted from it entirely; if he had even been able to leave home for a while, it might have helped some.

Quite possibly, he would never have forgotten Marian Parks, but at least he would have escaped the consequences of seeing her too often. He would have been able to achieve a more satisfying, normal sort of life; something a little nearer to that dream he had, of a house where gods might dwell, beautiful, entire, and clean.

But he could not go away, any more than he could have dropped for a time into oblivion. He had to stick to his folks, keep right on with his work, and fit in the details of his inner, personal life as best he could.

Matters at home were in pretty much of a mess. All through the winter and spring, the tension, the uneasiness, had gradually, subtly intensified; it had been like a strong, hidden current in the river that broke into turbulent rapids now and then. The Parkses had come home for the Easter recess, and there had been a repetition of the Christmas fracas — Morris lovesick, Elsie jealous, Hilda (with them for the weekend), sparkling with mischief, Graham admiringly responsive — and Charlie, who should have kept his head and laid down the law to ten or a dozen of them, had been actually sick with worry and repressed emotion. It had been a miserable week, but mercifully short.

Spring plowing and planting, and the exacting task of caring for the incubators, with their seething befeathered new life, left little time for Charlie to tear his shirt over love affairs; but with the coming of summer and the return of the college students, with the long, mellow evenings, the church socials, and the dances, things tightened up once more.

Marian had always liked the old-fashioned contra-dances, which she had never seen until the previous summer, when she had learned them with Charlie. She asked Tom Giles questions about them — wanted to know how and when and where they had originated; how long they had been danced to the same tunes he played for them; but Tom had been able to tell her little. He was an old man, and he had played those same tunes, called those same figures, for forty-odd years. That was all he knew. Green Mountain Volunteers was Marian's favorite. Its rollicking rhythm and abandon made it almost as much an athletic stunt as a dance. Marian usually laughed aloud over the figure she liked best — one column of couples whirling in the balance-and-swing, while the other stampeded off in a vigorous promenade.

How the girl could dance! She fell into the swing of it as if she had been born and raised in the hills, alive from head to heels with sheer love of motion and tempo, and evidently regarding Charlie for the most part as the obliging owner of a rugged arm to support her, and a pair of agile feet to keep pace with her own.

He sometimes wondered how she could be so indifferent to him; how she could notice him at all without knowing his state of mind — or lack of it! She was no fool. She must know that he was in love with her. Yet from her manner — her cool little-girlishness — he could have sworn she did not know.

Sometimes, that summer, she let him walk home with her. She loved to walk, and it was but a scant mile to Henry's. Charlie always made sure first that Hilda was under the wing of either Alf or Morris; he wouldn't have her gallivanting around nights with Graham Parks. And at first it had seemed as if seeing Marian home might be his own best bet. Local etiquette allowed him at least a good-night kiss, without question or obligation. But it was no use.

Marian would walk beside him, her shoulder sometimes brushing against him, or her hand grasping his as she stumbled over a rut, but he could not touch her. He never knew just why, but it couldn't be done. Even at her doorstep, when he would draw a deep breath and get ready to reach for her, she would say "good-night" and go into the house.

If he had seized and kissed her, she could have done no more than get mad, and any man ought to be able to laugh that off. But still, he never tried it.

As the weeks passed, he thought he would make an end of the whole business — after one more dance! No man with a real spine running up his back would go on and on, dancing with a girl, seeing her home, paying out his hard-earned cash for her ice cream, and not get so much as a kiss in return. But always, he put off the break.

He would have just one more evening with her — the years ahead would be long and empty!

But the affair kept Charlie in misery and suspense. After he had said good-night to her, and she had gone into the house and shut the door, he would tramp down the mountain side from the Parks place, and climb up the opposite hill to his own; and he would cool off some, thinking oh, well, he hadn't made it this time, but there was always the next. If he could get her in his arms and kiss her just one single time, then he would be able to quit. With other girls, he had always found that once was enough; after that he had always been completely fed up with them. He had only to try again, and watch his step. If he didn't get her too mad right at first, he could kiss her, get even with her to that extent for making a fool of him, and then he would forever let her alone.

Elsie was even more fussy that summer than she had been back along. Jealous, yes — but somehow it did not seem to be Morris' passion for Marian that made her so. She regarded that with a measure of scornful interest. She seemed to have scant hope that Morris would ever get along without making a show of himself. It was Charlie's state of mind that seemed the controlling influence over her own. It was Charlie that she watched, and fussed over.

He was later than usual in getting home one night. The moon was full, and Marian had been tantalizing as the devil; she had lingered on the porch, laughing and talking a blue streak, but each time he had got up his nerve to lay hands on her, she had held him off somehow. Why he had let her get away with it, he did not know; and after she had gone in, he had sat for some time on a fence rail, trying to study it out. If she didn't like him, why should she go with him so much? Probably her being younger had much to do with it. Kid fashion, she didn't look ahead and figure things out; she just acted on impulse, and that impulse told her that she would better not go too far with Charles Ashburn, since she would never want to pay the price of having to marry him.

When he let himself into the darkened house, he heard a rumbling snore from Pop's room, and a step overhead that told him Elsie was not asleep yet. She and Morris, Alf and Hilda, must have been in for some time. Why wasn't she quiet? Somehow, Elsie and her doings worried him all the time lately. He wondered if she had been listening to find out how late he stayed with Marian.

He got a drink from the kitchen pump, and as he turned away from the sink, he saw a glass of milk on the table, and a big slice of cake on a plate beside it. That was something new. Usually he went to the buttery for a snack if he wanted it before he turned in, but this time Elsie had left it out for him. Fussing over him again! He ate the cake and drank the milk, but he didn't like to be fussed over. "Damn it all, why can't she let me alone!" he muttered, as he stumped up the back stairs to his room in the loft.

Elsie had been changing in many ways. That was only natural. Nobody could expect her to keep forever the fleeting grace and freshness of girlhood. But as she grew older, and more settled down, there seemed to be nothing to take the place of that girlhood — nothing of dignity, or deepening intelligence, or increased broad-mindedness. She was accepted in the community as one of its solid, respected, dependable women. She could do things well, was mistress of a substantial household, and, as such, her time was pretty well filled with activity, of course. Her habitual silence was not that of formality, much less of curtness or unfriendliness. She merely had nothing much to say, and said it.

Vaguely, almost unconsciously, certainly without clearly formulated criticism or comment, Charlie understood what was taking place in the development of the mature Elsie. Her mind had reached its peak. She was not stupid, exactly, but she had grown intellectually just about as far as was possible to her. She was meagerly educated; she was totally without religion; she was strong and healthy in body, steady of nerve, methodical and capable in all things. What was left for her, by way of growth and change and variety of experience, except the emotions?

Routine makes up the most of every life. But routine must be leavened by something outside itself — some progressive and satisfying interest to give it meaning. For Elsie, there were the household and the two children — progressive, to be sure; but in her inmost, personal life there was a need. Morris did not satisfy it. His love for her did not grow with the years. Her love for him had been that of a normal young girl for a good matrimonial prospect. Their marriage was not holding up well, and the more emotional aspect of marriage was all poor Elsie had for color, variety, and intimate satisfaction.

This trouble was in no wise peculiar to her. Some women expend the fulness of mature womanhood upon their children; some, upon fanatical housekeeping, or a special handiwork; some find refuge and fulfilment in church work. Many indulge in poor health, either with physical ills as excuse, or without; well-educated women can read, or sing, or play an instrument of some sort; women with money can travel, and dress, and go to parties. For Elsie, nothing was left to absorb her naturally increasing energies and emotions but those very emotions themselves.

And if, lacking other expression, she flashed out sometimes in bursts of ill temper, it was not to be wondered at.

Things might even have been easier if anyone had flashed back at her. There would have been excitement, at least. But there was no one to scrap with. Pop was simply too lazy and amiably tolerant to answer back; the children knew when to keep out of the way — and really Elsie was not often crabbed; Morris could turn anybody from wrath by his keen yet gentle wit; and Charlie, while he might be boiling inside, would not express himself. Like the children, he knew when to clear out.

So, between Morris and Elsie there was no quarrel, no ill feeling; just an ever more encroaching indifference. They talked together, when Morris came home, only to settle some matter concerning the children or their simple finances; they shared the big south chamber, more from force of habit and because the house was crowded than from desire. And if, in Elsie's large brown eyes, there was at times a smoldering of discontent, or restless yearning, it was not directed toward Morris, and he did not see it.

But Pop did. Little escaped those keen, pale, deep-set Ashburn eyes; and when, sometime in July, Morris bought a bicycle and took to coming home oftener, it was only Pop who had any special comment to offer.

"Good thing you've took to comin' home more," he said. "Elsie needs ye."

"Elsie? Pshaw — she never misses me any," replied Morris easily. "But I guess, at that, it won't do her any harm to get out with me some — go to dances and times and like that."

"Sure. Dress her up an' take her around. Women like it. Keeps 'em contented, out o' mischief."

But Morris' plan of action was soon plain enough. He dutifully took his wife to dances, and, according to local custom, was her partner for the first three, the two intermissions and the last numbers. But the rest of the time he devoted, first, to several dances with Marian Parks, and then to the crowd in the men's room. He did not drink much, to be sure, and he always came back steady enough for the "Home, Sweet Home" with Elsie; but after those few dances with Marian, he had no interest in anything but the jug which inebriated without especially cheering him.

It disgusted Charlie. Drinking seemed to him a nasty habit, having no place in a decent life. And he pitied Elsie, sitting there with the women and the babies on the bench. He danced with her while Morris was with Marian, but it was slow going. She was getting heavy-footed, and she had a way of clinging to him, possessively, which he did not like at all.

The Ashburn tribe was getting altogether too deep into the muddle; hard work and economizing were easy enough to stand; it was the threat of shame, the suggestion of things that might best be hidden, that got under Charlie's skin.

One hot August night, Marian made things worse by appearing in a dress with a lot of ruffles about the feet and nothing much about the shoulders. Like a picture in a magazine. Charlie had never danced with such a dress before.

"Great scot!" he exclaimed, as his hand touched her naked shoulder blade, "what kind o' clothes do ye call that?"

"This?" Marian looked up, surprised. "Why, it's just an old thing I'm trying to get the wear out of."

"I don't like it."

"No? Shall I stop wearing it because of that?"

"Yes. You'd better."

That cool bare flesh had set him on fire. It wasn't quite fair for Marian to wear such a dress here at Henry's, but she seemed perfectly innocent about it.

A little later, Morris came along for his usual turn with Marian, and Charlie crossed over to sit on the bench beside Elsie. He did not want to dance. There was plenty of room on the bench, but Elsie moved close to him and rested her hand on his knee. Her fingers warmed and clung.

"Charlie, ain't that dress o' Marian Parks' the limit? Ye can see her whole backbone."

"Spose ye can, if you're interested," he admitted.

"Has Morris had a drink yet?"

"No. Not as I know of."

"I should say he'd had several," observed Elsie maliciously.

Charlie had been trying not to watch that couple, not to fret himself, not to be jealous, but now he looked to see what was riling Elsie.

No wonder she was sore! Morris and Marian had just waltzed by them, and Morris was plainly far more befuddled than hard cider ever got him. He was holding Marian close, her little brown head almost resting against his chest. He was bending over her, his half-closed eyes seeing nothing but that soft hair, that smooth cheek, rather more flushed than usual. Marian was annoyed. She was not enjoying this; Morris' ardor was getting too obvious, even for her innocency.

At last the music stopped and Charlie went to her.

"Go back to your own wife," he said to Morris in a gruff aside. "See if ye can't treat her decent for once."

"You go to hell!"

"You'll be there ahead o' me!"

Fighting with Morris again — going at each other like a pair of roosters—

"I would have danced with him longer, Charlie," protested Marian, "if it would keep him from drinking."

"That's good of ye, Marian, but it's no use. You don't need to be bothered about it."

Marian did not reply, but looked up at him soberly. She knew Morris was foolish about her, and she was worried.

The music began again, and Charlie took her close to himself now. It was his turn. Though not so tall as Morris, he too could look down at the top of her head, and his broad hand completely covered her tiny one. Probably Morris felt the same way — probably he, too, would have loved to take the girl up in his arms and travel — keep on going until everything familiar was left behind, keep on going until—

"Charlie — don't—" She was pulling away from him, and he came abruptly back to earth. They stood apart.

"Don't what? Did I hurt ye?"

She went to the open window and leaned against the frame, staring outside and twisting her hands together. Charlie waited. She was not going to answer him, but if she thought he would go away, she could think again.

Finally she spoke to him.

"I think there will be thunder," she said, "the sky seems so dark."

"Likely," said Charlie. "Well, we need rain. Hope it comes good and plenty."

The summer passed, and the day came when Charlie told himself, "It's the end. Tomorrow she will be gone."

He had, to his own astonishment, made a date to take

her riding on that last night. He had hired a team from the livery stable — their own old moth-eaten plug wouldn't do at all and a crazy sort of hope kept nagging at him. All his commonsense resolution would not put it down. He had seen her home a good many times, without ever getting a kiss or a tender word; but surely a ride in the moonlight would mean something, even to her.

It was a wonderful night, clear, mellow, brilliant, with the scent of ripening corn and apples in the air. Marian wore a dark cloak with a fur collar and no sleeves — sort of a cape, Charlie thought; and as he helped her into the buggy, his hand slipped through an opening in the side of the cape and touched her bare arm. As he took his place beside her, he saw that she had thrust her hands through these openings, and they lay white and small on her lap. Her face was white, too, in the moonlight, and softly framed in the fur and her own hair. He would kiss her tonight if it proved to be the last thing he ever did! She must be expecting it, or she wouldn't have come anyhow.

Gay and light-hearted, she sang as they rolled along the woods road, the sound of hoofs and wheels deadened by the matted pine needles in the sand. And she talked and laughed, about everything under the sun. When they passed Half-Moon Pond, like a silver sheet, she recited a poem, something about a "lake in the cool northern country, where I was happy, once, long ago!"

Happy! Charlie thought of the one other poem he knew, and of those words, "beautiful, entire, and clean." There was nothing ugly or unclean in his life as yet, but this girl was making a great, ragged hole in it, with her leaving tomorrow! Nothing entire except the hopelessness of everything. He ached all over.

Marian stopped singing after a while, and sat quiet.

He could think of nothing to say. And after all the cash he was paying out for this rig, there was a loose bolt in the buggy — it rattled some. The reins fell slack in his hands, and the horse, an old hand at this game, plodded slowly, nibbling leaves from the underbrush beside the road, now and then.

A mile or so beyond Half-Moon Pond, they came to the clearing under the big oak which marked the turn-off to the Falls. The sound of rushing water reached them, and the horse knowingly headed in the narrow, grass-grown side road. In the clearing, he stopped and fell to feeding. Across a deep gully, down the face of the opposite cliff, roared the Falls, all tumbling silver in the moonlight.

Charlie's hands shook as he wrapped the reins around the whip socket.

"It's lovely!" exclaimed Marian. "Will the horse stand, Charlie? We could watch the Falls a while."

"Sure, he'll stand. He's used to standin' here."

Marian laughed. "Oh, here's where you always bring your girls, is it?"

"Hell, no. I never brought a girl here in my life."

"You needn't swear about it. It won't make me any more likely to believe you."

"I didn't ask ye to believe me — it's just the truth, that's all."

Marian seemed lost in the beauty of the Falls, still and motionless beside him, as placid and content as Charlie was turbulent. That loose bolt in the buggy rattled again, and Charlie knew that he was shaking. Like a hot chill, it was. And there sat the girl, all taken up with the roaring of the water and the flood of moonlight, hardly remembering that he was with her. In a sudden fury, he seized her, held her tight against him. She had teased him long enough — she would have to take her medicine now—

For one short, dizzy moment he really thought she was yielding. He really believed that she had turned toward him as she gave a trembling, almost soundless gasp that was more of willingness than of protest. But it did not last. She kept her head, and she was too strong for him — stronger somehow than his iron muscle. She pulled free, and he felt her cool soft fingers loosen his own hands and lay them back in his lap, where they belonged.

"There," she said quietly, "that's much nicer, Charlie — much better manners, really."

By the eternal, she wasn't even mad! Just a thousand miles away from him, that was all. She couldn't or wouldn't play the game. She didn't even know what it was all about.

Speechless, Charlie unwound the reins from the whip socket and took out the whip, laying it unmercifully across the horse's back. The horse jumped and reared, but Charlie held him firmly in, raising the whip again. Marian grasped his wrist.

"No," she ordered, "no. Don't take it out on the horse. If you must whip someone, it should be me."

The fury ran out of him, and he looked down into her little white face, at the slim hand on his wrist. Why he should heed her was beyond him. There seemed to be a wall around her that he could neither climb over nor break through.

"By godfrey," he said, "you do need a good lickin'."

Weeks later, when she had gone, and he was settled again into doing the fall work to the tune of the summer's music, he remembered her moment of yielding — recalled what she had said, "Don't take it out on the horse!" Innocent, indifferent as she usually seemed, she was not unfeeling. She had understood what ailed him. Experienced, probably!

"The damned little flirt," he muttered. "Just likes to see a feller squirm, I guess."

Well, if she stirred all men as she did him, she must have plenty of amusement!

Chapter Ten

It was fall again – time for getting in the corn and apples and garden truck, time for cutting the hemlock banking for the house, for putting on the storm windows, for unpacking the woolens, time for tightening up generally, anticipating the cold to come, time for fires at night.

Something about it made Charles Ashburn lonely – lonely in a way the likes of which he had never felt before. The uneasy premonition that things were out of whack, and that they would be considerably worse before they were any better, was growing on him steadily. It seemed as if he really would have to strike out, and strike hard; yet he could not tell in just what direction to strike.

No use to get mad. No use to tear things loose. He was in love; he might just as well accept that and stand it the best he could. Nothing could be done to stop it; nothing would ever satisfy it. The cards had been dealt, and that was the hand he held. He had to play it out, and naturally he would try to play fair and square. No use to fuss.

He had been thinking along this way for several days that fall, and at the same time he had been giving some sort of attention to the work at hand. There were the pumpkins and squashes – he decided to get those in on a Saturday so he could take Young Morris with him. Little Elsie too, maybe; but it was the boy he thought of particularly. It was good for the youngster to learn how to do things, and to feel that he was useful, even though Charlie was always careful not to crowd him.

The boy was a chip off the old block – a true Morris Ashburn, tall and thin for his age, with white skin and black hair, and those small, keen, colorless eyes that saw things with an almost unchildlike coolness and detachment.

Little Elsie was different – a pretty child, small, round, and very feminine, with light brown curls and large brown eyes like her mother's. Her little red mouth drooped at the corners, and it worried Charlie some until, as the child grew and developed, he observed that her mother's chin had not been handed on to her – that Dennis chin that seemed so undecisive until some emotion or crisis revealed it to be downright stubborn. With a little encouragement, Little Elsie would have been a laughing, sunny-natured child; and Charlie and Morris, in their habitual unspoken agreement, did their best to supply the gaiety and spontaneous happiness which the mother so sadly lacked.

Young Morris had helped Charlie with the chores from the time he was big enough to walk alone, fetching and carrying willingly enough; and when she got big enough the girl child went with them, riding to Gag Corner on errands whenever Uncle Charlie went, snuggling on top of a load of hay, driving the cows to and from the pasture, or gathering eggs in small tin pails while Uncle Charlie carried a big one. Morris strutted with pride to feel that he was a man about the place, and Elsie, though silent, was always responsive to attention, her little three-cornered mouth readily lifting into a smile.

For Charlie, it was a good companionship, stimulating and satisfying, and as he went from one job to the other, in this getting ready for winter, he wondered if the children were comfortable – if Elsie had given thought to their winter clothes; if they would need new coats, and overshoes. Of course their mother was attending to all that. He had to hand her that much – she was always careful of the children. But Charlie would have liked to take more part in that care. That was the truth – he really wished he had children of his own, a wife of his own.

Well, since he didn't have, he could at least get some happiness with things as they were. He really loved these children, and had much else, too, to make him content. No use to fuss.

The day for getting in the pumpkins turned out to be cold – so cold that the ground was hard and the atmosphere thick and still with the threat of snow.

"Looks like an early winter," Pop remarked at breakfast.

"You never can tell," Charlie answered. "We'll be havin' a spell o' summer yet."

"Yep, I spose so." Pop tipped his chair back on two legs and hooked his thumbs in the armholes of his shabby vest. "Indian summer. Best time o' the year. We'll have it. Always do. By mighty, I've talked with men, in my lifetime, from a good many parts o' the country. Men from Canada, men from down south somewheres; you know – they drift by us every once in so often.

"Yes, they do for a fact." Charlie tipped his chair

back too. Pop didn't often talk, but when he did, it was well to listen. Elsie got up and began clearing the table right under their noses. She had her work to 'tend to – she had no time for conversation.

The fire was hot in the kitchen stove; the fragrance of the coffee and bacon and brown, crusty biscuits mingled with the reek of the beans that Elsie had set on to parboil. Funny how that smell of beans cooking would change during the day – plagued unpleasant in the morning, but rich and enticing toward night, when the flavors of the pork and mustard and molasses were getting well baked in, and a man was feeling tired and hungry.

The children sat back quietly. They had been taught to be seen and not heard, and they always wondered what their Grandpop might say when he got started.

It wasn't so much this time. "I've talked with men from all parts o' the country," he repeated, "and I never yet met up with one that didn't call October the best time o' the year, in his particular home state."

"Guess you're right," said Charlie. "I've never been out o' this state, and probably never will be. October's a good month, though. Sky's generally pretty."

Suddenly Young Morris spoke up.

"I like sky," he announced. "I like it when it looks deep. I like to keep right on lookin' up, when it's so deep you can't see the end of it."

"Well," said Elsie, "you can't see far today without comin' to the end. Get your things on, Morrie, and fill the wood box. Elsie, you be wipin' these dishes. If you want to go with Uncle Charlie you have to get your work done first."

That broke up the group around the table, but Charlie went out to the chicken runs with a good feeling inside him. Pop was that way. In a few insignificant words, he had given the world a brighter look, even on so threatening a day; had set Charlie and Young Morris, at least, to thinking of things deeper than the daily round of chores.

Yet what was the fall season but a part of the daily round of Nature's chores? It just depended on what was in the mind of each person looking on, whether the season was fair or mean. Take Old Man Stafford, for instance. Charlie had driven up there one day to buy a bushel of onions. He had had a failure of onions that year, for some reason – had planted them in a new place that didn't work out so good. So he had bought of Stafford, who was famous for his onion crop, year after year. Stafford lived way up on the mountain, and getting the old blind horse and the wagon up there was considerable of a tussle. But once there, it seemed worth the bother, on account of the view. You could see clear to Mount Washington, and follow the course of the river for miles; could even see the river shining in spots, here and there. Somehow, as you got to Stafford's place, and turned to look back, that view would hit you right in the eye. It was almost too much to believe. It made you think of God, and things like that. Well, on that day when Charlie had gone to get the bushel of onions, he had seen Old Man Stafford coming out of the barn, with a measure of grain crooked in his arm, and so he had waited right where he was until the old man came toward him. And all the while, Charlie had been taking in that view, and wondering what it must be to live right with it, year after year. Stafford had been there all his life – had been born there sixty-odd years ago, and never went off the place unless he had to. He hadn't even had to go courting his wife, it was said – she had come there to work for his mother, and had been willing enough to marry the son and stay right on. On that day Stafford had come toward Charlie with dignity and deliberation, and had said a brief "How are ye?"

"So's to be about," Charlie had replied. "Nice view ye got here."

"Think so?" Stafford had said. "Well, folks say 'tis. Can't say I ever noticed it."

Onions – Charlie had got his onions and gone home. But he had got more than the onions. He had seen so plainly just how much a man depended on his own state of mind for enjoyment in life. Stafford could have had that good feeling of exaltation any day in the week by just opening his eyes to the view, but he'd never done it. And his doing it wouldn't have hurt the onion crop a bit either!

Oh, well!

There came young Morris, wearing two sweaters, and overalls, tucked into the high boots he was so fond of, and an old cap pulled low over his head. Elsie'd seen to it the boy was done up warm. It was a pity that Little Elsie, trotting behind her brother, couldn't wear overalls too. But she had her black knitted leggings pulled up over her skirts and modestly covered by her last winter's coat. The coat was too small now, but the child's sweater underneath was pulled down over her wrists to meet her mittens. That was all right. Charlie never could bear to see a child with a red, chapped piece of bare wrist exposed, and likely enough he had said the same to Elsie more than once. At any rate, the kids looked comfortable for their day's work.

Charlie finished up at the henhouses and together they harnessed the old horse to the light wagon. Morris climbed up and took the reins, and Charlie lifted Little

Elsie. Then he put a wheelbarrow in the wagon bed. The pumpkins and squashes had been planted between the hills of sweet corn, which had gone to the corn shop weeks ago. Now there was just the stubble, dry and brown, and the wilted vines, and the great globes of yellow, and the crooked green squashes on the frozen grounds. They must get the crop all in today. Another cold night would be too much.

Morris kept his place for a while, and Charlie let him think it was necessary for someone to drive the old horse along the edge of the field. But after a time the boy got chilly and left the wagon, to help gather the smaller pumpkins into the wheelbarrow. Elsie did more looking on than anything else. That was all right. A little girl needed to learn things inside the house, but outside she might learn or not, as she chose.

"Leave that squash for me, Morris," Charlie admonished. "You've no business liftin' such a big one."

"I wish I could. Do you think I'll be as strong as you, Uncle Charlie?"

"Some day, most likely."

"Think I'll be tall as you?"

"Taller, like your Pa. Like your Grandpop. Tall, skinny. Strong, though."

"Teacher says drinkin' hard cider an' smokin' an' chewin' will keep a feller from growin'."

"Teacher's right. Want to pay 'tention to what she says. That's what ye go to school for."

"Well, Uncle Charlie, my Pa used to go to school, didn't he?"

"Oh, sure. He an' I went some. Had to quit, though, an' git to work on the farm." Charlie had never regretted this for himself, but often he had wished Morris could have kept on.

Young Morris was fixed on a certain topic.

"Well, my Pa, he must've quit when he was younger than me."

"How so? Seems to me he an' I went to school until we was bigger'n you are."

"Well, if my Pa had gone to school long enough, he'd have learned not to drink hard cider, wouldn't he?"

Charlie straightened up and looked at the boy. Elsie had cocked up her head and was listening. Evidently the two of them had discussed this before, and were set on getting an answer. Youngsters did beat all! Charlie sat down on a big pumpkin and thought it over. Morris the Fourth surely ought to get wise to himself and realize that his children had an eye on him.

Little Elsie stood close to his knee, and Charlie had to chuckle over her solemn expression, even while he was puzzling over an answer that would fill the bill.

"I tell ye what," he said at last, "you see, your Pa was gittin' so tall, he thought he might as well do somethin' to stop it. And sure enough, he hasn't grown an inch since he began drinkin' a little bit o' hard cider now an' then."

Elsie was satisfied, but not Young Morris. He said nothing, but in the Ashburn eyes there was a look of scorn for so slim an excuse, and Charlie had to do something about it. It would be a pity for these children to see their father as less than perfect – just yet, at any rate. He was a good sort of fellow, Morris the Fourth, but he had his failings. The children would be bound to see them as the years went by, but they must learn to love their father for the good in him and to minimize the weaknesses, just as the whole tribe had always done toward Pop.

Charlie drew Elsie to his lap and hugged her; no such show of affection was possible between him and the boy,

The Old Ashburn Place

but a little girl could be fussed over some without having her dignity outraged. In fact, she liked it, and she rubbed her soft face against Uncle Charlie's rough one. She seldom spoke.

"Well, Youngster," said Charlie to the scornful Ashburn standing there among the pumpkins, "you've never seen your Pa with too much aboard, now have ye?"

"No. I guess not."

"You take notice, and you'll see that he never takes too much. I wish he never touched it, but, take it by an' large, you could have a sight worse feller for a Pa than he is, now couldn't ye? Always good to ye. Always brings home money so's your Ma can pay the bills. Never gets hateful or ugly. And fun! By gory, we do have fun at home, now don't we?"

"Yep." Young Morris nodded his head, satisfied for the time being.

"I'm hungry," said Elsie. "Let's go get dinner."

Charlie set her on the ground and fished out the big nickel watch that he carried in his overall pocket, attached to the shoulder strap by a piece of heavy twine. Sure enough, it was eleven-thirty. Dinner would be hot on the table by the time they got back, and had put the horse up, and had taken off their things and washed.

There were a few of the pumpkins and two squashes yet lying around, so they made quick work of the loading and then went home.

As they drove into the yard, Pop unfolded himself from the roll-way door there in the sunny corner of the L and squinted appraisingly at their load.

"Guess ye got enough to last," he said. "Look pretty good, don't they? Watch out ye don't let none of 'em rest touchin' the cellar wall."

"I'll tend to 'em." Charlie had given Pop that

125

assurance once each fall, as far back as he could remember. He had never really believed that anything would freeze in the farthest room of the cellar, even if it did touch the wall; but every year he saw to it that there was the insulation of space, or sand, or sacking between that outer wall and the vegetables stored next to it. Some folks had to leave a lantern burning in their storerooms on the coldest nights, but the cellar at the Ashburn place was deep and well built.

Pop opened the roll-way doors, and Young Morris backed the old horse around so that the wagon stood handy to the cellar steps. Then he got down, wrapped the reins up over the hames, unhooked the traces and hold-backs, and led the horse to the barn, stopping at the trough for water. He liked doing this. Standing on tiptoe, he could unharness entirely and hang the rigging on its peg in the barn; he could turn the horse into the box stall and pitch down a forkful of hay, which would be enough until the night feeding of grain.

Dinner tasted good. It was a sort of pick-up meal, since Elsie had been baking all the morning, and scrubbing and cleaning up generally. They had some baked potatoes and fried salt pork, and slabs of cheese, and a big plate of warm, sugared doughnuts, and of course the pot of strong, bitter tea. Pop liked that tea "stout enough to rise right out o' the cup."

Elsie had let the children keep on most of their wraps, since they were going right out again. The kitchen was warm and pleasant with the odors of cooking – the spice of pies and cookies, the hot fat in which the doughnuts had been fried, the steam from the beans and brown bread that would be ready for supper, the appetizing smell of the salt pork scraps.

Elsie was rather quiet, as always, but good-humored

right now. She had evidently accomplished much, having the house to herself all the forenoon, and when she was feeling satisfied she was nice enough.

"I read somethin' in the paper last night," she remarked. "Blest if I could see what it was all about. Somethin' about food values, it was. I read it all through, but it struck me if you just eat what comes off the place, right along, you get everything."

"Teacher said something like that," Young Morris cut in.

"Guess you've been listenin' to that teacher plenty," Charlie said. "Does she ever mention readin' and sums?"

"Yep. Course she does."

"Well, I do'know," said Elsie. "Seems-so they mention a good many things I never heard of when I went to school. Food values – Humph – "

"Now keep your shirt on, Elsie," remonstrated Pop, mildly. "Think o' them Sandy-Landers down by the river. Good fields down there, best in the township, maybe. And what do they raise? Nothin' but more kids."

"Kids look like grass that's grown up under the woodpile – white, sickly," Charlie assented. "Spose they raised what they could, if they wasn't so damned lazy. Raised it, and cooked it, and ate it. Maybe their kids would look more like these."

As he rose from the table, Charlie gently pinched Little Elsie's cheek, and watched the color come flooding back into it. Good, sound, firm flesh, smooth and pink. Good food, good warm clothes, long nights of sleep. That was what children needed.

After dinner, they all pitched in to store away the morning's harvest. They took the wheelbarrow down cellar and passed the big luscious gourds from the wagon, down the stone steps of the roll-way, and loaded them on the wheelbarrow. Then Charlie shoved each barrow load back, through the main part of the cellar, into the frost-proof storeroom.

That storeroom was always a beautiful sight in the winter, packed full with the fruits of fields and orchard – cabbages, root-crops, apples; barrels of salt pork and of cider; crocks of pickles and mincemeat; two swing-shelves suspended from the overhead rafters and laden with glass jars and jelly tumblers, all neatly labeled and dated. Elsie was a good housekeeper, and both Pop and Charlie were watchful that she had plenty to do with. The Ashburns would not skimp their women-folks.

Ben Sparks, now, was a skinflint. He was well fixed, but he made that old aunt that kept house for him can all her fruit without sugar, and put in the sugar when the jars were opened for use. That way, there was a minimum of waste in case a jar went bad. There wasn't much risk about Elsie's canning, anyhow; she was careful.

The day went well enough. The stint of work was completed; the chores were finished off; Morris the Fourth came home in time for supper; it was settling in cold, with sure promise of a freeze, so Pop and Young Morris filled the wood box full and the routine of baths was got through with early.

A good day, all told; and yet, at the close of it, Charlie felt let down and gloomy. Elsie asked him what was the matter, and he said nothing was the matter. It made him mad that she should notice. What business was it of hers? Couldn't he even sit and think without her having something to say? Probably she even knew what he was thinking about – knew the constant gnawing hunger of his heart, the spasmodic and almost savage restlessness and rebellion which he put to it to conceal. Elsie was dumb, and no mistake, but sometimes it seemed as if she knew his state of mind and resented it.

"Steppin' tonight?" Morris asked, as he settled back on the big sofa with his after-supper pipe.

"Nope. Turnin' in," replied Charlie.

"Got in a good crop o' pie timber, today," Pop reported.

"Apples?"

"Pun'kins."

Morris blew out a long, comfortable puff of smoke and blinked his eyes dreamily. Elsie cleared away all litter of daytime activities and brought her stocking basket and sat close under the lamp, mending. Pop rather indifferently flapped about the pages of the daily paper and occasionally adjusted his glasses and read a line or so. Then he would take the glasses off entirely and really read a whole paragraph, perhaps. Charlie believed that those glasses were worthless; probably Pop's eyes were better than most people's anyhow, and certainly he could read better without the glasses than with them; yet there they always were, on the window sill by the rocking chair, and if by any chance they were mislaid, the whole tribe had to hunt until they were replaced. "Can't read a word unless my specs are right there where I can reach 'em," Pop always maintained.

Saturday night, it was. Just a few weeks ago, Charlie had been with Marian Parks. He closed his eyes now and thought back to the summer nights, warm and full of soft sounds and fragrances. He recalled the music and the motion of the dance hall; Marian, alive in the curve of his arm, her hair shining in the lamplight, her little hand warm and content in his.

Charlie drew a deep breath and shivered as he opened his eyes again and brought his mind back to the present. Elsie was watching him furtively.

Morris rose to put another chunk of wood in the stove and to refill his pipe, and while his back was turned, Elsie muttered,

"You can't tell me nothin's wrong with you, Charlie."

"Gosh sakes, I'm all right!"

Elsie just looked at him, her big brown eyes saying that she knew better, that she knew what ailed him, and would do her best to make him happy –

Morris came back to his place on the sofa; Elsie took up her darning again; Charlie rose and yawned and stretched himself.

"Guess I'll hit the hay," he said.

He lighted his small hand lamp, and with a gruff good-night, he left the warm, hospitable kitchen, crossed the woodshed and climbed the back stairs to his room.

It was cold there, but it was a fresh, clean sort of cold. The lamp threw his shadow grotesquely on the low gabled ceiling. The room was neat and comfortable enough. There was straw matting on the floor, a clean, bright patchwork quilt on the narrow iron bed; the one full-sized window at the end of the room had just the plain shade, which he seldom had to lower, for he shared Pop's contempt for draperies, and this room could not be seen from anywhere outside. The other window, a single sash hung with hinges close under the eaves, had not even a shade. An old-fashioned dresser stood against the wall opposite the larger window, which was the only space big enough for it; a small table for the lamp, a rocking chair, and a compact iron-framed washstand completed the furnishings. Charlie had an oil heater that he could bring up if he chose to, but it seldom seemed worth while.

Now, he quickly undressed, blew out the lamp, and

got into bed. The clean, smooth sheets felt good, and he thought he might be tired enough to go right to sleep. But he wasn't. Or maybe it was that second cup of tea he had taken at supper. Sometimes it did seem to keep him awake. He turned over a dozen times, and punched his pillow around different ways, but it was no use. He couldn't get to sleep. So as a last resort, he got out of bed, wrapped a quilt around him, put on his shoes, and pulled the chair over by the larger window.

It was nice there. Cold, very dark, but fresh and still. Charlie leaned his elbows on the window sill and his chin on his hands. He would have cut quite a figure sitting there wrapped up like an old woman in the quilt, crouching and doing nothing but think. But he was absolutely unselfconscious, and it was dark, and there was nobody there to see him anyhow.

Yes, he was in love all right, and with a girl who never, under any possible circumstances, would marry him. That was tough, but it had to be borne.

How best to bear it, how best to make the most of the situation, and get some happiness out of life in spite of it – that was what he had to think over, and keep thinking over until he got somewhere with the problem. Probably the best way would be to get married. Then, with a wife and some children of his own, he could just not think so much about Marian Parks, not let his memory dwell on her. Living a normal life in every way, he would be comfortable and finally content. Live to be an old man most likely, and all this unrest would be worn out and forgotten. Suppose he did marry – what would the rest of the family do? Elsie, of course, would take the children and go to live somewhere with Morris, and that would be a good thing.

Elsie was an all-right sort of woman. He had to do

her justice. She wasn't even so bad to look at, though she wasn't improving any with the years. If only she hadn't taken to fussing over him this way, he would have kept right on being rather fond of her, accepting her without complaint or question as an agreeable part of his daily routine. But she had been for some time, he realized, gradually spoiling all that.

If Morris had been at home more, or had been more interested in Elsie when he was at home, it would have helped. His attitude of kindly and gentle tolerance was a mask for his indifference. He did not love Elsie any more; he did not dislike her; he showed no evidence of wishing to be free of her. His interest was in the children, and in a sort of inner life which he lived during the days and nights he spent apart from the family. All that ought to be changed, and maybe would be, if Charlie got himself a wife, and Morris and Elsie set up housekeeping, making that branch of the Ashburn tribe a coherent and united whole.

But who in time could Charlie bring himself to marry?

He thought about Nell Simms. The years were using Nell kindly; she was just about the same as she always had been, colorless, quiet, and capable, still living with her mother in the little story-and-a-half white house down the road, still working out for the neighbors in time of need, still very plainly yearning for matrimony. Why not?

Plenty of reasons why not, the main one being that Nell bored Charlie to the point of murder. Yes sir – probably most of the gruesome and morbid crimes committed in such backwoods places as this were the results of boredom – of people getting so unbearably on each other's nerves, with so little of variety and outside interest to relieve the friction, that reason gave way under the strain. Charlie could understand how it might be, and he had no mind to let himself in for a long life of constant irritation. Nell would be a nice housekeeper, but with her there would be no solace of companionship.

He thought of Maud Ripley. Maud would have him – he was pretty sure of that. She was not a yearner like Nell, but she probably would take any decent man with a good farm and honorable intentions, and her genuine liking for Charlie was unmistakable. It had been so since they were children in the school back of the mountain.

Maud was a strapping, handsome girl, with loud, free manners, Hail-fellow-well-met, and a notably good housekeeper here in a community where a self-respecting woman dared not be otherwise. Yet, in her easy freedom with men, there was none of the subtle come-hither that characterized such women as Fleta Carmel, for example.

Fleta and her kind offered no relief to Charlie. They made him sick at his stomach.

Maud couldn't even be thought of that way. She was clean, and honest. Let's see – he had thought of her as a handsome girl. She was getting on, to be called a girl, and she wasn't really handsome. But she was likable. Charlie could remember her as a child, sturdy, self-reliant, noisy, good-humored. He had never kept company with her. He had never thought of it, to tell the truth. Had she ever had a beau?

Of course, there had been some buzzin' around her. There must have been. But, aside from Ben Sparks, who liked the women well enough but was too stingy to marry one, and poor little Pukey Burrows, who had worshiped her all his life but who just wasn't man enough for her, Charlie could think of no one. Funny. Maud would make a might fine wife for somebody.

The night air grew chillier, and the quilt was not

quite enough to keep him warm, so Charlie got back into bed. He seldom was wakeful like this, but before now he had found the old dodge of counting worked pretty well, so he tried it again. Slowly, methodically, he counted off by tens, setting each ten away in his mind until when he had about a dozen of the tens lined up, he was asleep.

Chapter Eleven

The thought of Maud stayed with Charlie as the fall days went by, and he grew more and more pleased with the idea. Maybe she really would be glad to come and take the place of poor old Elsie, who was watching him all the time, fussing over him, mollycoddling him.

It would of course be too obvious for him to call on Maud; it would set the whole town talking and he would like to avoid that until he had a chance to decide just what to do.

He would have to find out somehow if he really could warm up to her – could bring himself to go through the motions of courtship.

So he made an errand. It took some thinking, as the Ripley place was a good three miles away, up the river valley. Old man Ripley had no tools he could borrow; it was the wrong season for buying the seed potatoes which Ripley usually had for sale. Charlie himself had nothing to offer for barter or cash. Therefore it seemed like an act of Providence when he got an unexpected order for eggs, and had not enough on hand to fill his cases. He would have to buy outside, or disappoint a customer; he knew that Maud Ripley kept her own flock of hens.

Charlie made scant preparation for the trip. He was not going courting by a darn sight, so he merely washed up and harnessed the old horse and started.

The blaze of autumn glory that had been running like fire over the hills for weeks past was now rather dimmed; its smoky richness lay smouldering, drowned in the melting frost as the sun penetrated the woods and underbrush. Charlie leaned back in the buggy seat and let the reins go lax in his hands. A feeling of peace stole over him with the strengthening glow of the sun.

It was a good world after all. He would be a fool to let a chit like Marian ruin it for him. This frenzy of wanting her would let up some if he had a wife of his own, a hearth fire of his own; if he had that "house where gods might dwell, beautiful, entire, and clean." His own children would be even dearer and more absorbing than Young Morris and Elsie; if his own wife fussed over him, he could tell her to quit it.

Or let her go ahead – that might not be so bad if the right woman did it!

The horse was climbing steadily, and from the hilltop Charlie looked off toward the northwest where Mount Washington was a pale blue shape clean cut against a paler sky. The horse spied a bit of belated green by the roadside and stopped to browse. Charlie turned toward the south, with its sweep of diminishing hills, and the crooked line of the Saco valley winding toward the distant and invisible sea. It was like a crazy quilt of heavy, silken patterns, only it was richer, grander than anything human hands could make. Soon it would lie black and white, with the pines and the bare hardwood trees etched against the snow. And then it would quicken to life with the tender green of spring. After that summer would come, and the years would follow each other –

Why should he be such a fool as to let Marian Parks spoil the hills for him, to let the thought of her make God's own beauty hateful, to let her make happiness and satisfaction just a tormenting mockery to him? He picked up the reins and got the horse back into the road.

"We got to git goin'," he said harshly.

Down the hillside, and further along the river road, he came to the Ripley place. The big, old, low-posted house, white against the thinning russet-gold of the maples, was welcoming and comfortable in the sunshine. A big dog ran out and barked at him dutifully, wagging an enthusiastic tail as Charlie rubbed his head. Maud herself came to the door before he had a chance to knock. She stood there, tall, ruddy, wholesome in her clean gingham dress and apron. A streak of flour whitened one firm cheek.

"Well, if it ain't Charlie Ashburn!" she cried, her voice loud and cheerful. "For the land sakes, what put you in the notion to come here? I ain't seen you around this way for a long time."

Charlie took off his cap and stepped in at the door so hospitably opened for him.

"Just passin' the time o' day," he said. "Where's your folks?"

"Papa's gone to the Corner; Mama's around somewhere. Want to see her?"

"No – no. You'll do. The hens is yours, I take it."

"Why, yes. I been raisin' 'em ever since I quit school."

"Well, it's nice to have a crop o' your own."

"Yes, it's something o' my own to tend to, still I can

stay on here with Papa and Mama."

"I guess they need ye."

Maud was wary. "Not exactly need me, I spose," she said. "But they like me to stay with 'em."

"Well," Charlie came to the point, "I need about four dozen eggs. Got an order I wasn't lookin' for. Thought maybe you'd help me out."

"Why, sure," Maud met his sidewise glance with a full, frank stare. "I've got some to spare. But couldn't ye have found four dozen eggs without traveling three miles and back to git 'em?"

"I might have, if I'd a-wanted to," replied Charlie.

"Oh," said Maud. "Well, just a minute, till I git this batch o' cookies out." She turned to the stove, and Charlie stood watching her. The warm, pleasant kitchen was her domain, her background – sunny and homelike, with geranium slips struggling toward life in the south window, whose panes glittered with soap-and-water cleanliness, and the smell of spice and of rising yeast bread, the crackle of the wood fire in the stove.

"I don't want to keep ye from your work," said Charlie politely.

Maud removed the cookie sheet from the oven and overturned it on a white and blue towel on the table. Then she filled it again from the thin-rolled dough on her board.

"Just a minute till I git these in, and I'll git your eggs," she said.

Charlie sat down. It was a pleasure to watch Maud's swift movements, to rest there feeling no need to make conversation, to be at home in that kitchen. The cookies, when she passed him three on a china plate, tasted as good as they smelled. Charlie wondered if Marian Parks could cook. Probably not. Why should she?

Maud slammed the oven door.

"Now," she said, "just a jiffy, and I'll have those eggs for ye."

While she was gone, Charlie had time enough to think, but he was too comfortable. Maud was a nice woman; she would be sensible, easy to get along with. Comfortable – but when she came back, the basket of eggs in her hand, the sunshine pouring over her ample figure in the doorway, he felt no least stirring of the pulse, no trace of the wild desire that the mere thought of Marian gave him. Maud was a comfortable woman.

In the following weeks he saw Maud sometimes – in the store, at Grange meetings, on the road – and each time he stopped to talk with her, gave her marked attention.

"I hear ye're shinin' up to Maud Ripley, Charlie," remarked Morris, one night when they all sat around the kitchen stove, the chores being done, the children in bed.

Elsie looked up sharply from her mending; Charlie knew she was watching.

"Not specially," he replied easily. "She's a nice woman, though. Easy to look at, easy to talk to."

"She's easier to hear," snapped Elsie. "She's got a voice like a foghorn."

"More like a hen that's laid an egg, I'd call it," corrected Morris, chuckling. "Sharp, kind of. Foghorn's heavy, and low, ain't it? I never heard one."

Pop stretched himself and yawned. "Don't matter which she sounds like – I bet she never gits a chance to yell around this place."

"Well, now, you never can tell," said Charlie. Whatever he might or might not do in the end, it was fun to give Elsie a jolt like that.

"Gosh sakes, Charlie, you wouldn't – " Morris, who

had begun the talk so casually, sat bolt upright, and stared.

"Wouldn't what?" queried Charlie.

Elsie had forgotten her mending, and her glance went from one brother to the other. Morris leaned back again.

"Oh, nothin'," he replied.

"Did ye cover up those tomato vines?" Charlie inquired of Elsie. "It's fixin' to freeze tonight."

Elsie took up her needle again. "Yes. That makes everything under cover now. Let it freeze."

Thanksgiving came along, with Elsie engrossed, as usual, in preparations for the family dinner, with the first powdering of snow, and the feel of holiday in the whitened air. Lights were bright in the Parks place across the valley, that Thanksgiving eve, and Charlie knew that Marian was at home, and that he really did not wish to see her.

He had been winning out to a sort of resignation, had been thinking with increasing seriousness of marrying Maud, and he resented the possibility of being disturbed and set back again. He had steadfastly resolved that, when Marian came, he would stay close at home until she was gone again; would steer clear of the store and the highway and, above all, stay away from the dances. He would cling to such beginnings of peace as he had won.

But it was no use. Here was Thanksgiving eve, and he was shaving himself by the mirror over the kitchen sink, heating water for his bath, dressing with care, even to a new necktie, and hustling off to Henry's with the rest of the family.

Marian was sweet and cool, as ever, and, evidently remembering the happenings of that late-summer ride, she was just a little distant and impersonal, not only to him, but, he gloatingly observed, to the infatuated Morris.

Her attitude was maddening, yet it stiffened his resolution, and he succeeded in staying away altogether on Saturday night. She would not have another chance to freeze him out!

A few days before Christmas, Elsie came home from the store, red-cheeked and snow-powdered, and laden with bundles.

"Who do ye think I saw?" she said, as she took off her coat and turned to put away her groceries, not waiting for any reply. "Marian Parks and her beau. They came in for the mail while I was in the store. They was on snowshoes. At first I thought it was Graham with her, but when they got inside, I saw he was bigger'n Graham – a big, tall, dark feller, Charlie, and not so very good-lookin' either. He had on a dark blue sweater with a big white letter on it, and when he pulled off his stockin'-cap, his hair stood up all over his head, thick, black as coal."

Charlie said nothing, as he fumblingly got some wood from the box, put it in the stove, fussed around with the dampers. Of course. It was to be expected. He had had it figured out for some time now. It was right. Marian was probably engaged to the chap, or soon would be. Engaged to someone that belonged to her own world, one of the fellows she went to college times with, a fellow that didn't get all upset over a low-necked dress, a fellow that could kiss Marian Parks and get away with it!

Charlie suddenly slammed down the stove lid and went out, bareheaded and coatless into the snow. Dusk was falling.

An hour or so later he came back, wet, shivering, and weary. He couldn't eat his supper, and Elsie fussed over him. Pop sat there in the corner, looking too wise altogether. Charlie escaped to his own room, hoping that he had really done all his chores, though he had scant memory of what he had been up to, out there in the shivering dusk.

He was sick in bed for a week – something that had never happened to him before. It was hard for everybody. Alf had to spend all his vacation working, and Pop and even Elsie had to help outside. Hilda took the children to Gladys' with her, so there was no Christmas celebration in the house. It was dreary business.

He was sitting up at last, wrapped in a shawl by the kitchen stove, when Elsie, finishing off a long telephone visit with her mother, announced that the house-party at the Parks place had broken up.

"Pity you didn't git to see Marian's beau, Charlie," she said. "They've been all over the place – Marian and this big chap, Ham Witham, his name is – Graham and a girl from Boston. We had to miss all that, with you laid up."

Charlie shivered as if a draft had struck him, and Pop said: "Lay off him, Elsie. He don't want to talk, sick as he's been."

Good old worthless Pop – he always did understand.

Charlie soon regained his strength. It would take more than an attack of grip to knock him out for long; and, besides that, Elsie's fussing soon drove him out of the house. She watched him, waited on him, raised a holy row about his working so soon.

"Hell," he raged at her once, "what do ye take me for – a woman with a new baby?"

Work, work, work – that was what he needed. That, and Pop and the children, whom he loved, helped him to keep going, to be sane and sensible in spite of the dull pain, riven by sharp agonies of jealousy, which seemed to be all there was to living.

But with his strength, his poise returned, and after a

while he began taking Maud Ripley around some. She was a passably good dancer; not like Marian, of course, but fairish, and she dressed neatly. He had no need to be ashamed of her. Her voice, loud as it was, had a likable, hearty sound, and she was never vulgar. Charlie could have done a sight worse, and he knew it. People talked. They guyed him at the store, and he answered amiably. But he was noncommittal with Maud, and treated her respectfully. She had no claim on him yet, and until he was dead sure what he wanted to do, he meant that she should have none. Being with her was comfortable; they were good friends. But toward spring, he began to be more conscious of her; to pay heed to the soft curves of her figure, the fresh color in her face, the shine of her eyes and the silkiness of her light brown hair. He began to think it was time to make love to her – they had never indulged in the casual kissing that was customary among the younger fry – that he was ready to ask her the big question, the answer to which he took for granted.

It was on an afternoon in April that his plans got knocked galley-west again. He was at the depot after his empty egg crates; the train came in, and he ran up the platform abreast of the baggage car to get them as soon as possible. He wanted to get home and look after his incubators. He had just retrieved his crates and hoisted them into the wagon bed when he turned about and nearly fell over Marian Parks.

"Oh, Charlie!" she cried, laughing and clinging to his arm. "Are you going to give me a lift home? I came a day earlier than I'd planned, and I didn't wire Dad. I thought somebody would be here –"

"Sure — sure—" Charlie rallied from the shock of seeing her and tried to laugh, too. "Little bird told me you was comin'. Got a trunk? You won't mind ridin' in the wagon?"

"Of course not. And there's no trunk. Just these two suitcases."

"Where's Graham? Have ye seen Alf? He's comin' tomorrow, I guess."

Charlie threw the suitcases in beside the egg crates and then lifted Marian to the wagon seat. She was light. She seemed to have springs in her heels.

"Graham's going to Boston, Charlie, and I saw Alf yesterday. He had used up his cuts, and couldn't get away any earlier. Oh, it's good to get home again! There's no place, anywhere, that smells as good as Parkston township. Pines, and fresh wind – " She drew a deep breath of it. It had been a melting sort of day, and now the slush under the wagon wheels was beginning to stiffen as the darkness came on. In the woods there was still the utter silence of winter, riffled only by the hushed moaning of the pines.

"I was sorry you were sick at Christmas, Charlie," said Marian. "I wanted to see you."

"Guess ye didn't miss me much. You had company, I hear."

"Oh, well – but I did miss you, Charlie, and it's too bad for anyone to be sick at Christmas anyhow."

"That don't make any diff'rence to me. Christmas is for kids – and for happy people."

"What makes you speak so? You're happy, aren't you?"

"Me? Happy? What about?"

"Why, Charlie!"

Charlie looked down, sidewise, and Marian was looking up at him, soberly and a little perplexed. He could not cut his glance short, as was his habit, so he had to speak, to break the magnetic pull of Marian's dark eyes.

"Graham didn't come, you say? Then I spose you won't be at the dance Saturday night."

"Well, I hadn't thought of that. I suppose I can't go."

"Pity ye didn't bring a partner with ye."

"I hardly thought that would be necessary!" Marian laughed right in his face. Charlie stiffened up.

"Sorry I can't take ye," he said. "I'd like to, first rate, but I'm – " He started to say he was taking another girl, but his nerve failed him, and he finished lamely, "I'm not goin'."

"Not going? Why, you never miss a dance."

"Never used to. But I'm workin' hard now. No time for foolishness."

"Nonsense!"

"That's what it is – nonsense. Dancin' all night and havin' to git up and git to work before you've had a chance to git to bed. Hate to meet myself comin' downstairs."

"Oh, well." Marian turned her face away. "I can stay at home – or send for Ham Witham."

"Yep. You'd better do that."

Again, that crazy jealousy, that utterly brainless rage that had driven him, half dressed, into the December storm, got hold of him. The horse was toiling up the steep hill to the Parks place, and Charlie jumped out over the wheel, as if to ease the load. The reins slack in his hands, he plodded along in the freezing mud and slush, longing with all his soul to strike out and hurt somebody, even as he was being hurt.

At the horse block he lifted Marian down. Evidently no one in the house had seen or heard the team, and he had her there for a moment.

"Thank you for bringing me home," she said, "and

you're sure you won't take me to that dance?"

He was still holding her, and he hugged her close.

"No – no, Marian," he protested. "I tell ye I'm not goin' – I tell ye I won't –" He hardly knew what he was saying.

She pulled away from him easily enough, and stood there straightening her hat while he unloaded her bags.

"Well, good-night, Charlie – and thank you!"

She went into the house.

Chapter Twelve

For two whole days, Charlie stuck to his resolution, and on Saturday it was still solid. Nothing could induce him to make a fool of himself any more; nothing should set him back in the headway he had made with Maud Ripley, nor in his fight against his own idiocy. Marian Parks could look elsewhere for her amusement, and lord help the man she picked on – it wouldn't be Charlie Ashburn!

And he resolved to settle things irrevocably.

Gradually he had learned much of Maud Ripley's routine, and he was usually able to save himself a trip to her house or an embarrassing telephone call – party lines are not so well adapted to the needs of courtship! – by timing a visit to the store to coincide with her regular buying days. So, at about noon on Saturday, he was on hand, and helped the storekeeper load the sacks of grain into the body of the Ripley wagon. This task he was soon tactfully left to accomplish alone; a storekeeper knew when he was not needed.

"How about the dance tonight, Maud?" asked

Charlie.

Maud hesitated and stood thoughtfully smoothing the mittens on her capable hands, her head bent slightly.

Then, "Charlie," she replied, her usually strident voice softened and slow, "you don't want to take me to this dance; don't you know your other girl is home?"

She looked up quickly; their eyes were on a level, and rather close. She waited, studying him. Now was his chance; in spite of the public place, now was his time to tell her that he had no interest in anyone but her, to insist that she go with him, to clinch forever his independence of Marian Parks, his captaincy of his own soul.

And he faltered. His face reddened miserably, and he could not for the life of him meet Maud's frank, comprehending gaze, much less lie to her. He stooped and lifted the last sack of grain, and heaved it into the wagon.

"I wish ye'd go with me, Maud," he repeated.

"Well," she answered tartly, "I won't. I've got eyes in my head. I thought maybe you'd got over that crush on Marian Parks, but I see now ye haven't. Maybe ye never will. I ain't hankerin' for a place as second fiddle."

"Sure ye mean that, Maud? It ain't as if I had a ghost of a chance with that girl. There's just nothin' to it, ye know, Maud. You and I – we've both got a long life to live."

"Listen here, Charlie," Maud stepped closer lest someone overhear. "I'm goin' to tell ye somethin'. Years ago, I'd have married – a certain man – if he'd asked me. He didn't. I got over it. But ye see I know somethin' about what it's like. Until ye do git over it, it's no kind o' use to try fillin' in with second best. It wouldn't make ye happy. See what I mean?"

"I was goin' to ask ye to marry me," Charlie said.

"I know. And I was thinkin' some of sayin' I would. I might do it yet if ye really put that girl out o' your mind and still want me to. But if ye was to ask me right now, I'd turn ye down flat."

She climbed into the wagon and took up the reins as Charlie untied the halter and looped its end over the hames.

"I wish things was different, Maud," he said.

Maud clucked to the horse. "There's one good thing about ye, Charles Ashburn," she said. "Ye couldn't lie to save your soul."

When Charlie came in from his chores that night, Elsie was moving about the kitchen in her methodical, purposeful way, getting supper on the table. She wore her second best wool dress, with a big apron over it, so Charlie knew she had been to visit with someone – her mother, probably.

The children came and fell all over him; they were always glad to see Uncle Charlie come in at night, and he hugged them, pinched Little Elsie's cheek and pulled Young Morris' hair. Pop got up from his rocking chair and folded his newspaper. Supper would soon be ready now that Charlie was in. The room looked pleasant, and warm, and homelike.

Beautiful, entire, and clean; it seemed that way, but it wasn't. He thought for the thousandth time that he, not Morris, should have been the married man, and thus been shielded from loving the wrong girl. This home might then have been wholly his; these children might have called him father instead of uncle.

But that didn't hold water. Morris, safely married to Elsie, had not been protected from a passion for Marion Parks. Elsie was not enough to satisfy either one of them. The mischief was done anyhow, and nothing could be gained by such thinking.

Elsie poked the fire and put in another stick of wood.

"I got hot water ready, Charlie," she said. "Your white shirt's there on the dresser. I sewed the button on."

Charlie said nothing. He washed at the sink, and combed his fine, thin hair. Even had he been a college man, Marian wouldn't have cared for him – he was getting bald already! He looked like an old man at twenty-eight.

Elise was speaking to him again.

"Takin' Maud to the dance?" she asked, as she wrapped a clean towel around her hands and poured the beans from the earthen pot into a serving dish. Charlie drew up a chair and took his place at the table.

"I may not go," he replied.

"Well, that mean's you're not takin' Maud," Elsie stated, her tone electric with curiosity. "I spose you're figuring on havin' Marian Parks for a partner again."

"Oh, I dunno. Is she home?" asked Charlie innocently.

"You ought to know. You drove her up from the depot," snapped Elsie.

Charlie speared a slice of brown bread. "You've been to your mother's," he said.

"What if I have? If you won't tell me the news, I've got to git it somewheres else. Well, I guess Morris won't be home tonight – he hasn't phoned or anything. But I've got your bath water and your clean clothes ready, Charlie, so you can go to the dance."

"I said I wa'n't goin'."

"I wisht ye would. Seems to me I ain't been to many dances since you've been buzzin' Maud. Morris seems to've lost interest in 'em."

"Well, I'm not goin' tonight."

"Why not?"

"I just don't feel like it."

Pop spoke up. "Maybe Elsie would be glad for ye to take her," he suggested not quite approvingly.

"Let Alf do it. He'll probably be in pretty quick."

"Alf hasn't got back from the Corner yet. He said he was goin' to pass the time o' day with some of the fellows there."

"Well," said Charlie, "that's too bad."

Supper was finished in silence. Alf came in before they were through, and announced that he had been traveling all the afternoon, seeing different people, and he was tired. Going right to bed. That seemed to settle the dance.

But Charlie started. While Elsie was busy with the children, upstairs, he sneaked the hot water and the clean white shirt to his room, bathing and shaving in the chilly, badly lighted place. Then he eased down the back stairs directly to the stable, and harnessed. There was no time for getting a livery rig – the old shabby team would have to do.

The lights were bright at the Parks place; it was plain enough that they had company. Was Witham there? Had she sent for him? Charlie was about to lose his nerve and drive away when the door opened and Marian stood, framed with the bright light at her back.

"Hello!" he called, half sullenly.

"Oh, it's you, Charlie! I thought I heard a team. But you said you weren't going to the dance."

"I thought I might's well, if you wanted to. But I see you got company."

"Well," admitted Marian, "we have. It is just some of the older folks – I could go with you – but see here, Charlie, why don't you come in? Dad and Mother would love to have you, and so would I."

"Aw, sho', Marian. I couldn't do that. I'd never fit in there, with your folks, and company too."

Marian left the lighted doorway and stepped down beside the buggy, one hand resting on the dashboard. She was such a cute little trick. It always seemed as if something ought to be done about it – as if she ought to be kissed, or grabbed and run away with. It wasn't good sense for her just to stand there, all by herself, shut away from him –

"Come on in, Charlie," she was urging. "I never do have any callers of my own while I am at home. Really, I need someone to liven things up. Not even Graham here to play with!"

"Marian, you're crazy. Come on and go to the dance with me. That's bad enough."

"Bad enough? What do you mean?"

"Oh, never mind. Come on. Git your coat."

She had been standing there in the dim light, one hand on the dashboard; now she put the other hand on Charlie's knee and looked up at him teasingly.

"You know," she said, "I hardly ever really make up my mind about anything, but when I do – watch out! You are coming in and spend the evening with the Parks family."

Charlie groaned. "You little devil!" he muttered.

"Come on," insisted Marian.

She went to the horse's head and took the bridle, leading the team to the hitching ring at the corner of the house.

"He can stand here all right," she said. "Come, get out and put on his blanket!"

Dumb, rebellious but obedient, Charlie hitched and blanketed the horse, and followed Marian into the house.

He was scared stiff. What in creation was he letting himself in for? Would they snub him? Or would they talk down to him? What would they think – these older people – of his calling on Marian this way? Would she take him to a different room, where they could be alone? His heart lurched at the thought, yet he was neither surprised nor disappointed to find himself in the big Parks living room, seated beside Marian on a sort of settle at one side of the great fireplace, and feeling far more at home than he would have thought possible.

It had been easy enough. He was pretty sure he had got by all right. There was Marian's mother, plump and small, with keen, dark eyes like the daughter's, and smoothly dressed gray-brown hair. She was a homelike, plain-spoken person, and she had welcomed Charlie as if he had been coming there all his life. Dr. Parks, rotund, lusty-voiced and laughing, had been equally easy to meet up with; and the other two – an elderly couple who seemed to be relatives – had noticed him just enough to be courteous. That Marian should bring in a friend was apparently of no great interest to them. They took it for granted. So the quartet had taken up their conversation right where the interruption had left it, and before long Mrs. Parks had said:

"Marian, bring the little sewing table, dear. We still have a job ahead of us, showing these people we haven't forgotten our whist."

"Mother," Marian replied, as she unfolded the table, "you really ought to cut out this duplicate. It's stupid, and everybody's playing bridge now, you know."

"Yes. I've heard. I've even gone so far as to play it. But this won't even be duplicate. It will be just plain whist."

The card game had left Marian and Charlie almost as

good as alone, there in the firelight. The girl was sweet, and quiet, and looked happy. She had on a dark silk dress, and she sat perfectly still, relaxed, her hands idle on her lap. She didn't fidget. She didn't try to make talk. It was fun just to sit there beside her.

Suddenly she smiled and looked up at him.

"I hear you've been courting," she said. "Can't I turn my back without your hunting out another girl?"

"It takes a lot o' girls to keep me happy," he countered.

"I believe you. But where is she tonight? When you told me you couldn't take me to Henry's, I suspected something – then I heard about you and Maud, and I thought of course you were taking her, and leaving me at home with the old folks."

"I did ask her. She turned me down."

"Not really! And I'm second choice? Charlie, I'm mad at you!"

She laughed as she said it, with such frank good humor that, even though he had to laugh with her, he felt sore. She really was indifferent to him. It really meant nothing to her at all that he loved her, or that he was trying to get over it, or that he was thinking to marry Maud Ripley.

In the silence that followed, Marian slid one hand into Charlie's and, staring thoughtfully into the fire, she spoke, rather soberly.

"Maud is nice," she said. "I should think you would marry her. I mean, it really would be a good thing all around. Don't you think so?"

"It might be – if she'd have me. She won't."

"Oh, Charlie – surely she would. Why don't you ask her?"

"I did."

"You did! And she refused? Why, I would have thought, from all I've heard, that she would jump at the chance."

"Nope. She didn't. Nary a jump."

"Well, she's foolish, that's all. But don't you care, Charlie – "

"That's just it, Marian. I don't care. And Maud knows it."

"Oh-h-h!" Marian nodded her head wisely, soberly, as if now she understood something that had been puzzling her, and at the same time she tried to draw her hand away from him. But Charlie held it tight, and she made no protest.

The whist was going on rather noisily across the room. Dr. Parks came and threw another log on the fire, giving them a keen, humorous glance as he did so, and went back to the game.

At last Marian stirred and pulled Charlie to his feet.

"Let's go to the kitchen," she suggested, "and make some pop corn. They'll be wanting something before they finish, and I know the fire's not out yet."

"Suits me."

The Parks kitchen was big, of course, but it differed from the typical farm workroom in being painted white all over, with white furnishings, and bright linoleum on the floor. The few pots and kettles that were visible were shining like silver – the new aluminum ware, he supposed. Marian opened a drawer and took out an apron, and slipped it on. It fastened behind, and she turned to Charlie and asked him to button it. His hands shook. The soft silk of her dress was warm from her body and, as he touched her, he sensed the faint, clean fragrance that was always a part of her. Adroit as usual, she slipped away from him just in time, and set about stirring up the fire, and ordered him to bring some wood.

While the stove was heating up, they shelled the corn by rubbing the ears, one against another, and put a handful of the hard, shiny kernels into the wire popper, carefully fastening the cover down.

Marian drew a high stool up near the stove and perched on it and motioned Charlie to bring another chair from the adjoining breakfast-room – as she called it – and they sat there, idly talking while the corn got warmed up. As the first grains began to snap, Marian gave him the handle of the popper.

"You tend it, Charlie, while I get the bowl ready, and some butter."

Charlie complied, sliding the corn popper about on the hot stove-top, while he kept watch of Marian. She seemed sufficiently at home in a kitchen after all. She brought a big, deep white basin for the corn, and a small saucepan with a chunk of golden butter, which she set at the back of the stove to melt.

"There," she said. "Now, that's ready, and that popperful is done. Give it here."

"No. You'll burn ye."

"Well, here's a holder."

Charlie took the folded towel and opened the lid, pouring the light, snow-white kernels into the big bowl. Marian poured on some of the butter, sprinkled the salt generously, and stirred the whole with a long-handled fork.

Charlie was still and spellbound. A dozen times her hands touched his, or she brushed against him. She was sweet and familiar in her apron, working at the homely task. How many times he and Elsie had sat together by the fire, had worked together thus, yet what a difference! Blindly, Charlie let himself go, gave up the struggle to keep a level head, and reveled in happiness.

When the bowl was heaped full, Marian bade him carry it to the living room while she followed with a handful of saucers and paper napkins. The card game halted while she served the elders, and conversation became general. They did not snub Charlie, nor talk down to him. They seemed to assume that there was no reason for them to. Charlie liked them all, and was enjoying himself even while he wondered how he was to get away when he must, and if he would get a word with Marian alone.

They made that easy, too. He did not know how it happened, but a little after eleven o'clock the group naturally broke up, and he said good-night. Marian followed him to the corner of the house, where the horse was hitched, and, emboldened by this, he tried to kiss her.

"Now, now Charlie," she admonished, with no great heat. "You know I don't care for that sort of thing at all."

"You claim you don't. Give yourself a chance. You might like it."

"Don't be silly. It just won't do, and you know it."

"Maybe not. But you won't get away this time."

As he held her so, he could feel the sudden throb of her heart, and her quick, indrawn breath. But the struggle she made was not physical. She was perfectly still, but absolutely unresponsive, and before he knew it, her strong will had beaten him again, and she was free.

"Good-night, Charlie," she said. "We had a good time, didn't we!"

He did not go directly home. It was too early for him to have come from Henry's, and he wanted to cool off anyhow. He drove to the Falls again, and heard the roaring water, felt again that swift, breathless yielding of a summer night. Marian was not cold – far from it. It was just that she kept herself behind that stone wall, kept her real self clear of entanglements. She would never give in to any man until she got good and ready to. Her mind ruled her – not her passions.

Hours later, with weary body and hair-trigger nerves, he reached home, put up the team, and stumbled into the kitchen. Elsie was waiting up for him, sitting there by the stove in her bright-colored wrapper, with her long hair, smoothly brushed, in a braid over her shoulder.

"Hello. You still up!" He felt ugly.

"Yes. I'm still up."

He got a drink from the pump and took down his lamp from the shelf.

"Go to bed, Elsie. I ain't hungry, and even if I was, I could get my own snack. No need for you to wait up.

Elsie followed him to the door. She was crying.

"Charlie, I wanted to go. I thought, when you wasn't takin' Maud, you would take me."

"Morris is the one to take you around – not me."

"He is never home any more, and besides, I'd rather go with you than Morris."

"Oh, what in hell do ye talk like that for? You married Morris – why can't ye stick to him and leave me be?"

There, he had said it – fired at her point blank a question he had until now barely formulated in his own mind.

"Morris don't care about me. He likes Marian Parks as much as you do. She's a hussy, that's what she is – makin' fools out o' both o' ye."

Charlie raged, but it was no use to say anything. Elsie's mind was not capable of taking in the situation at all. She would never be able to understand Marian's ways of living and thinking.

Of course Marian did raise the very devil, but she was just a kid. Probably she was sound asleep right now, never dreaming she had started anything like this. He spoke up in her defence.

"Marian don't aim to make a fool o' me or anyone else. I know what I'm up to." He turned to go, but Elsie held him back.

"You saw her tonight?"

"Sure."

"Who took her? Graham ain't home."

"Is it any o' your business?"

"I'll bet ye didn't even get to kiss her," jeered Elsie.

"What makes ye call her a hussy then?" he flashed back.

Elsie's voice rose. "I call her a hussy because she don't pay for what she gits. I know you're never satisfied. She's rich, and educated, but she does somethin' I'd never do – she takes, but she won't give!"

"Nonsense!"

"It's true, and you know it."

"What does she git from me but a dish of ice cream once in a while?"

Elsie came closer and grasped the front of his coat with both hands.

"You're givin' her your whole life, and you're such a fool ye don't even know it."

Charlie stood rigid. That sounded as if perhaps Elsie could do a better job of thinking than he had given her credit for.

"Nonsense," he repeated. "I git all I ever expect to. I know what I'm about."

And then Elsie shoved the whole matter aside with a movement of her soft, heavy body. Her arms were warm about his neck.

"Charlie – Charlie –" she whispered.

"Devil take it – Elsie – behave yourself – "

He struggled to the table and set his lamp down for safe keeping, but still she clung to him, yielding, warm, generous. She had served him faithfully for years, and she asked so little – only to give herself again.

Charlie thought drowning must be something like this. She was smothering him, sapping away his resistance, his self-respect, his family loyalty. The whole world was a mess, a grim practical joke played on man by a heartless god. Why struggle against it all the way along?

Those warm arms would not let him go. Charlie was at the end of his rope.

HE FAILED TO wake up the next morning until Pop had called him – a thing which seldom happened. He felt queer, as if he were seeing things with eyes not his own. As he went down the shed stairs, he noticed for the first time in his life the exquisite luster of the familiarly smooth wooden rail, naturally polished by generations of Ashburn hands; yet he observed this with the detached interest of a stranger. The morning sun slanted, rose-colored, through the dim, small panes of the shed window. He could hear Pop stirring around in the kitchen, could hear the warm crackling of soft pine wood in the stove, as he opened the door. There was the smell of coffee, and the hissing song of the blue enameled double boiler, steaming with the breakfast cereal.

Pop was not often up ahead of Elsie, but when he was, he started things going. Charlie was relieved now that she had not come downstairs just yet. He dreaded seeing her. Dreaded the days ahead, when he would have to live side by side with her and his shame.

As he stood by the sink, pumping cold water into the basin, he knew Pop was watching him. Was guilt written in big letters all over him?

"The teakittle's hot," offered Pop.

"Don't need it – this is all right."

"What's the matter? Marian treat ye rough last night?"

"No worse'n usual, I guess." Charlie kept his back turned. Never before in his life had he been afraid to face Pop; never before had he felt the need to hide from those all-seeing, deep-set eyes. He doused his head and neck with the cold water, trying to quiet his jumping nerves.

Pop filled his pipe and lighted it studiously.

"Seems to me I heard a rumpus last night," he observed.

Cold fear gripped Charlie. "Rumpus? Where?" he muttered.

"Just sort of a rumpus. Hope a skunk didn't git into the roost."

Charlie buried his face in the roller towel.

"Guess not. I got the skunks pretty well cleaned off this farm."

Elsie's step could be heard now overhead. Pop glanced upward.

"Don't be too sure about that, son."

"About what?"

"Skunks."

"What's eatin' ye this mornin', Pop?" he rasped. And then he chilled again. That fifth stair from the bottom – had it creaked, as it usually did, when he came down last night? And with Pop's room right next to that front staircase –

"Elsie's a good worker," Pop went on, "and she

treats me good. I ain't got a word o' complaint to make about her. But I tell ye she's got a shifty eye."

"What's that got to do with –" Charlie couldn't quite bring himself to use the word.

"With skunks?" Pop rose, and went to the stove, lifted the lid and spat thoughtfully. Then he sat down again.

"Your ma always wanted we should hang together, and live decent." He spoke quietly. "I guess 'twould be just as well if Morris came home oftener. I wa'nt born yesterday, and I ain't dead yet – not quite. But I hope to God I never see a day that I'd be glad your mother didn't live to see."

The old man crossed his bony knees, hooked his thumbs in the armholes of his vest, and leaned back, eying Charlie thoughtfully.

"Pop, what in the devil are you drivin' at?"

The fifth stair creaked as Elsie came down. Charlie grabbed his hat and went out.

Chapter Thirteen

Charlie's dread of too close communion with Elsie and his own conscience was swallowed up in the turmoil and grief of the next two weeks.

The weather was warm, melting, intoxicatingly beautiful with the sights and sounds and fragrances of winter-bound New England awakening to fresh life. Pop loved the spring. It was the season when his thoughts went back to the springtimes of his young manhood, when, as his own father had expressed it, he was so "wide awake an' full o' hell." Young – he had been – spirited, eager, daring. He had stepped high, wide and handsome; and his father, while seeming to understand him well enough, and to be reasonably tolerant, had despaired of ever making him work. Morris the Third had always had brains enough – ability enough; all that had been conceded; but he lacked not so much ambition as the grace to connect ambition with practical accomplishment.

Pop could remember his youthful dislike for manual work, his total lack of interest in the labor which produced the food he ate, which earned the clothes he wore. Always he had loved the farm deeply, but he had loved it as a home, a sanctuary, a refuge from the self-created furore of his life. He did not then love it as a life work, or medium of self-expression. After his sisters, Sarah and Hannah, had married and gone, and his parents had died, leaving him as the only son in possession of the homestead, he had settled back easily, cultivating just enough ground to keep body and soul together, spending his days in little labor and much thought, and his nights, all too often, in carousing. He had not been lonely.

Not lonely until the years began to stretch long ahead, until he was no longer young, no longer quite so attractive to the girls, no longer sufficiently well-to-do to buy what he wanted. The time came when he was no longer "full o' hell," but began to long for the peace of a well-ordered life.

At this period, questions had begun to intrude themselves more and more on his thinking. Such questions as these: Of what use is your life, to yourself or anyone else? What have you ever done to pay your way – to justify your existence? And why try to justify it anyhow? Do you really care to live? Would you wish to die? Why were you, or anyone else for that matter, ever born anyhow?

It was at this stage that he had begun to suspect a lack in his hitherto highly colored life. All the women, for instance – he had never really loved a one of them. He had always thought pityingly of the few really faithful married men he knew. They had seemed to him to be the victims of domineering wives, afraid to call their souls their own, tied hand and foot to a domesticity they hadn't guts enough to break lose from. Now, he began to doubt. Could there after all be something about a woman that a man could love for years on end, could cleave to for a lifetime? If so, he must have missed it.

Morris the Third had always liked children, but had never come in intimate contact with them. His sisters, of course, occasionally brought their families to call on him, but not often, and they never stayed long. Sarah tartly and frankly disapproved of him; Hannah always regarded him with a sympathy and tolerance which rather softened her disappointment in him. But both lived in different townships, and worked hard, and were absorbed in their families. The Ashburn ties were weakening, just as the old place was running down, and Morris the Third hadn't the git-up-and-git to do anything about it.

Then Hilda Bowers had come to teach the school back of the mountain. Hilda – tall, strong, energetic, vital – she had startled him to life the first time he saw her, had fired him not so much with passion as with ambition, purposefulness, a yearning for such self-respect as he had never really known. This, he had thought, was what he had missed in life; this woman was the symbol of home, children, orderliness, comfort – of the very sort of thing which he had been regarding as tame and humdrum beyond all bearing. He had been a fool.

But maybe not. Suppose he had met Hilda Bowers while he was still a youth, helling around generally. Suppose she had been willing to marry him then, before he was really ready to settle down. He would have made a mess of things, probably, just as other men did – drinking, chasing women, staying out nights and so on. He would have loved Hilda through it all – he could see that – but he would have broken her heart with his restlessness.

It was a good thing, of course, that he had sowed his wild oats and reaped enough of the harvest to become satiated before Hilda came. Their years together had been good. He had taken pride in his work, his home, his children. He had never felt the slightest temptation to be unfaithful to Hilda; she had satisfied him utterly. Even the lash of her tongue had never troubled him, for it had either been amusing or the wholesome rebuke which he had consciously needed. Take it by and large, he certainly could not regard as wasted all the footless years which had prepared him to appreciate his Hilda.

Pop was worried, these fine spring days, about Charlie and Morris and Elsie. He wished with all his soul for Hilda Bowers' counsel and companionship. That was why he took himself to the barn, and sat there on a slab of stone with his back to the silvery-gray shingles on the south side, whittling idly sometimes, yet mostly lost in thought, and smoking constantly.

The sun was warm, and he took off his coat, letting the sunlight soak him to the bone. Yet it could not burn away the chill of an uneasy dread.

He had never trusted Elsie. Too well he knew her sort – all emotion and no brains, no sensitiveness, no firmness of moral principle. Elsie was not bad; she was not good. She merely got what she wanted, and did not think of analyzing her own wants. Hilda had always taught the children that anything which was not right was wrong; that a sharp cleavage existed between right and wrong. Probably Elsie had never heard of such thinking and teaching.

You couldn't blame her for that. She hadn't asked to be born, any more than anyone else ever had; she hadn't had the choosing of her own character, her own surroundings. She had had to take life as she found it, just like everyone had to.

Pop had known from that very first winter, when Morris took the team to the woods, that Elsie was in love with Charlie; what he had never been satisfied about was the possibilities of the infatuation. What would Elsie do about it? What would Charlie do if he ever got wise to it? Pop had sometimes wished he could have watched the drama unfold from a disinterested point of view. It would have been fun to watch, if only he had not loved the two boys so deeply – if only it had been happening under his observation but not in his own home.

Morris the Fourth was to be pitied. He was sensitive, Pop knew, and though he might be foolish, he would never be base or mean. Charlie, until the Parks girl had got him, had been a reliable old sober-sides, tending to his work and knowing little else . . . It would have been mighty nice if Charlie had fallen in love with some local girl, who would have married him. Charlie deserved to be happy – but who, of all the girls that would be likely to have him, would the poor chap care for now? This affair with the Parks girl had set a mark on him, and he was not a man that could forget. As for Elsie – well, Charlie was a normal, healthy, male critter. He could stand just about so much.

Pop sank back lower against the south side of the barn. The whole mess was sickening. It had always seemed possible to put up with anything that might come so long as the children were happy and full of courage. Now, here were two of them miserable, and sinking into a mire of sin and deceit. What was the use of anything?

All the restless questionings of his bachelor years returned now to Morris Ashburn the Third, and he turned for refuge to the same comforter – Hilda. Where had she gone? And why had she gone?

A passer-by would have seen just a shabby old man in his shirtsleeves, loafing in the April sun; would perhaps have envied him his leisure, his apparently placid reveling in the quickening springtime. But here was a lonely soul in torture, reaching out in aching desperation for the strength and courage and companionship of one long dead. Reaching out through the darkness of the future, struggling toward eternity – and Hilda.

The sun went down, and Pop was chilly. He got himself together and went into the house, but he couldn't seem to get himself warm. Elsie made him go to bed, and brought him some hot soup for his supper. Later, Charlie got some cider from the cellar, but still nothing warmed him much. Pop wanted Hilda – not little Hilda, but Hilda.

It was plain enough from that night that in sitting out so long in his shirtsleeves, Pop had overdone things. Just a cold, they all supposed, and a cold usually wasn't so bad. But he sure did feel peaked with this one. It failed to yield to Elsie's homely treatment, so they decided it must be the grip. A few days more, in which Pop got no relief, but grew worse and worse, drove them to sending for the doctor.

The doctor raised a fuss because he had not been called sooner, but he guessed the old man would pull through all right. They sent for Alviry to help out, but took pains to keep her busy in the kitchen. It would not do to have Pop worried.

Still there was no improvement, and the doctor began to look serious.

"Hasn't much gumption, has he?" he remarked.

"Well, he must be pretty sick," Charlie defended him.

"Sure, but not so bad, seems-so, as to make him lie like that. Wonder how old he is?"

"I never did know," Charlie answered, "but he must be pretty well along. Why, he was all of forty-five when he and Mother were married."

"Well – we'll see. Maybe he'll snap out of it, but I don't know."

Charlie went about his chores with a heavy weight on his mind. He was pretty sure Pop had heard that fifth stair creak. All those two or three sunny days when he had been so busy holding up the south side of the barn, Pop had been unwontedly silent, his eyes deeper than ever, his thoughts too far away to break out in his habitual terse comments. Probably all along he had been aware of the undercurrent of discontent, of stifled passion, of aggressive yet subtle uneasiness, that was disrupting the Ashburn tribe. Pop had always known everything. No one had told him, yet he had known it was Marian Parks Charlie had been with that night. He had known that Elsie waited up. He had known the whole vile business, and he had said he wished to God he might die before he saw things go any further.

Maybe he was about to get his wish.

Nothing much was said, but somehow, that week, the family was all at home. It was a strained and silent household. None of them could put it in words, but they all knew that Pop's time had come; yet, knowing, they could not believe. It seemed to Charlie that the old man was done with life, and was deliberately availing himself of the first chance to get out of it. Who could blame him?

Of course, the doctor called it pneumonia, and that was the report given out to the neighbors. But Charlie knew better. It was heart-break, disappointment, discouragement. It was age.

The Ashburns were not much given to tears, but several times Charlie caught Gladys drying her eyes, and Hilda was openly frightened and rebellious. She threw herself on Alf and stormed.

"Pop's got to get well, I tell you. He's got to get

well!"

Alf took her on his lap and tried to soothe her.

"We hope so, Hilda. We're doing all that can be done."

"And it won't be enough?"

"We're afraid not, Hilda," said Alf, and tucked her frowsy little head down on his shoulder as she cried.

Pop had been sick about ten days when the doctor told them the end had come. Pop knew them all, as they gathered around him with white, stricken faces.

"Don't fuss so – " he muttered. "It's all right – my time – that's all – comes to everybody – bein' born and dyin' – "

The downstairs bedroom was still, and its stillness was emphasized by the metallic clamor of the nickel alarm clock on the shelf behind the heater. Pop lay there, a wasted shape in the big, ugly black-walnut bed, whose ornate carving had always seemed to the Ashburn children so rich and beautiful. This was their mother's room – their mother's bedroom set. Here on this bed they had all, in turn, sent up their first protesting wails, and here their mother had died.

A grim crayon portrait of her hung above the mantel where the clock was making such a fuss. This portrait had been drawn by a traveling artist from an old photograph; and, while it was not a good likeness at all, it was the only one they had.

The room was rather disorderly now for, even in good health, Pop had never cared what it looked like. The carvings on the massive bureau and bed and washstand were faintly dim with dust; the brown marble slabs, on which Pop could never tolerate even a linen towel, were stained and littered with glasses and medicine bottles. The bowl and pitcher of heavy porcelain were chipped at the edges, and their gay colors dimmed by years of rough and ready handling. Even the scattered homemade rugs on the painted floor were shabby, and the cushions on the two small chairs were faded and worn.

Yet this was a pleasant room. The shabbiness was not that of neglect, for Elsie Ashburn was a good housekeeper. It was the shabbiness of steady use and familiar occupation. Here Pop had had things his own way, and Elsie had never interfered. She had seen to it that the sheets and spread were smooth and snowy white, and the towels always clean; and, except for the high reaches of the carving, the furniture was dusted every week. Twice a year, Elsie had dusted even that, though Pop had always told her to leave it be, since she had enough to do without tearin' her shirt over that.

The present disorder was merely that of the emergency; nobody had the heart for cleaning up, with Pop lying there suffering, and indifferent to anything earthly, except the faces of his loved ones.

There was Gladys, leaning back against the wall, with Hilda clinging to her, both of them, usually so trim and neat, now red-eyed and unkempt. There was John Freeman, big, calm, serious, watching his young wife with a solicitude that did not see her untidiness. There were the always inseparable Herb and Alf, sitting together on the old chest in the corner, the one tall, lank and careless, the other compactly slender, almost dapper, the one really handsome Ashburn. There was Elsie, crouched alone by the bedside; and there were Morris and Charlie, closer than ever before as they leaned on the foot of the bed waiting. Had they known how, they would have prayed for their father's peace and comfort.

Alviry, openly crying, hovered at the doorway. Hers was the thankless task of keeping the three grandchildren out of the way. She could see no sense in that – but the tribe had agreed to spare the little chaps as much as possible; to screen from them the grim realities of suffering and death. But in spite of her grief and her duties, Alviry was not missing a thing.

At last it was over. Pop had almost eagerly breathed his last, his spirit seeming visibly to leap forward into the unknown. The doctor had silently closed the no longer all-seeing Ashburn eyes, and the tribe had quietly filed out of the downstairs bedroom where Pop had spent every night of his adult life.

He had moved into that room when his own father had died. He had slept there alone throughout his long bachelorhood; he had slept there for years with Hilda, his wife, in the broad old wooden bedstead, or on a sofa drawn close to her side as he cared for her and her new-born babies through the night. There had been a few years when the baby Hilda had been there with him, when her infant needs had been a solace for his bitter loneliness; and then the years of nightly solitude, now ended in this forever silence.

Pop was done.

And it was to the Ashburn tribe, returning from the cemetery, as if the bottom had dropped out of the world. Herb and Alf went off on the night train; Gladys and John and the little Jack drove back to East Parkston, taking Hilda with them; Morris stayed around for a few days, but his presence was small comfort. His usual hilarity was doused in sadness, and the moodiness that had been gradually growing on him was more pronounced than ever.

It was bad all around, and what with one thing and another Charlie had little time to think of the thing of which he was so bitterly ashamed; but as the household settled back into its routine, and became accustomed to seeing the rocking chair in the kitchen vacant, the horror came to him again. It was especially bad, since Elsie mourned for Pop sincerely, and would have turned to Charlie for consolation.

She was a queer make-up – Elsie; so good and faithful in some ways, so rotten in others. Probably if Morris had ever taken pains to keep her interested in him, she would never have turned to Charlie.

Any man, Charlie thought, might get into an affair with a woman, and get out again. It wasn't that part of it that bothered him. It was the fact that she was his brother's wife that made it so bad. It was dirty, incestuous; and it seemed to have cut him off forever from the ideal of cleanliness and beauty that had always haunted the back of his mind. But it was over with, he told himself; she would never catch him that way again.

Spring work was hard, as always, and he was glad of it. If he kept going late enough every day, he fell asleep at night as soon as he hit the bed. He simply did not see Elsie at all; that was the easiest way. Their old partnership was ruined, and as the raw newness of grief wore away, there was no need for him to speak to her, to pay attention to her at all. He had a hard time not to despise her; but she had a right in the house, and he had to be decent about it.

Sometimes she touched him, coming near as she poured his coffee, or passed him in the doorway; but he had no slightest desire for her. Once in a while he did manage a kind word or two, for he pitied her. The day she broke Pop's old moustache cup, knocking it off its hook as she cleaned the cupboard shelves, he came in to find her crying bitterly as she gathered up the pieces. Something about her bent shoulders and her childishly wrinkled face as she cried made his heart turn soft.

"Ye miss Pop, don't ye!" he said.

"Yes. Nobody knows how much. But I'm kind o' glad the old cup's gone. It always made me feel bad to see it."

"Well, it's no use to keep mullin' things over. 'Twas his time to go, and Lord knows this ain't such a hell of a happy world. Don't quite see how anybody should want to stay in it over time."

Elsie dried her eyes and looked up at him gratefully, wistfully, and Charlie fled to the barn. Work – work – that was about all a man could do. He and Elsie between them had killed Pop, but there was no help for it now.

Chapter Fourteen

Alfred Ashburn's graduation, that June, was too great an event to be dimmed by the family's recent sorrow. It was so big, in fact, that all of them but Herb shrank from witnessing it. Gladys would have liked to go, but she felt too much tied at home for such an undertaking — one which would involve not only her absence from her youngster and her housekeeping, but the buying of new clothes which she feared might not be just right.

"Spose I should get all dolled up," she said, on her Sunday visit to the farm, "and then make a mistake somewhere — the wrong gloves and hat with the right dress, or the other way around? It isn't the money — John would let me have that. I just would rather stay at home than make Alf ashamed of me."

"I guess you're right," Charlie agreed. "I feel some that way myself, but I thought perhaps you'd make a go of it. But if you ain't sure, maybe it's best you don't try it."

"Someone ought to go."

"Herb would be as bad a rough-neck as I am."

"Still, he's got nerve," suggested Gladys. "He wouldn't give a hoot whether he made a show of himself or not. He'd laugh it off somehow, and make Alf laugh it off too. And Alf could make sure his clothes were all right."

So the next time Herb came home, the matter was broached to him, and he was unexpectedly in full agreement.

"Sure, I'm goin' to see Alf graduate," he said, grinning. "We've had that fixed up for some time. Oh, 'twas way last winter Alf wrote me to be bankin' on it."

Elsie, coming to the butt'ry door with a smoothly shaped loaf of bread dough in her hands, spoke with the edgy tone that was becoming habitual with her.

"I guess he'd be ashamed to have the rest of us come, hicks that we are," she said.

"Well, he'd have room to be," retorted Charlie.

"Aw, rats," scoffed Herb. "Alf's no snob. Here we've been diggin' down in our jeans to give him a chance to be somethin' we never can be. When he gets there we've no room to gripe."

"Well, I notice you ain't plannin' to take me along," jibed Elsie.

"No, nor anybody else," said Herb. "I'll have all I can do to walk the chalk myself. If you and Morris want to go, manage it yourselves."

"Well, don't worry, I'm not goin'," and Elsie retired to the bread making.

Herb, as usual, had money enough for his project, and he cannily left his shopping to be done in the city under Alf's supervision.

The paths of these two had lain far apart for four eventful years, and their meetings had been seldom. Yet the bond between them was strong, and diversity of interests had never yet affected it perceptibly. Herb felt that his trip to Orono was the great adventure of his young life, and yet he would have perished rather than have even Alf suspect how he felt about it.

Travel to the railroad brakeman was nothing new, but there was decided novelty in traveling as a passenger. He even blew himself to a parlor car chair from Portland to Bangor, and sat outwardly blasé and at ease, inwardly feeling like a fish out of water and wondering if he looked as idiotic as he felt.

Alf met him at the depot in Bangor, and together they did the shopping. Herb was gratified to find that his suit would do. His lank figure was well proportioned, and he had paid enough for his ready-made blue serge to get by in it. There remained the details of shirts, shoes, collars and ties. Even the underwear and pajamas, Alf had his say about, for Herb was to bunk at the frat house, and nothing could be hid that should not be revealed.

Alf saved the worst blow until the last.

"Now," he said, "we'll go around and see about hiring you a claw-hammer for the Ball."

"A what?"

"Claw-hammer— soup-and-fish— full-dress suit."

"You're crazy!"

"No such thing. No use for you to buy it — you'll never wear it again maybe. But you can't go to the Ball without it."

"Who said I was goin' to the Ball?"

"I did. I've even got you a dame to take. Sort of a friend of my girl."

"Rats!"

"Oh, it's all right. She's a swell girl. Not hard to look at. Good dancer. I couldn't have got her for you if my girl hadn't helped out."

"She'll be sore, havin' to go with a hayseed like me."

"No, she won't. Beth — that's my girl — said Evelyn understood all about it, and thought it was sort of a sporting proposition. You can dance with the best of 'em, Herb, and you don't have to talk if you don't want to."

"Hell and hardtack," replied Herb fervently. Then a glint of fun and a sudden set of the jaw showed Alf that the battle was won.

"Come on. Here's the place," he said.

They got the dress suit, and then hied them to a barber shop. The haircut was over and the shave under way when the second battle was staged.

Alf was adroit. While Herb was swathed in a steaming towel, he beckoned to the manicurist, who settled down and took Herb's great paw in her hands. Herb started up and snatched at the towel.

"What the—" he muttered, and rolled a wild eye at Alf.

Alf grinned encouragement and signaled him to submit.

"You can't step out with mits like that," he said.

Herb groaned, and then as the towel was removed, he lost himself in contemplation of the fluffy peroxide coiffure bent over his hands. The soft fingers, so smooth and so skillful, intrigued him, and when the girl threw him a swift glance of knowing coquetry, he chuckled. He was having the time of his life.

Finally, laden with boxes and suitcases, they took the trolley to the campus, and it was night when they got in. The frat house was alive with lights and laughter and music, if such it could be called. One small, pale chap was sitting at the piano, slamming away at the keys and producing such "rag-time" as made Herb's feet twitch even in these strange surroundings.

"Hi there, Hayseed!" yelled someone, and Herb stiffened.

"It's all right," whispered Alf, "he means me. That's what they call me." Then, in the direction of the voice, he called, "Come on up, Monkey-face."

Bundles and all, they made their way upstairs to a small, overcrowded room which it seemed Alf shared with three other fellows. Herb stared in bewilderment at the narrow cot.

"I s'pose ye take turns sleepin'?" he inquired.

"Wait till you see the ram pasture," answered Alf.

That, to Herb's relief, proved to be the third floor, stark, unfinished, with windows opened wide, and twenty-four narrow beds in orderly rows. Some of the Freshmen had gone home, leaving room for a few visitors and alumni.

Herb weathered the week-end very well. He had only to follow the crowd, he found, and speak when he was spoken to; he knew his table manners were not above reproach, but as he looked about he could see others as bad off as he was. Alf's roommates were good guys; one of them seemed to have a slinking eye, and to hold aloof, but that didn't matter. The good-fellowship of the others made up for it.

The baccalaureate sermon seemed impressive to the lad who could count the sermons he had heard on the fingers of one hand. The man, whoever he was, in the voluminous silk gown with its colored hoods, spoke what sounded like common sense. He didn't pound the Bible once, though there was a tremendous Bible right under his fists. Herb liked him.

He liked the long rows of graduates, in caps and

gowns — his brother Alfred was among them — and he liked the scattering of co-eds, a mere handful among a hundred and fifty men. You would not know they were there except for the froth of white under the gowns, and the soft hair under the mortar boards. He had never seen a crowd like this, so quiet, so well dressed, so much all of a kind.

"High class," he thought.

After the service was over, he stood among the crowd and watched the graduates file out in a long double line which dissolved and mingled with the visitors on the green slope of the lawn. He saw Alf go by, walking with a co-ed nearly as tall as himself, a good-looking, clean-cut girl whom Herb supposed to be Beth Nichols. If so, he was to meet her later in the day. He spotted the big, dark fellow who had been in Parkston at Christmas, but he was walking with another man, not with Marian Parks. She came farther down the line. Alf saw her as she came out of the chapel, the sun in her face. She seemed oblivious to the man at her side, who was not oblivious at all. Herb watched them a moment, and thought of Charlie. A good thing he had not come — he would not have liked this at all — Marian sober and preoccupied, and the slight, pale, rather scholarly man beside her, looking down with all his eyes at the little, black robed figure, as if he would never look elsewhere as long as he lived. Herb pitied him, then wondered if pity were in order. The girl might like him after all. She would never wear her heart on her sleeve even if she were in love for good and all.

Afterward, dreaming over this colorful interlude in his prosaic life, Herb remembered best the Commencement Ball. The days and events leading up to it had been rather hectic; he had had to get used to the frat house, with its devil-may-care ways; to mannerisms and customs which seemed to him so smoothly sophisticated; to the girls — sisters, sweethearts, college widows, co-eds — all so different from the girls he knew.

He believed he had been well accepted. His gaucherie apparently made little impression on anyone; indeed, probably few of the people he met paid enough attention to him to perceive it. The few with whom he became really acquainted were Alf's roommates and their girls. It struck him that they formed a protecting group around him, and treated him well because he was Alf's brother. Only the one with the shifty eye was a bit supercilious, but Herb didn't mind that. He could see that this fellow was less popular among his fraternity brothers than was Alf.

Herb enjoyed the Class Day and the Commencement. Much of the speaking went clean over his head; the jokes and hits of the class prophecy and the bestowing of gifts were too subtle for him. But he was alive and interested every minute.

He had met Evelyn Chase, and had gone canoeing with her and Alf and Beth on the turbulent river which looked as smooth as glass yet gripped the paddles with a wicked force. He had been befriended by her at the "open house" at the women's dormitory — "The Coop," as it was called. She had been nice about that, had steered him to the receiving line, piloted him down it, towed him along to the punch table, and introduced him to the girls as Hayseed Ashburn's brother. She was so jolly and nice that he didn't notice her looks. He just liked her.

But it was different at the Commencement Ball.

Herb felt like a fool in his dress suit, and he suspected that he looked like one.

"Alf, see here," he pleaded, "if I look anything like I

feel in this damn fool rig, I'd better stay right here. I don't want to ruin everything this last night. I've got by all right so far, but this—"

"Aw shut up," replied Alf reassuringly. "Let me tell you something. Half the fellows that will be there never had a dress suit on more than a half dozen times in their lives, never until they came to college. Look at me. I never saw the inside of one until last year, you know. You look all right. Just forget about it."

"Forget this armor plate? Forget these—" He held out his big, white-gloved hands in disgust.

"Aw, come along. Be a sport!"

Unfailingly Alf had chosen the right plea. Herb was a good sport, and he was sure that once he got to dancing he would be all right. Any Ashburn could dance.

They called at The Coop for the two girls, who came down in their long, pale-colored cloaks, with scarfs over their hair. Neither one seemed to see anything odd in his get-up. He was reassured. Evelyn pressed his hand to her side with her elbow.

"You look great," she whispered.

Herb was never to know at first hand just how much the ways and customs of Commencement Balls might change in two decades. That June night, just a few years before the outbreak of the World War in 1914, stayed with him as a framed picture hung in memory.

The girl, Evelyn Chase, dressed in a long, sleek sheath of pale blue satin with a frivolously stately little train, and blue slippers and stockings that showed occasionally; the great gymnasium draped and decorated with banners, green boughs from the college woods, and sprays of roses; the thick, moving mass of delicately colored dresses and the rigid black and white of dress suits; the throbbing and wailing of a hidden orchestra; the lights that sometimes shifted and changed their hue — it was a fairyland scene to the brawny young brakeman from the White Mountain Division. He might not have fitted in at all had he not lost all consciousness of self in the enchantment of the Ball.

"See here, Herb," Alf instructed him, "here's your dance order." He handed over a small white paper booklet with a silken cord and a tasseled pencil. "You see, you have the first, last, and two intermissions with Evelyn, just as we do at home. I made out your order for you. I thought you'd rather stick to just a few partners, so you'll have four others with Evelyn, two before and two after supper. I'll see that she gets her partners. She knows 'em all anyhow. You'll make out all right."

"Sure; but what do I do with this damn thing?"

"Vest pocket, and don't lose it. Your gloves will soon be a wreck, but don't dare take 'em off until after the first supper dance. And if your shirt front wilts you just have to let it wilt. We're all in the same boat that way."

"Gosh," said Herb.

"Be sure and fan your girl between dances. Just grab her fan and go to it. All set?"

Herb moaned, "I guess so." Then again he was lost in a wonderment which he would have died rather than show. In spite of the soup-and-fish, he believed he was going to like the Ball.

Evelyn Chase was really quite a girl.

"You can dance!" she exclaimed. "Alf told me you could, but really you are better than he is."

"I like it more, I guess. Alf was always more for readin' and studyin'."

"I know. Beth talks about him. She likes him a lot."

"Does she?"

"Yes. Oh, there goes Marian Parks. You know her, don't you? She's with that little shrimp Haverford tonight. Why on earth she turned down Ham Witham, for him, I fail to see."

"Did she turn Witham down?"

"She must have — he hasn't any other girl on the string, and Marian hasn't been anywhere with him for weeks."

"You know her well?"

Herb was thinking of Charlie, and of all the talk at home.

"Well enough to know that she carries a picture of your brother Charles in her History of Western Europe. I sit near her in that class. It is a snapshot of him in a cow's-breakfast and overalls. She uses it for a book mark."

"Well, you know all about the Ashburns." Herb grinned at her.

"I room with Beth. She and Alf have been going together for two years."

"We didn't know that."

"Alf is a clam," said Evelyn.

Herb met a few more girls, whose names were scrawled on his order. He couldn't remember the names, but he discovered that he had only to dance and the girls would do the rest. At intermission, they strolled back to the frat house for ice cream and cakes and punch. The punch was mildly spiked, and Herb liked it; but Alf and the girls drank from the water cooler in the back hall.

"Co-eds won't touch anything with a stick in it," Alf explained.

Plenty of the other girls did, though Herb was impressed with the sobriety of the party. No rough stuff, no "fussing," much laughter and fun. He had heard that college men were pretty gay and reckless, but there was no sign of it here. Alf explained that, too. No matter how the fellows might behave otherwise, when there was a house-party, there was the utmost decorum. No excessive drinking, no spooning; nice girls were entertained in a nice way, for the honor of the fraternity.

The Ball was even more fun after the intermission. Gloves were taken off and stowed away in coat-tail pockets, and everyone felt more free and easy. The music was better, too. Probably the orchestra had had spiked punch. Herb was dancing with a small blond girl, whose name he could neither decipher on his order nor remember, when the lights went dim, silver-blue like moonlight, and long streamers of colored paper and showers of confetti rained down from the rafters. He and his little partner were entangled with the streamers, wrapped around with them, as they waltzed in the glamorous light. Herb felt bold. He drew the girl close and asked, "What's your name?"

"Pat."

"Well, Pat, you're a sweet thing!"

"So are you!"

Herb raised her hand and kissed it quickly, as that seemed the logical thing to do. She giggled; so he stooped and kissed her bare shoulder.

"You know your way around, don't you!" said Pat, giggling again. Herb felt sophisticated.

But even at the sad, sweet throbbing of the "Home, Sweet Home" he did not try anything of the sort with Evelyn Chase. He knew that it wouldn't do at all. They said good-bye at the doorstep of The Coop, and the June sun was showing faintly pink in the east. It had been fun. The girl had been kind and understanding — a good sport. She reached up and patted his cheek almost maternally.

"Let me know if you ever get married," he said. "I want to send you a present."

"I will," she promised. "I know you'll send me something nice."

They took an early morning train for home. And as they sat in the Portland depot, waiting for the Mountain Division train, Alf spoke for the first time of his affair with Beth Nichols.

"Say, Herb, no need to make any talk about Beth and me there at home, what?"

"No? Sort of secret?"

"No secret about it. There's nothing to tell, that's all. Nothing to hide either. Just nothing."

"Kind o' looked like somethin'. Evelyn told me you'd been keepin' company for two years."

"That's what folks would hardly understand. She and I've been good friends, and it's a good thing to have a girl to take around. It's like skating on thin ice sometimes, of course, with a square shooter like Beth. But Beth's got ambition. She wants to earn some money. She's been poor all her life, and worked hard. She wants to try easy street for a spell."

"Nothin' so easy about earnin' your own livin'," Herb suggested.

"She'd be independent, anyhow. And it's all right with me. None of you have ever said a word about getting your money back that you've spent on me, but I'd like to make some of it good. I'll bet not a one of you knows how much each has put in.

"Oh, gosh sakes, Alf, who cares? Mother wanted us to get educated. You are the first one to do what she wanted. That's enough."

"I've got a job for next year."

"What doin'?"

"Teaching. Instructor back there." Alf jerked his head in the general direction of Orono. Herb whistled.

"They must think well of ye."

"'Tisn't so much. But it was handed out — thought I'd better take it."

"Why, sure. Mother'd like it."

"Well, just keep mum about Beth, will you?"

"Of course."

There was hilarity when they got home. Gladys and Hilda had come to hear about the graduation, and Morris showed up after supper. He chortled over the dress-suit episode.

"Good gosh, Herb, to think you'd come to that! Bad enough for Alf. Spose he really can't help himself, bein' educated and all. But you—"

"You never did tell us anything about the girl you took, Herb," Gladys reminded him.

"Aw, gee, she was a peach. Wa'n't she, Alf? Swell dresser — I tell you, I've had myself a time!"

"And what about Alf's girl? I bet he hasn't even got one," teased Hilda.

Alf looked bored and dull, suddenly. Herb came to the rescue.

"He's got too many; that's what ails him. This one I took was one he had to turn down. Sort of consolin', I was. He just picked the best lookin' one in his string and I took next best."

Elsie had to get in her say.

"Did either of you dance with Marian Parks?" she inquired.

"Sure, we both did. She was with a different fellow — not the one that was here Christmas."

"I spose you got an awful crush on your girl, Herb."

"Aw, sure. Never shall get over it, most likely."

"Don't talk like a fool," said Charlie, speaking almost for the first time since they had got home.

Chapter Fifteen

Naturally, everyone knew that Graham and Marian Parks came home at about the time Alf did, and Charlie was distinctly conscious that Elsie was watching him jealously, wondering what he would do about it. He kept away from the house as much as possible.

The season had started out well. The strawberries, his latest innovation, had begun to bear, and a few were ripening already. He had started an asparagus bed, too. It would not be ready to cut until the following spring, but the family were all watching it lovingly. It would be something good to eat at the dry time of year, before the "garden sass" was ready. Such crops were becoming Charlie's recreation; sort of a change from the serious work of corn and potatoes, cows and chickens.

Alf helped him some. And one day, when they were resting at noontime on the stone wall near the barn, Alf spoke of Marian.

"Seen her yet, Charlie?"

"No."

"She's changed. Looks older, I guess. They say she

and Ham Witham had a falling out. Some chance for the rest of us, maybe!"

Charlie saw red; but then he realized that Alf meant no harm; that he did not see what went on at home nor hear all the talk. So it was best to just laugh it off.

"Fat chance!" he scoffed.

He had made up his mind to one thing, however — he would have guts enough to stay away from that girl this summer, or know the reason why. He did pretty well for a week. He would see her sometimes, a figure diminished yet clear-cut in the mountain air, coming and going about the old Parks place. He had often longed to go over there, yet had not dared. Dancing with her had been about all he or the town gossip could stand.

One rainy day he took his tools and went down the road to mend a break in the fence. There were usually about a dozen such fiddlin' jobs waiting for a rainy day, when it was too wet to work in the fields. The fence wasn't in such bad shape and he took his time about it. The softly drizzling rain was nice to be out in, and there was something different, intimate, about the chirp of the birds and the rustle of water-laden leaves. Why couldn't a man just grow roots, and so be at peace? Or like the animals, run nature's course and not keep tearing his shirt over it? Look at all the little lives and homes, all around him, beautiful, entire, and clean. It seemed to take a man, with his notions about advancement and civilization, to step in and cover things with smut. Man's dirty cities — man's dirty machinery — man's dirty morals.

Charlie picked up his tools and began to think about going home — back to his own particular nastiness — and as he straightened up, he saw that Marian Parks was coming down the road afoot, right toward him. His heart turned over. She was slim and cute enough in her green rubber coat, tramping along in the mud. He would have known her anywhere by that free, swinging gait, head held high, back straight as a ramrod. Maybe if he hurried, he could get into the road ahead of her and keep ahead, pretending he had not seen her.

No, it was too late for that. He drew back further into the tall underbrush, hoping she would pass without seeing him. It wasn't every day a man got to watch a girl so closely without her knowing it. She was so small, yet so wiry and strong. She liked the rain; didn't mind the mud on her heavy tan boots. She was almost within arm's length before she saw him.

"Goodness, Charlie!" she exclaimed, "what are you hiding there for? I didn't know you for a minute."

"Didn't mean to scare ye. How are ye?"

Her hand was wet with the rain, but it was warm, and he kept hold of it, so that she was near him, looking up into his face. There were beads of mist on her eyelashes, and on the curls that her cap didn't cover. She said, "I am glad to see you again, Charlie," and he knew she meant it. Then she asked, "Where were you Saturday night? I saw Alf and Herb at the dance, but I missed you."

"Oh, I was home."

"That's no explanation."

"Do I have to explain?" It was unlike Charlie to be so sharp. A puzzled expression on the girl's face gave place to one of comprehension.

"I was so sorry when I heard about your father," she said. "I would have written to you, but there's never anything to be said, it seems to me."

"No. Not a thing. Death's a part of the game. Talkin' won't stop it; grievin' won't bring anybody back. And anyhow, what would anybody want to come back for? Tell me that!"

Marian shivered and drew back, putting her hands in her pockets; there was a far-away look in her eyes, as if she could see through the clouds and mist.

"I'm beginning to think," she said, "that this life is nothing much but a disagreeable, complicated mess."

It was so exactly his own idea that Charlie was startled. "Where'd ye git that notion?" he asked roughly.

"I'm not the first person to have it."

"No, by the Lord, you're not!" Marian shook herself and smiled.

"Be a sport and come to the next dance, Charlie!"

"No, I'm done with all that."

"Oh, no!"

"Sure thing. I'm too old for such foolishness. I got to have my sleep."

"I've heard you say that before."

"I mean it this time."

She took a step nearer him.

"But I can't have any kind of a vacation without you, Charlie!"

"By godfrey, you may have to!"

"Well, well, what are you cross about? Something gone wrong? Can't you tell me?"

"No."

She laughed again. "Well, since you don't like me any more — nor want to dance with me—"

She turned and walked away. Maddened, Charlie was after her, grabbed her by the shoulders and faced her about so that she was in his arms.

She was cool about it.

"Well, what next?" she asked.

He had acted without thinking, and he had no idea what next. Any other girl, he would have known what to do with; but not Marian, mocking him with her eyes, calm, unmoved, miles away from him. He let her go.

"That's better," she approved. "I'll see you Saturday night."

And she walked off down the road, and left him standing there like a fool.

And like a fool, he went to that dance. He went afoot and alone, leaving Alf to bring Hilda and Elsie with the team. Morris had not come home, and it was high time he did come. He had stayed away for weeks now, and it worried Charlie. But he would not be hanging around Marian — and that was one good thing.

There were nearly as many automobiles as horses huddled about Henry's dance hall now. Times were changing — a good, high-stepping horse no longer got a fellow anywhere with the girls; it had to be a car. And of course Graham Parks had got him one. Charlie saw him drive up to the hall, Marian beside him, with everyone standing around pop-eyed at the sight. It reminded Charlie somehow of the night she had worn the low-necked dress. She was always doing something that made the gulf between them wider and deeper. It would be a long, cold day before the Ashburns would have an automobile.

The music began, but Charlie lingered in the men's room. He had some idea of easing off gradually, dancing less and less with Marian, and finally stopping altogether. It might be the handiest way to do it. So it was not until well along in the evening that he went to her.

"Oh, hello, Charlie! You're dancing after all. I'd begun to think old age and rheumatism had surely got you."

She was laughing at him, as usual, but there was a hard tone in her voice, as if she had to try to get that laugh out. He slipped his arm around her, loosely at first.

Long ago he had discovered that trick — if he was easy about it at first, and then gradually tightened his hold, she seemed not to notice; while if he grabbed her suddenly she hated it. Talking always helped to distract her too, until he had got her as close as he could hold her.

"I see you and Graham are puttin' on style," he said.

"Just keeping up with the times, that's all. Why didn't you come around for the first dance, Charlie? Graham was sore. He had been planning to ask Hilda for his partner, and he had to stick by me instead."

"Hilda?"

"Yes. He had a high time with her last week — you missed the show. Hilda is going to be a very, very attractive girl, Charlie. How does she get on with the singing lessons?"

"Pretty good, I guess. Freeman wants her to go to Boston and study as soon as she's through high school."

"Freeman? Well, I suppose as she lives there so much, he is interested in her."

"He'll do more for her than I can," replied Charlie, a trifle bitterly. "I don't see what Graham wants to buzz around her for. He has girls enough other places, hasn't he?"

"Oh, Graham likes Hilda. He told me so. He says she has more sense than most girls twice her age, and that she can dance like a dream."

"Oh, well— Gorry, Marian, but you're thin! Have ye been sick?"

Getting her close, it seemed to him that there was nothing left of her at all. It was almost pitiful.

"No, I'm all right. What makes you say that?"

"You don't weigh more'n half what you used to — and that never was much."

"I'm all right," she repeated.

But she wasn't. He saw what Alf had meant by saying she looked older. As the evening went by, she was lively as a cricket one moment, and dull and sober the next. Not like Marian at all. Pitiful — yes. For the first time since he had known her, he pitied her; wished to do something for her to make her happy. It would be wonderful if she really needed him!

At intermission, she leaned back against the wall. He had never seen her tired before.

"Want I should take ye home?" he asked.

She sat up straight. "Heavens, no! Too many hours before daylight!"

"Don't ye sleep good?" Charlie could understand that dread of a long night, and poor Marian didn't have even the comfort of hard work to wear her down and bring the solace of sleep!

They stayed until the last dance, and he wished they might have stayed longer, for Marian was sweet to him, and not even Morris was there to cut in. Even the goings-on between Hilda and Graham failed to worry him; he was too preoccupied with this serious, wistful mood of Marian's to care for anything else.

At last it was time to go, and as Charlie helped Marian into the automobile, Graham and Hilda joined them.

"Got your team, Charlie?" asked Graham.

"The family's got it. I walked."

"Well, Alf can drive it home, then. You and Hilda hop in with us."

Hilda was visibly thrilled. It would be her first ride in an automobile, and Charlie could not have denied her, much less let her go alone with Graham.

The crowd around the doorway was watching the proceeding; the noisy cranking up, the sputtering, the pistol-shots, the rattling crescendo as they got under way — probably everyone hoped they would get stuck, but it was getting so that cars really would run most of the time. They were being improved every year.

Marian settled back wearily as they chugged along the dusty, moonlit road.

"How about a spin down the river road?" asked Graham.

"I don't care if we do," answered Marian. "Are you and Hilda in a rush to get home, Charlie?"

"No, I guess not.

He thought of the night he had taken her buggy-riding. Never again! And with all he had on his hands, he could never hope to own a car.

Marian was very still and, watching her sidewise, he saw her put her hand to her face once or twice. Sure enough, she was crying! He got hold of one hand.

"Tell me, Marian," he urged. "What ails ye? Have ye been sick? Did ye have some trouble?"

"Oh, Charlie, I've been so miserable!"

"What about?"

She straightened up and put away her handkerchief; then she laughed in that hard, queer tone.

"I'm suffering," she said, "from the pangs of unrequited love!"

"Huh?"

"Don't you believe me?"

"I don't know what you're talkin' about. Neither do you."

"Oh, yes. I know what I'm talking about. I know what it's like to be perfectly wild over someone that doesn't care a cent about me."

"Fun, ain't it!"

"Charlie — sometimes I've wondered — since you

were at our house that night — you remember?"

"Yes. I remember."

"Well, Mother seemed to like you, and she told me you were too good for me to play with. She said it wasn't fair for me to go around with you so much — that it was selfish and mean of me."

"Nonsense!"

"Charlie, I might have known you'd say that. Of course it's nonsense. What is selfish or mean about our being friends? You've always understood me. You don't really care, do you — except that we have such good times?"

It was pitiful to see her so troubled, with her little face so solemn and white in the moonlight.

"There, that's all right, Marian," he said. "We've been good friends; had a lot o' pleasure dancin' together. That's all there is to it, o' course."

What a whale of a lie! And Charlie had always prided himself on being truthful.

"That's what I've told Mother. You have too much common sense to—"

"To lose my head over you? Well, I've got common sense enough, if that has anything to do with it."

She leaned nearer and put her hand back in his.

"I like my friend Charles Ashburn," she said.

Funny — that he could be so near her and yet feel only this pity, this tenderness.

"Maybe ye just don't understand this feller — Witham, I spose it is," he suggested.

"Yes — Hammond Witham."

"Maybe ye just had a little fallin' out; and it'll all come around right in time."

"I wish I thought so!" She leaned against his shoulder, much as Little Elsie did when she was tired.

Marian liked her friend Charles Ashburn — she had just said so. She was in a gentle mood, longing to be loved. It was a lonely road, and the pair on the front seat were busy with an exchange of jibes and teasing that would keep them absorbed for some time. A little urging, and Charlie was sure he could have made Marian love him — for a while, anyhow. Why he did not take advantage of her mood and satisfy himself with holding her while he could, he never knew. Perhaps because it would have been like hitting a man when he is down.

It was quite a distance down the river road and back by way of the cross-road over the mountain; and all the way he kept one arm around her, and held the little hand. Her loose dark hair blew up against his chin, but he didn't even dare to smooth it back. He held her, and yet, she was miles away!

Tired as he was, when he got home to bed he could not sleep. The fever that had been subdued by Marian's childish clinging blazed up again at the unsatisfying memory of it. With her, he was held down by that severe reserve of hers, by the fear of arousing her anger or filling her with disgust of his roughness. Away from her now, and remembering that slender body, the soft, waving hair, he was nearly crazy. He got out of bed and crouched in a chair by the open window, his head braced by his clenched fists. He was there when Elsie came, creeping up the shed stairs, tiptoeing across the floor. She had him cornered.

"Look here," he raved, "what in hell do ye keep after me for? Why don't Morris come home and look after ye?"

"I don't want Morris. I want you."

Elsie was not pretty, any more; she was not clever. She was not much of anything, one way or the other. But she clung to him, sapped away his strength, ruled him through the one weakness of his flesh.

Chapter Sixteen

All that summer, Charlie was beset with perplexities, most of which had to do with the women-folks.

In the cool of the mornings, out in the dew-drenched orchard, over on the slope where he had located the chicken runs, going his rounds before Elsie called the tribe to breakfast, he would try to figure things out. It could not go on — if the beauty and completeness of home were not for him, at least he must manage to stop the growth of this foul thing that was his foremost worry. He must keep the home clean for the children, anyhow. He often wondered how it was that he could face Marian Parks, with so besmirched a conscience; but he did face her, dangled around her, as idiotically as ever. He was getting hard, shameless, and he despised himself for it. Elsie was different.

She was not the out-and-out hard-boiled kind. Had she been that, Charlie would have been repelled rather than tempted by her. She was just an average sort of woman, neither plain nor pretty, neither stout nor slender, neither dark nor fair. Her hair was getting just a little gray, and her hands showed the marks of years of labor. She had glasses now for sewing, and for the occasional reading which she did. Nobody seeing her about her work, or dressed in her good clothes at Ladies' Aid and Grange meetings, or even at Henry's on a Saturday night, would have suspected her of any irregularity of conduct. Her round, fresh-colored face with that slightly receding chin was usually expressionless. She seldom spoke, and never said anything especially interesting or significant. She was, to all appearances, a good, decent, hard-working woman, devoid of complexities, finished long ago with passion.

But Charlie, to his sorrow, knew her better.

Morris had never really loved her; she had loved Morris but briefly. The elemental woman in her, always her strongest characteristic, was lavishing itself now on Charlie. She had loved him long, and deeply; loved him more than she loved herself, or her own peace of mind; loved him with a stark, demanding simplicity.

Charlie understood her well enough — too well!

"She don't give a damn," he thought. "She just don't give one single damn about right and wrong, so long's she gits what she's after."

He thought rebelliously of pulling up stakes and leaving home — trying his luck in some other part of the state. He might hire out on a farm, or get work on the roads, or with the brown-tail moth commission. Just step out and leave everything; let the rest of the tribe do as they pleased with the place.

But if he did that, Elsie might get after Alf, or Herb, and that wouldn't do. They were too young to be nagged that way. Perhaps Elsie would go and live with Morris; but then Hilda would have to come home to keep house, and then, what of their plan for her education — high school first, then Boston Conservatory? Nothing must interrupt that! Yet wouldn't anything be better than letting this dirty business go on? Maybe time would serve to show him what was best to do.

For the present, Gladys was expecting again, and really needed Hilda that summer. Charlie never had any worry about Gladys; rather did he find solace in her strength, her common sense, her kindliness. Having another baby was no bother to her — she felt fine and was utterly happy. But she was a little concerned about Hilda. She came to the stone wall by the barn one day, when Charlie was treating himself to a Sabbath nap far from the houseful of holiday confusion. They talked a while of this and that, and then Gladys said, "Charlie, what do you know about Hilda?"

"Hilda? What do ye mean? Anything wrong?" Charlie sat up and scratched his head drowsily.

"She's growing up, Charlie. Do you spose she'll get boy-crazy?"

"Any signs?"

"Boys enough, if that's any sign."

"Oh, gosh, she's just a baby!"

"She's going on fourteen, and old for her age, for all she's so small."

Charlie could see no cause for concern.

"There's boys hanging around, Charlie. I'd have sent her home this summer but I really need her, and she'll have an easier time with me than with Elsie, even with my tea-party coming. Jackie'll never miss me if he has Hilda."

"Well, what's wrong with boys? Don't all girls have 'em around?"

"Charlie, I don't want her too interested in any of 'em. It's all right for her to have fun, and gad around some, but she's got more ahead of her than these small-town fellows. You know that. And then there's Graham Parks—"

"Pshaw — no—"

"Charlie, I've watched him., He don't know it yet, but he's interested. Of course he thinks of her as just a kid, but don't you see? If we do right, and see she gets educated, and has her voice trained, and all that, it might work out—" Gladys flushed. It was a delicate matter to discuss.

Charlie chewed soberly on a straw. He thought of Marian, of the tragic differences that kept that stone wall between himself and her. Was Hilda in danger of running into such a mess as that?

"You keep her with you, Gladys. Better a dozen small-town boys than one Graham Parks."

"What's wrong with him?"

"Oh, nothing — not a thing. But she'd better stick to her own crowd, her own age, for some time yet."

So though Hilda was safe in East Parkston, Charlie rather had her on his mind. His heart was tender toward her, and he wished she might never know pain and disappointment.

Elsie, and Marian too, kept him in a stew all the time. Both made demands on him. He could understand Elsie all too well — Marian was another proposition.

She was planning to teach school in the fall. She had joined a teachers' agency, and kept writing to apply for places, wondering what she would get, disappointed when some turned her down, relieved when others did the same. It wasn't worrying her. There was plenty of time, and she was sure to be signed up before September.

Meanwhile, she wanted to be on the go all the time. She flirted with Charlie; not in her natural, little-girl innocence, but in a hard, deliberate way he did not like. She knew just how to torment him, knew that she did torment him; yet she kept holding out the bait, snatching it back again the moment he overreached. Then, having goaded him all the traffic would stand, she would penitently relapse into simple friendliness, with the wall of reserve around her that no lover could have got through. She was using her own emotions, and his, as playthings; her mind always ruled.

As luck would have it, there were more dances than usual that summer. The Grange was trying to raise money for repairs on the hall, and sponsored a series of Wednesday night hops. There were plenty of summer boarders within driving distance, especially now that everybody was getting a car. The floor at the Grange Hall was good; the one at Henry Church's better. Crowds came from all around. Marian would not miss a dance.

"Oh, I'd go wild, Charlie, day after day, so still — so dead — I just have to dance or I couldn't stand it."

"Pity ye don't have to work," he retorted.

"I do work. I cook, and sew, and wash dishes. But what's that? Just my hands busy, and not my head."

"Too bad — but see here; ye used to like the quiet. Said ye liked to be peaceful, and look at the hills. Don't ye ever go up to the big ledge any more and lie under the trees?"

Marian shivered. "No — it's too peaceful; that's the trouble. It makes things worse than ever. Nature's something like you once said holidays are — for happy people."

So twice a week they danced. Graham no longer acted as his sister's keeper; Charlie went after her and took her home again. It was a short mile to Henry's, a half mile to the Grange Hall, and Marian loved to walk.

Often she ran ahead of him, laughing and slipping away just as he was about to catch her.

"Sometime," he warned, "you'll go too far with this nonsense and then I'll — probably make ye mad as fire."

"Oh, no, you wouldn't. You're altogether too nice."

And like a fool, he was "nice." And no matter how late he stayed out, walking with Marian or sitting on a fence somewhere trying to cool off after he had left her, he more than likely would find Elsie waiting up for him.

Elsie was sly about it. There was Pop's downstairs room, vacant unless Morris came home, and the younger folks were always asleep upstairs. It was too damnably easy.

Morris came home very seldom. He told Charlie he was steering clear of Marian Parks.

"I used to dance with her a lot," he admitted, "but not any more. 'Tain't healthy, for me, or for you either."

"I'll look out for my own health." Charlie was gruff. He could not feel free with Morris any more; there was too much black and hidden sin between them. Once they did have a talk, and agreed that, now Pop was gone, Elsie would better live with Morris somewhere near the shop, before folks got to talking; but she rebelled, and Morris said to leave her be till fall. While Alf was home, there would be no gossip.

"Better settle it right away," Charlie warned, but Morris only sighed.

Blueberry season always came along just as the haying was done, and before it was time for the late summer and fall work to begin. Of course the berries ripened sooner in some places, so that enough were picked to have for supper now and then. It was fun to see them change from light blue to deep, rich purple when Elsie stewed them. But the real blueberry picking was a serious matter. It meant one day off, devoted to that alone, and while the young fry regarded it as a picnic treat, housewives thought of it as a necessity. It meant full purple glass jars on the swing-shelves in the cellars, and deep, juicy pies through the winter months and in the spring after the apples were gone. A good housekeeper must have blueberries.

Elsie usually made out to go herself and see that the job was well done. There were plenty of places to go. Wherever a forest fire had once swept away the tall trees and left the fallen logs and stumps, there the berries grew, some the high-bush, with large, blue-black fruit in heavy clusters, and some the low-bush, whose luscious sky-blue globules were covered with a silvery bloom.

One morning, when Hilda had come for a day at home, Elsie hurried through with the morning work and packed a lunch in two school dinner pails. Then she called Alf to harness for her.

"What's on your mind?" he asked.

"Blueberryin'. Want to go?"

"Don't care if I do. Hilda going?"

"Yes. I'm going to do up a few cans for Gladys."

Elsie and Hilda both were dressed in their old clothes, for the day ahead of them was an arduous one. It struck Alf that Elsie was certainly going off in her looks, yet there was about her a firm and competent vitality, and an inarticulate sort of consciousness of womanhood. Dumb, silent as she was, Elsie knew what she was up to most of the time.

Hilda was cute; even her shabby cotton dress, her shapeless sun-hat, her childish, ribbed black cotton stockings and her run-over shoes did not stop her from being sweet, and lithe and graceful as a kitten. as she swung up over the wagon wheel to the seat between Elsie and Alf.

Alf gathered up the reins and clucked encouragingly to the horse. They had the old horse, who was no longer any good to work, but who liked to go places once in a while. He looked like a rack of bones, but the whole tribe loved him.

As they went rattling down the mountain side, Alf could see, across the valley, two figures strolling somewhat aimlessly down the lane from the Parks place. Marian and Graham, evidently, enjoying the morning sun.

"Hey, Elsie," he said, "how about asking the Parkses to go. They might like it."

"No, they wouldn't." Elsie was positive.

"Why not? I'm going to ask 'em, anyhow."

Hilda chimed in, "Charlie'll take you apart if you do that."

But Alf was not to be turned from his purpose. He watched the couple coming nearer, and he wondered. What was on the Parks girl's mind? Did she realize what a sap Charlie was about her? And if so, did she care? What had happened between her and Ham Witham, and would she ever marry that other fellow that had been taking her around some in the spring term? And where did poor old Charlie come in?

Still speculating, Alf reined in just as the brother and sister were too close to them for Elsie to make a protest. Hilda was visibly interested and expectant.

"How about going along with us?" Alf invited. "We're going after blueberries over in Dan Chadwick's old pasture."

Graham glanced at Hilda, and then back over the wagon bed, at the lunch and milk pails and the measure of grain for the horse.

"You're pretty well loaded," he observed, "and we'd have to get our feed bags too."

Marian was interested. "I tell you what, Graham," she suggested, "we'll get the car, and something to eat, and follow them."

"Bad road for a car," said Elsie sourly.

Alf covered her curtness. "Do that," he urged. "You can leave the car at the corner and ride in with us on the wagon. You'll overtake us before we get there."

Elsie didn't think much of the arrangement, and said so as they drove ahead.

"She's too stuck up, that girl. How'll she feel when she finds out what she's in for — scratching around in all that mess of underbrush?"

"That's just what we'll find out," answered Alf, smiling amiably. For some reason it always tickled him to get Elsie riled. He hadn't a thing in the world against his brother's wife — he just liked to plague her.

The car overtook them just before they reached the intersection of the highway and the deep-rutted, grass-grown road that led to the old Chadwick pasture. The car could go no further, so Graham and Marian put their pails in the wagon, let down the tailboard and jumped up to ride, their feet swinging in the tall grass as the horse plodded on.

There was little left of the original Chadwick homestead — just the chimney and the cellar hole, with a thicket of lilac bushes, and the gaunt, satin-gray hulk of the barn with one great overshadowing elm tree.

They left the team, the horse tied to the spoke of a wheel, and set off across the pasture with their kit — a ten-quart milk pail and a small lard pail apiece. There was no need even to climb a fence. The stone wall was crumbled and the loose small rocks were scattered along the lines in the underbrush. The coarse, sun-baked grass was slippery and brittle to walk on. The rich dark green of the sweet ferns sent up faint fragrance, and Alf showed Marian how to pluck the tiny, nutsweet seeds out of their softly fuzzy burs.

"Oh, I never knew they were good to eat!" cried the girl, delighted.

"Plenty of things to learn, here in the hills," said Alf.

He was watching Graham Parks. Sometimes Alf reminded himself of Pop, with his intense interest in people, his tendency to observe and analyze.

Graham was walking ahead, between Elsie and Hilda. He was tall and lank, and rather good-looking; tanned, his medium brown hair bleached on top from the sun. His face was thin in profile, the nose rather too big perhaps, but the chin decisive enough to keep it company. And when he smiled, his teeth were an even white flash across his face. His shoulders were good — square under the silk shirt he wore. Alf did not resent that shirt, for it was torn at one elbow, and tucked into flannel trousers that were old and stained; Graham's sneakers, too, were obviously the veterans of many jaunts such as this. Elsie had been wrong — the Parkses knew something about roughing it; knew what to expect of a blueberry bog.

There was a sudden burst of laughter from ahead. Graham was strolling along, suiting his stride to Hilda's shorter steps, and had been talking to her with a sort of quiet absorption quite alien to his habitual sophisticated gaiety. But the little girl was lively enough for two, apparently.

"Hilda's a cute thing," said Marian, "Graham seems quite smitten."

"Hilda's a baby," retorted Alf.

They were beginning to find the blueberries. Gaunt,

charred tree trunks and fallen logs marked the ravages of fire, the pitiful ruin being softened and covered by the greenery of smaller growth.

Bees hummed loudly, and near the dampened brim of a spring they found a deer track. They set to work, the big blue-and-silver berries falling with metallic clamor into the empty lard pails. Soon the small pails would be filled, emptied into the larger ones, and filled again, and again, until the harvest was enough to satisfy Elsie's needs for canning. Gradually, the workers drifted apart, each following what seemed a likely path through the thickets.

The morning wore on; the sun climbed higher; the heat became intense. Alf slackened his pace and looked about. Marian was not far from him, bending over the low bushes. She had torn her dress, and her soft, pale shoulder was reddened with sunburn, but she was indifferent to that. She straightened up.

"I'm a sight," she said, "but look — my big pail is half full!"

Alf smiled at her enthusiasm. "Don't wear yourself out," he said. "There's no rush. Want to sit and rest a while?"

"O-Oh, but I'd love it!" She rubbed the back of her neck and wriggled her shoulders to loosen the aching muscles, then hoisted herself up on a fallen log and took off her hat, letting the damp little curls about her face get a breath of the passing breeze.

Alf drew himself up beside her.

"I love it, don't you?" Marian continued. "I've torn my dress, and scratched and bruised myself unmercifully, but myself doesn't seem to mind."

"No — it's all in the day's work. The main trouble is the danger of breaking a leg when the underbrush fools you. I've been down a dozen times this morning, when I thought I was going to step on solid ground. Hornets been after you?"

"Oh, I don't mind hornets. They never bother me. I just sit perfectly still and let them buzz around until they get bored and go somewhere else."

Alf liked that. It was some like Beth Nichols. Most girls yelled at the sight of a hornet, or a bee, but Beth never yelled about anything. He wished she were here right now, to enjoy the wild isolation of this place — its magic, humming stillness.

Elsie was far away. He could barely see her huddled down and almost lost in the foliage. But there came Hilda, tripping along, looking back and chattering to Graham, who was close behind her carrying their pails. Hilda was the most voluble of the Ashburns. Her vitality seemed to break into speech as well as to express itself in her dancing footsteps and her songs. Now, as Alf watched, she turned quickly back toward Graham, and stepped into treacherous footing, falling in a little heap at his feet.

Alf was not alarmed. Falling was nothing to fuss about. But Graham was concerned. He set down his load and took the little girl up in his arms. Unconscious of any observation, he bent over her and spoke to her, then set her on her feet, his arm still about her, and smoothed back her hair.

Hilda laughed. She was not hurt. Graham took up his pails again and followed her to the log where Alf and Marian were sitting.

Graham Parks was sunk. A muscle in his thin cheek was twitching still, and his hand, as he helped Hilda to the log, did not want to let her go again. Alf knew better than to form any opinion as to how serious this might be, or how long it might last. He had seen plenty of such affairs come and go, and neither party any the worse for it. That's how things might work out with Graham and Hilda. She was young; the years ahead would be many and eventful; there was just no telling. But Charlie and Gladys were right about one thing — Hilda must stick to her schooling, and go away to the Conservatory. They could manage it among them.

Graham pulled out his watch. "My tummy and my time-piece," he said, "are in perfect agreement. 'Tis noon."

"Right," said Alf, and they called to Elsie and followed their trail back to the team.

There was water. Where once a trough had been a spring still sent up a freshening little pool, cold and sparkling.

"It has nearly as much git-up-and-git as apollinaris," Alf remarked, and Hilda wanted to know what apollinaris was. Elsie merely looked dubious. This was just cold water, to her.

Elsie was more than ordinarily silent, which Alf believed was scarcely necessary. Her hostility toward Marian was too pronounced for comfort. As soon as they had eaten their sandwiches and cake, and the boys had smoked their pipes, Alf took Marian aside.

"Elsie's sore," he whispered. "She's sore because Morris used to shine around you so much. Just for fun you pretend you are all taken up with me, and maybe she'll feel better."

Marian was doubtful, but she let herself be led around to the farther side of the old barn, where the great elm tree stood as a symbol and a memory of previous habitation. Here they settled themselves with their backs against the tree, and Alf refilled his pipe.

"I guess we've worked enough," he said; "how about it?"

"I'm sure I have. I don't seem to yearn for any more berries right now." Marian blinked her dark eyes sleepily, and snuggled her hands into the grass. She was not pretty, exactly, Alf thought, but nice. She looked like a square-shooter, and yet — well, there was more than one thing he wanted to find out, and now would be the time to do it. He had only to wait, and be alert, and the girl would spill it herself.

The pasture and the near-by woods were quiet and very warm. The rest of the party had returned to their work. Close to the foundation of the barn, a clump of raspberry bushes dropped crimson fruit upon the grass, and Alf rolled over indolently to gather a handful.

"By way of variety," he said, as he gave Marian half of them.

"Alf," she said, "I wish Charlie could have come today. Why didn't he?"

"Picking berries is work for women and children, you know."

"And which are you?"

"A combination of both, perhaps. Lily-fingered!" he spread a stained and muscular hand before her.

"One could hardly accuse an engineer of being lily-fingered," she replied.

"A bachelor's degree doesn't make an engineer, as our worthy Dean so carefully explained to us. It merely makes, in my case, a pedagogue."

Marian took his hand and turned it, palm upward, on her knee.

"Your hands are thinner than Charlie's," she said, "but much the same. Square, practical, but more sensitive; that's the student in you. I like hands. They seem to be an index to character."

"Well, Charlie's practical as all get-out, and he's certainly no student."

"Might he not have been?"

"I doubt it. But he's nobody's fool — he's keen as a whip."

"I know." Marian was thoughtful, seemed ready to lapse into dreams with Alf's hand still in hers. He sat up.

"See here, while we're at it — let me look at that heart line of yours."

She laughed and surrendered her hand. "It's like a feather duster!" she exclaimed.

She was right. The heart line in her soft palm was broad and chain-like and ended in a cluster of fine smaller lines.

"If there's anything in palmistry, you're a terrific flirt!"

"Well, happily it's all bosh." Marian was sure of that.

"Is it, now? It strikes me, if you don't mind my saying so, that you're playing fast and loose with two or three lads I might mention."

"But of course you wouldn't mention them."

"Certainly not!" They grinned at each other understandingly. Alf was enjoying this, and he could see what it was that captivated Charlie. It was her simplicity, her frank good fellowship, that was ready at any time to withdraw into dignified detachment, or to break into coquetry. A fellow couldn't be sure which it was going to be. What was she, anyhow? What did she feel, and what did she think about?

"Oh, no, no!" Alf murmured, "I wouldn't mention any of them, but how I'd like to!"

Marian turned toward him. "You're a good scout,

Alf. Sometimes, since I've known Charlie so well, I've wished I knew you better. But college is such a rush, and you've always been so taken up with Beth Nichols—"

"Now who's mentioning names?"

"I am, and I don't care."

"Neither do I. Go ahead."

"Well, I'm glad to have this day with you, and Elsie and Hilda. So is Graham. You see, we have always wanted to be on good terms with Parkston people — not to be thought of as just summer folks, but as neighbors. Sometimes it seems to work pretty well, and then again, it gets complicated."

"Yes, complicated — as when two brothers, one of them a married man, fall in love with you, and you fall in love with someone far away from Parkston, and have a scrap with him, and then come home—"

"And try to figure things out. And someone proves to be so kind, so understanding, so faithful, such fun to be with! You know, Alf, he is the best sort of companion, and yet—"

"And yet of course it would never do. He is poor, and unlettered, and not so young, and certainly not much to look at—" Alf recited Charlie's failings with merciless candor.

Marian protested. "All that wouldn't matter, if only I really loved him. But I don't — not that way."

"You couldn't, as things are. But without his handicaps, you might find it quite easy to love Charlie," Alf insisted.

"No." Marian jumped to her feet and threw out her arms with mock theatricalism. "No, I could never love him, for alas! I love another!"

"That so? Well, sit down and take it easy. No need to get all het up about it."

Marian sat down, and seemed for some time almost to regret her free speaking. Alf waited. There was more to come, he knew.

Finally, "Tell me, Alf — why does Elsie hate me? It isn't on account of Morris. There was nothing to that."

"Wasn't there? Elsie may think differently."

"No, I'm sure it isn't that. I often know things without being able to reason them out, and that's one of them. She hates me because of Charlie — maybe she thinks I'm mean to him. But why should that worry her?"

"She's fond of Charlie. He's a brother to her. She may think he is not very happy."

"It's not that. I've seen it in her eyes — just today I've seen it. I can't make out—"

"Oh, well, don't worry. Whatever it is—"

Alf did not finish. Graham and Hilda came crashing through the thicket and threw themselves down on the grass.

"We're fagged out," said Hilda.

"Speak for yourself, woman," retorted Graham. "A midget like you can't stand much. But me—" he slapped his broad, flat chest and then relaxed, stretched himself full length on the ground, and closed his eyes. As he did so, Alf saw him slyly reach out and grasp a fold of Hilda's little gingham skirt, and hold it.

Hilda had been eating berries. Her mouth was stained with purple; her hair was flying every which way; her face and hands were dirty, and she didn't care if they were. She was an impish, unkempt country child, fourteen years old. But she was a woman-child, and Graham Parks, one of the more prominent students at the State University, equally at home in the classroom or the ballroom or on the athletic field, well versed in the mysticism of Greek letter life, reached out to touch her dress as he lay down to rest.

They lingered there in the shade of the elm until Elsie came with her big pail full to the brim, and announced that it was time to be goin'. She was glum and silent, but nobody cared. She drove the team back to the highway while the others walked, and then the party separated.

"Graham and I haven't so many berries," Marian remarked. "Not so many. But we surely have had fun getting them."

"Glad ye call it fun," said Elsie. "I'm all tuckered out, myself."

Chapter Seventeen

As soon as Alf had graduated, and announced himself ready to go it on his own, Charlie had felt free to spend a little money; and he had installed a grain mixer, run by a gasoline engine which also, on occasion, could be used in place of the old windmill to pump water.

"Ye know," Morris had suggested when the engine had been tried out, "next thing to do is to git a bathroom put in. Have faucets at the sink, hot water and all."

"Think we could make a go of it?" Charlie had asked.

"Sure thing. We got water enough. Got the engine. All we need is some sort o' storage tank that won't freeze. I'll figure it out."

That would be a mighty good thing, they all agreed, and perfectly possible if things kept on as well as they were going now. The hens were doing fine. The grain mixer would be a real saving in the end, as they could now buy in larger quantities and mix in no time at all. Some different from mixing with shovels on the barn floor.

Charlie had the thing going full blast one day, when

a sudden shadow on the floor made him turn around. He was paralyzed for a moment — Marian Parks stood there in the doorway, Marian in a little gingham dress, and a broad hat in her hand, Marian with her dark hair damp and curling around her face, and her eyes laughing at him through the din of the whirling machinery. Even then, he knew something had happened to her. She was more like the little girl he had loved first.

He reached for the lever to stop the mixer, but Marian protested.

"No, no!" she cried, "I like to see it go!"

"All right, but keep close to me. Ye mustn't get hurt."

Hot and dirty as he was, Marian seemed not to mind keeping close to him, and he pointed out the workings of the contraption, explained the formula for mixing the grains. Then he shut off the engine.

"Can't keep yellin' at ye like that," he said, as the noise died away. "Come on outside here, under the apple tree, where it's cool."

Marian sat down on the grass and looked up into the tree.

"These aren't ripe yet, are they?" she said.

"No. But before ye go, I'll git ye some that are. Unless you have plenty."

"We haven't any right now. I'd love some. But what I came for is this — I had a letter from Ham today."

"I thought so."

"What made you think so?"

"Knew you was feelin' good about somethin'."

Charlie was decidedly not feeling good, but it would never do to let her know it.

"You're right — and I'll tell you about it if you promise not to tell."

"No — I won't tell."

Charlie looked at her sidewise, just once, and then sat there beside her, his elbows on his knees, carefully breaking a twig in half, and then in quarters; then taking another twig and beginning all over again. He was wondering just how much he could stand.

"It all goes back to early in the spring, after the Easter vacation," she was saying. "You see, it wasn't just Ham — there were two of them, and I went to the junior Prom with the other one. Ham had been too cocksure I'd go with him. He didn't say a word about it ahead of time — just took me for granted. So when the other man asked me, I accepted. And Hammond Witham was wild!" She laughed.

"Yep. I guess he must have been." Charlie was glad Witham had suffered. He wished the guy had killed himself.

"Yes — he was furious. And we got to talking, and said a lot of ugly things to each other, and Ham just couldn't get over it. I was beginning to think he never would. But today I had a letter from him." She paused, remembering that letter.

"And it's all fixed up? You're goin' to — marry him?"

"Probably. He's just graduated, you know, but he has a job already, so we may be able to marry right away. But until he gets my letter, I suppose I'm not really engaged to him, so don't tell anyone just yet, will you?"

Charlie did not answer, but Marian seemed not to expect him to. The sun was beating down through the branches overhead, and the drowsy hum and the mellow fragrances of late summer filled the air. Marian drew a deep breath of it. Her very happiness seemed to be a part of it. A world of happiness and content, of fulfillment —

with Charlie forever left out!

"Well," he said finally, "I spose ye won't want to be bothered with me any longer."

"What an idea! I'm not going to give up all my friends and good times just because I'm engaged."

"Maybe not, but I tell ye right now, I'm quittin'."

"Charlie!"

"Don't you go Charliein' me! Seems to me all I hear lately is women yellin' 'Oh Charlie' at me."

Marian laughed. He wished he could choke her and stop that laughing.

"All the women after you, are they?" she teased. "I never did see a man yet who wasn't worried about the women being after him. But you needn't be afraid of me. I've got a man of my own!"

Harshly, Charlie laughed too. He might as well — just let the whole thing pass as if it meant no more to him than to her.

He threw down his handful of broken twigs and turned toward her, fighting down that aching dread of the time when she would be there no more. He reached for her hand, and it was firm and responsive in his grasp. She was watching him, her eyes dark and gleaming with genuine feeling of some sort. He had never before been sure of the color of her eyes; now he knew that the color changed. They were blue today because the gingham dress was mostly blue. By lamplight they were black. With her green raincoat, and with her dark winter dress, they had been green. There was everything in Marian's eyes as she watched him now — her own happiness, her fondness for her friend, Charles Ashburn, her regret that he was so hurt, her suddenly matured woman's consciousness of the wrong she had done him, and her remorse.

They sat for some time under the apple tree, talking or silent as the girl's mood shifted, but she was sweet to him. There was no more teasing, no more deliberate tormenting. Just that gentle friendliness and understanding that he had read in her eyes.

At last, with quick kittenish grace, she got to her feet and said she must be going; and, as he stood beside her, wordless, she lifted her hand to his shoulder.

"Don't do that," he said. "Witham would beat you up if he knew it."

"He won't know it," she replied. "I guess I can do as I please with so good a friend as you, Charlie. Listen, Charlie — do you know, I shall miss you when I go away. You've been so good to me, all this awful summer. I — thank you—"

She had gone too far. In her softened mood, she had forgotten her habit of aloofness, had come out from behind it, where he could reach her. He had her in his arms, and she could not get away. Not this time. Not until he had kissed her, and kissed her again—

"There," she said. "That will be all—"

"No!"

"Yes, really — not again, Charlie — I mean it!"

Yes, she meant it. He knew that, knew that she was stronger than he. He let her go.

"You just meant to say 'Thank you,' " he stated with bitterness.

"Well, perhaps — Charlie, do you know, sometimes I wish there were two of me — one to go away, with Ham, and one to stay right here in the hills forever."

"Not with me?" he suggested, starting toward her again.

"No — no — I suppose not. I wouldn't fit into your life, nor you into mine, any more than just as it has been these past few years. But I do like you so much, Charlie!"

"Well," he told her grimly, "you have to call a halt to a thing like that, ye know. It can't go right on, year after year, just the same."

"I suppose not. Well, good-bye, Charlie!"

It was not until he saw her in the distance, on her side of the valley that the full bitterness of it swept over him. He would have to stay away from her now. He wouldn't be able to stand it. Of course, she had never belonged to him, and he had known she never would; but neither, until now, had she belonged to anyone else. Good God, what had he ever done to be punished like this for — to be in love with a girl who was marrying another man? This punishment had come before the sin of which he was so ashamed. Indeed, that sin itself, and its aftermath of shame, was all a part of the punishment for loving Marian too much. Yet what wrong was there in that love? He could not help it; never could have helped it.

He was glad he had known her, anyhow, even if she had spoiled his liking for the sort of girl that would be likely to marry him. There wasn't another girl anywhere, in these back woods or out of them, that could compare with her; not one that could stand up so straight; not one with such cute, independent ways; not one that could keep a strong, hot-blooded man so completely under her thumb. She was a tormenting little vixen, but she was good, too; honest, decent — and not for him, not ever!

After supper one August night, Charlie harnessed up and went to see Gladys. He sometimes did that. It had been a trying day; he was feeling decidedly down in the mouth over things in general. He hardly wished to talk, even to Gladys, but he had to go somewhere, had to dodge Elsie with her watching and her fussing, had to have time to himself which the six miles over and back again would afford.

He began to feel some better as he drove through the woods. It was a hell of a world, of course, but there was something still and peaceful — something maybe like heaven would be, if a person ever really got there — something calm and grand about the woods at twilight. The sky was glowing red through the tree trunks, and a big star was beginning to show up plainly just above the feathery tops of the pines. A hermit thrush was singing. Maybe if a church could have a singer like that thrush, people would come, and get some religion.

And the thrushes would always sing — they always had sung in the woods at sundown. All kinds of cussedness might come and go for men and women in this world, but forever there would be this much of heaven — the thrushes, and the pine woods, and the gathering restfulness of night.

Gladys was comforting, as usual. He could tell her nothing, of course, of what Marian had asked him not to tell, but then, she knew enough. She knew he was heartbroken, and she could easily guess why. So Gladys talked mostly about herself, and her affairs, and about Hilda, who was out with some friends and would be in before he left, she said.

Freeman was there. "You really ought to smoke, Charlie," he remarked. "It's real sort of soothin'."

"Maybe, for some," admitted Charlie. His trouble could never be smoked out, that was one sure thing.

He stayed late, wishing to see Hilda, and also reluctant to go back. That was bad — an essentially home-loving man, dreading to go home. It was far from right.

A crowd of youngsters came chattering along the

street, stopped by the front gate a while, and then went on, still talking and giggling as if there wasn't such a thing as misery in the world. Hilda came up on the porch and sat on Charlie's lap a few minutes before Gladys sent her to bed.

"She goes out like that often?" Charlie inquired.

"Not so very. Don't you fret — I've got my eye on her, Charlie."

"So has young Parks," Freeman said.

"He been around?"

"Some. Gladys seems to think she's quite a hand at managin'." Freeman was more than half serious, and Gladys answered defensively,

"I don't see any harm in tryin' to make things right for Hilda. Want I should drive a nice fellow like Graham Parks away from her?"

"No — no." Charlie was cautious. "Don't say's you should drive him away. But spose he should be just foolin' and triflin'? "

"Well, even if he is, Hilda's got her heart set on the Conservatory. She's safe." Gladys was quite positive in that, and Charlie started for home with nobody's worries but his own to bother him.

But the woods were dark, and lonesome, and he thought of another August night when he had not been riding alone — when a little face, white in its frame of dark hair, had been beside him; little hands, white on the laprobe; little soft body, yielding for just one short breathless moment against his own—

The return trip was not as quieting as he had hoped it would be, and he was still sore and despondent when he opened the door and tiptoed into the dark and silent house.

"Charlie!"

It was Elsie, drat her — Elsie sitting there in Pop's old chair by the south window, waiting up for him. She was forever doing that. She seemed to know just what he was thinking about, and how he was feeling. Dumb as she was about most things, she was keen enough about that! It was low-down — it was contemptible — it would have to stop—

But not now. Charlie was too tired to fight.

It was well toward daybreak that he heard someone groping at the kitchen door, coming stealthily in. Doors were never locked in that neighborhood, for there was never any need of it.

"What do ye spose 'tis?" whispered Elsie fearfully.

"Hush up. I'll go see."

He turned on the light in the entry between the bedroom and the kitchen, at the foot of the stairway. A man's figure loomed in the corner by the sink. It was Morris, searching for his matches and his tobacco can with his pocket flashlight.

Here was a pretty how-do-ye-do!

"Hullo, Morris. Where'd you come from?"

"Been to Cross Corners, wirin' a house. We stayed late to finish and went to a dance over there. They dropped me off on the way home."

"Well, that's nice. Better take my room. I'm bunkin' down here tonight."

"Oh, I'll just turn in with ye. Too much work climbin' those stairs, this time o' night. Anything to eat?"

"Help yourself."

This was a sorry mix-up, and no mistake. Desperately, Charlie tried to think of a way out. He never had been any good at lying; even if he could have thought up a good one, he wouldn't have been able to make Morris believe it.

Morris would find out in time anyhow; why not face the thing right now and have it over? Charlie stepped back to the door of Pop's room. Morris was rummaging in the butt'ry, but it would be no use to try to fool him. Elsie must pass through the entry to get upstairs, and the doors were all open. The one between the kitchen and the stairway was even propped open with a chair to keep the wind from slamming it.

It was only a step, though — maybe Elsie could make it—

"Who is it? Morris?" she whispered.

"Who'd ye think it was, Santa Claus?"

"Oh — Charlie—"

"Shut up and get upstairs. He's getting something to eat — he may not turn around—"

It was a bare chance, but really Charlie almost hoped she would fumble it. And she did. Hastily gathering her wrapper about her, she tiptoed to the door, and just as she did so, Morris came from the butt'ry, a piece of pie in one hand and a glass of milk in the other. They faced each other, the width of the kitchen and entry between them. Elsie was frightened, sullen, half defiant, unmistakably guilty. Unlike Charlie, she could have lied, could have covered the matter up somehow, if she'd had more time to think it over. But there was nothing to be done now.

"Elsie," Charlie ordered, "git upstairs."

Hurriedly, she obeyed. Morris stood, open-mouthed, incredulous.

"Well, for gosh sakes—" he began. "What in tarnation — how long since—" The situation seemed to dawn upon him by degrees, and Charlie felt as if he had to break through somewhere and clarify it fully. Anything would be better than the hell of the past muddled weeks.

"Too bad there ain't any shells for the shotgun,

Morris," he said. "Want me to go git the hoss-whip?"

"Charlie — you—"

"Want I should git it for ye?"

"What?

"The hoss-whip."

"What for? Good God, no!" Morris sat down abruptly, splashing the milk on the table.

Charlie stood there in the doorway, feeling like a fool, suddenly conscious that he must cut a pretty figure — a homely, bald-headed old moss-back in a cotton nightshirt — stealing another man's wife! He, Charles Ashburn, turning out to be a devil with the women! If it had been anybody else, he would have laughed outright. Scandals like this made rich telling at Gag Corner. Lord knows he'd heard enough of them in his lifetime, and often they had seemed comical. But when it happened to the Ashburns, he would laugh out of the other side of his mouth entirely.

"You ought to want to do something about it, I sh'd think," Charlie suggested. Was Morris just going to sit there, hard as nails, and eat that pie? Was he taking this all in the day's work, going to shrug it off like he did everything else that bothered him? Didn't he care a hang—

"I don't want her," said Morris, apparently losing interest in the pie and the glass of milk. "I never did want her. I've kept on because she was good to the kids, good to Pop. I didn't want to cut loose when everybody was satisfied but me."

"I thought as much."

"Yeah. You know, Charlie, Pop and Mother would turn in their graves if there was a divorce in the family."

"I know it."

"But if you want her, I spose that's the way out."

Morris looked almost hopeful. Charlie felt as if the jaws of a trap were ready for him.

"Gosh sakes, Morris, you don't think I want—" He couldn't say it. Morris stared at him, and then gave a short, ugly laugh.

"Wrapped herself around you, too, did she, Charlie? That's the way she got me!"

It was a raw thing to say, but it was true and they both knew it. And as always, the understanding, between them was deep, and strong, and as old as their life together. Morris was an irresponsible sort, sometimes; he was more a care to Charlie than a help; he had muddled things one way and another all along; but they were brothers. Charlie had been a fool, and a wicked one; he had broken the commandment and his shame was a bitter thing; Morris could have killed him then and there and been well within his rights. Charlie was sure that, had Morris turned on him, he would not have even put up a fight. He would have been glad to pay for his sin with his life. But here they were, talking it over in the old farm kitchen as they had always done. Bad as things were, they would figure it out somehow. They always had. Words came to Charlie's mind, from somewhere — words vaguely familiar — "Passing the love of women" — where had he heard those words?

After a long time, Morris broke the silence.

"Once in a lifetime," he said, "ye find just the right kind o' woman. After that, there just ain't any other one."

"That's right. Once in a lifetime."

"She'd never have had either one of us."

"No. She's goin' to marry that feller that was here Christmas. She told me so."

"She did?" Morris thought it over. "Well, that's right. Suitable. Say, it's too bad you wa'n't educated, like

Alf. You might-a had a chance then, Charlie."

"Me? Old, homely, pretty near bald-headed? Humph!"

"She always did like ye."

"Oh, sure. She likes me. Likes me fine. Likes me like a friend. Hell and hardtack—"

"Well, now, Charlie — havin' a friend ain't so bad. Considerably better'n nothin'."

"Maybe so. But see here, Morris, I wish we could git this business settled somehow. I can't stand lettin' things drift. I've tried to git ye to take Elsie away, before folks got to talkin'. Now we're in this mess. How's it goin' to work out? Darned if I see."

"I'll have to make her go with me," Morris replied grudgingly. "I hate it, but I do want the kids to have a square deal. Divorce would be hard for everyone. Wouldn't do any real good."

"You could come back here, and I'll clear out." The thought was not new to Charlie, but it was a hard prospect. He really loved the place — would be utterly lost away from it. Life elsewhere would seem utterly impossible to him, yet if that was the right thing to do, there were no two ways about it.

Morris' reply was reassuring.

"I don't want to farm, Charlie. Elsie'll have to bring the kids and keep house with me. We'll tell her tomorrow."

That seemed final enough. Hope began to grow up in Charlie's troubled soul, and a sort of clean-washed peace that stilled for a while all doubts and questionings. It was queer — but out of every perplexity there always came, in time, this compensating sense of satisfaction. Always there was a nugget of gold, once the dross was melted out. This time, it was inviolate brotherhood that shone so bright.

"Morris!"

"Well, Charlie?" It was like pulling teeth for them to speak what was deep down in their hearts.

"Morris, I want ye to know one thing. I wouldn't have robbed ye — I couldn't have done that — by God, I don't want to throw the blame on her, but—"

Morris reached over and gripped Charlie's shoulder. His big hand was steady and warm.

"Aw, shut up, Charlie. Haven't I had chance enough to find out what she's capable of? It's all right between you and me."

A while longer they sat there, until dawn began to shame the light burning in the entry. They did not talk much. They had been buddies for a long, long time.

Finally, Charlie remembered Elsie, and the family, and impending chores.

"By george, Morris, go up and talk to Elsie now. She's probably throwin' fits up there, wonderin' what next."

"Go yourself," retorted Morris. They grinned at each other sheepishly. It was one hell of a situation; but there was no use to be too squeamish about it. They ended up by retiring to Pop's room for a couple of hours' rest. Alf would come down and build the kitchen fire and do the milking. He must find nothing out of the ordinary, of course.

Chapter Eighteen

The Ashburns were naturally and traditionally a straight-forward, honest tribe, close-mouthed and unemotional, yet not secretive. Deliberately to hide things, or to dissemble, went very seriously against the grain with Morris and Charlie; but for the sake of Morris' children and of the family reputation for clean and orderly living, they were determined to put it through. They must manage to set things right without fuss and bother, without making talk. It was the least they could do to square themselves with each other and with the memory of their mother.

Breakfast the next morning was difficult. Elsie was frowsy and nerve-wracked, her eyes bloodshot with weeping, her dress untidy. She was silent, and Morris and Charlie ill at ease and self-conscious. Alf stared somewhat thoughtfully from one to the other — of course, he realized that something had gone wrong. The children as yet noticed nothing. They merely assumed that Mama was having one of her cross spells; a state to which the past few months had well accustomed them.

Charlie was the first to leave the table. It was a relief to get outside, in the freshness of morning, to escape to the poultry yards, to the sort of female fussing and cackling, he grimly thought, which was decent and profitable.

He was in one of the farthest pens, busy with the distributing of dry mash and water, when he saw Elsie come through the gate and close it behind her. Once more she had him cornered.

"Charlie!" She was a sight. He turned sick at the thought of having to deal with her.

"Well, what do ye want?" he asked.

"Charlie — what—"

"Hasn't Morris told ye what?"

"No. I didn't speak to him. Alf and the kids were there."

"Well, then I'll tell ye what. This is the end. You're leavin'. Morris wants ye to keep house for him."

She stared in blank amazement. "Morris — wants me—"

"Yes. And you're damn lucky that he'll take ye."

Almost overwhelmingly, Charlie realized how true his statement was. He wondered that he could ever have seen anything lovable about her; wondered at the great changes there had been since the days when he and Elsie had really been friends, partners, co-workers on this farm. Why in time had it all had to be spoiled like this? Now, he could only grit his teeth and stand it until she should be gone.

But as he was thinking of this, a change came over Elsie. In her dull and reddened eyes, amazement merged into incredulity, and then hardened into stubborn resistance, as she stared back at him.

"I won't go," she said. "You can't kick me out like that."

"I ain't kickin' ye out. Your husband is makin' a

home for ye, that's all."

"I won't go. I'll make him divorce me. Then I can stay here."

"You can do no such thing! Great scot, Elsie, don't ye see we can't keep this up? It ain't decent. Think o' the kids."

"But if Morris will divorce me, you can marry me, Charlie; you'd have to."

"No, by God!" Charlie hurled it at her like a cannon ball, and she recoiled; but she was not done yet.

"You'll have to," she repeated stubbornly. "It'd be on your account that he'd divorce me—"

By mighty, what a mule the woman was! She had been playing a game all along, leading up to this. Behind all that silence, that apparent stolidity, she had been scheming to get her own way. Who'd have ever thought she had brains enough, feeling enough, to put it through? Charlie was learning things every day he lived, it seemed. But if she'd cornered him time and again, he was wise to it now; he could, now that he saw more clearly, dodge anything she might attempt.

"No, ma'am," he said grimly. "No, ma'am! Your little game ain't goin' to work. He'll tell ye the same. He don't want a divorce; and I don't. I wouldn't take the gift of ye. Can ye get that through your head?"

"I won't leave here," she persisted, tears streaming down her swollen, sallow face. "I won't go. The kids and I — we like it here, with you, Charlie. This is home—"

Charlie reached past her and opened the gate; shoved her through it and followed her into the open field.

"Now you git along and leave me be," he said decisively. "I'll never lay hands on ye again, so help me God. You tell Morris you're ready to do as he says, ready to be sensible, and patch things up the best we can.

There'll be no scandal and divorce for us Ashburns, Elsie."

"You don't love me at all, Charlie!"

"Gosh, no! Who ever said I did?"

Love her? Love Elsie? Great heavens, who ever could think it even a possible thing? Charlie was sick at the thought of his ever having given in to her demands. He must have been out of his mind, crazy with worry and grief and loneliness. It was all a nightmare — it could never have really happened — and yet it had happened; and the stain of it would always be a dark blot on his life — on his self-respect. Well, anyhow, it would get no worse. They would, the three of them, keep their mouths shut and do their best to repair the damage.

Nothing more was said for a day or so. Morris went back to Brownvale to work; Elsie kept to her routine tasks, pale and (what was utterly new to her) unkempt and careless. She and Charlie scarcely spoke to each other, but he assumed that everything had been settled; that in time she or Morris would tell him their plans.

Meanwhile he had to make some explanation to Alf, as he would later to the rest of the tribe.

"Now that Pop's gone," he said, "it don't look just right for Elsie and the kids to stay here. Soon as you go, Alf, she'll have to live in Brownvale with Morris."

"That would be better, considering the way talk travels," Alf agreed. "What does she think about it?"

"She's been raisin' considerable fuss."

"Who'll keep house for you, Charlie? Hilda? Or Maud Ripley? "

Maud! In his weeks of storm and stress, Charlie had almost forgotten Maud Ripley. Maud had said that she might marry him if he ever got over loving Marian Parks. It would be a solution, a comfortable, respectable one. It would never do for Hilda to give up her schooling. Maybe, after a while, he could get himself in hand, and then Maud might be willing to come. Until then, matters could take their own course.

He had really decided not to see Marian again. So far, he and Morris were the only ones who knew of her engagement to Witham, but before long she would either go away to teach, or marry the fellow; and the sooner he got right down to forgetting her, the better. It had to be done, or he would go crazy.

But on the following Wednesday night, he overheard a conversation at Gag Corner, where he had gone for some postage stamps, which rather changed his intention.

The late summer twilight was thickening when he came out of the post office, and he saw a knot of loafers, standing in the shadows under the big maple tree. He was about to join them when the sound of his own name halted him. They had not seen him.

"Guess Charlie Ashburn and the Parks gal will be steppin' it out as usual tonight," one said.

"Yeah — they understand each other, I bet ye!" guffawed another.

"Charlie's a fool."

"Huh — don't ye think it! Charlie gits what he's after."

"What about that guy that was here Christmas?"

"Well, ye notice he didn't come back again."

"No—" They all laughed hoarsely. "She don't really need him, with Charlie on the job."

Charlie, drawn back close to the thick tree trunk, was seeing red. It would be fun to step out and knock their teeth down their throats, but what would be the use? Even if he were to succeed in licking the daylights out of every one of them, they would not believe in Marian's innocence. Their dirty, back-woods minds were incapable of comprehending her. If he raised one bit of fuss, they would merely be all the more certain that the girl was his property to fight for.

The damned old women in pants — they were not to be blamed, perhaps; and one of them was right; he, Charlie Ashburn, was a fool. Even so, he would have to stand by Marian a while longer — until her engagement was announced, or until she went away. That would end the gossip naturally, quietly; while his quitting her now would set the whole township buzzing. By mid-September the whole thing would be ended.

Charlie found himself anticipating with some impatience the time when he would be alone on the place. He knew he would miss the children, but with Marian out of town, and Elsie out of the house, he surely ought to get some peace. Meanwhile, his days were bad and his evenings with Marian little better. He was trying his best to be decent, to resign himself to her marrying Witham, to be gratified to see her so happy. He really was glad she was happy, but he was a long way from being happy himself.

August lagged along into September. Morris came home once, but said nothing about Elsie's moving. Alf returned to Orono, and still nothing was changed except that Morris came home again on the battered bicycle, and said he would come every night hereafter. It proved to be rather hard on him, but he made no complaint.

The Portland papers came out with the announcement of the approaching marriage of Hammond Witham and Marian Parks, and after that Marian came to the dances no more. She was getting her trousseau ready, she said. She asked Charlie to come to the old Parks place to see her, but he would not go.

The whole thing was over.

The crisp nights and mornings of September were but the beginning of severe weather to come, and Charlie decided to have another talk with Morris. The daily bicycling would soon be out of the question, and some action was necessary. He brought it up as they were sitting late by the kitchen stove one night.

"Well, Morris, when do ye move?" he asked.

Morris sat sucking his pipe a moment.

"Elsie don't seem to be doin' any movin'," he replied.

"She don't seem to be, but she'd better."

"Well, I've told her. I've found two houses that might do, and told her to come over and take her pick. But she keeps puttin' it off. Doggone, it's a mess, tryin' to deal with a mulish woman."

Mulish — she was worse than that. How she could endure it, staying here in the same house with the two of them, remembering all that had taken place, and knowing that Morris knew it, was beyond Charlie. Of course, he was standing it himself, and so was Morris, and probably they were putting it over all right so that nobody else suspected a thing. But he and Morris, though they hated the mess, had a definite object to stiffen their spines, while Elsie had nothing to back her, nothing but her own stubbornness to give meaning to the performance. He thought of other women he knew — of his mother, of Gladys, of Maud Ripley — not one of them could have lived in such an atmosphere, he was sure. Of course, not one of them would have been capable of getting so involved; but, even granted they could, they would have been impelled to make a clean break of it some way. They would never have muddled around like this—

"Say, Morris, she must have a hide like an elephant

— livin' here this way. How can she? Gosh, I don't claim to be dainty, myself, but it's pretty near more'n I can stomach."

"Same here," confessed Morris. "Ye see, Elsie — she just don't see things the way we do. They say folks is born free and equal. Maybe so; but they sure are born a lot different in their ways of thinkin'!"

"Seems-so. Well, you talk to her. Make her do it. She's your wife."

Morris took his pipe out of his mouth and regarded Charlie intently.

"Is she?" he inquired.

Abruptly Charlie was on his feet. "By Godfrey, I didn't think you'd throw that at me!" He stood irresolute, hurt to the quick. "Why, I've done my darnedest — I took care of her the best I knew, for years, while you gadded around free as air. I worked with her, talked with her, watched out for her; now when she goes and gets out of hand, you blame me for it. I tell ye, I don't feel any call to take that from you, Morris."

"There, there, Charlie, don't git hot under the collar. I didn't mean that — you know I didn't. Sit down, now."

Charlie sat down. He knew Morris hadn't meant it. "It's just what I'm tellin' ye," he explained. "This business is makin' us do and say things we wouldn't otherwise. It's no way to live — in a houseful o' dirt and stubbornness and hard feelin's."

"Well, I spose it's up to me," Morris admitted. "I brought her here, and I left her here. I'll git her away again."

So it rested, and a few days later Elsie spoke of it herself.

"I guess I may as well go, Charlie," she said, sullenly. "I guess you don't want us here any more." She had been crying again, and Charlie could think of no one he would want there less.

"I'll miss the kids," he replied truthfully.

"I'll stay till I git things ready for winter," Elsie told him. "Then I'll move into that biggest house, near the shop."

"Go any time," Charlie invited. "I'll make out all right."

"I can't git ready right off. It takes time." Elsie stood close to him and looked up with her large, round eyes; there was in them a gleam of desire and of hopefulness. Charlie turned sick. She hadn't given up after all. She was deliberately putting off her going, still of a mind to wear him down, and get her own way. He set his teeth. He would show her who would wear down first.

The line storm came a little early — about the middle of September. For three days the wind raged and the rain came in a steady, unremitting downpour. It was hard on the children in a way, for they had to get to school just the same and it was almost impossible to get there dry. Elsie took them with the old blind horse and the wagon; they had the heavy robe for warmth and the rubber blanket and big carriage umbrella to keep the water out, but the best they could do, it was dampish.

Of course Gladys' baby took this time to be born. Alviry predicted it the first day of the storm. She had come in, you would have thought, just to pass the time o' day with Elsie, but as usual she had something special on her mind, and that was it.

"This kind o' weather," she remarked, "makes the babies uneasy. Saw the Doctor at the store this mornin', an' he says, says he, 'Sure's the line storm comes along, I'm busy as a pup with fleas.' And I've noticed it myself. Usually, I don't pay no attention to those old sayin's, but you'll see — when is Gladys' time?"

"'Longabout now," Elsie told her.

And it was the second day of the storm that Hilda called up and announced the arrival of young Ashburn Freeman.

"That's all the name he's going to have," she stated. "Gladys says it's name enough for anybody. If she has a few more, she'll start naming them for the boys, right down the line, but she's making sure of getting an Ashburn, anyhow."

As soon as the storm was over, Elsie dutifully went to see the baby and Gladys, and to return with all the news for the delectation of her mother and Alviry and a dozen others who called or telephoned. Charlie overheard the full details of the confinement retold until he was sick of it, and marveled again at the women. You would have thought they'd like to forget such details as much as they could, but it didn't work that way.

He would go over himself, of course, as soon as Gladys was home again and settled down. She was getting on all right; Hilda was there, and they had a hired girl, and John could make out to be at home much of the time to help when he was needed. Charlie never had to worry any about Gladys. She could manage her life.

Alf, back at the university, wrote that he was getting adjusted and thought he would like his teaching. It was his absence, and the storm, which led to Morris buying an automobile.

He had always wanted one, but never could think up sufficient excuse for the extravagance. The bicycle had served to get him home each night, as long as good weather lasted. But now Morris figured that he must come home regardless of weather, and the cycling was pretty bad. He found he could get a car cheap — one of the doctors in Brownvale thought he'd rather sell than keep the thing all winter, when he had to use a horse anyhow, so the dicker was made.

Charlie had hoped it might make Elsie sit up and take notice, and perhaps think more kindly of her position as Morris' wife. It did help some. She insisted upon learning to drive and though most women balked at cranking a car, she didn't mind. She was husky enough, and what she wanted to do she usually did somehow. It was not long before she felt she could handle the car by herself, and after that she often kept it all day, taking Morris to the train in the morning and going after him at night. This trip by train was not so convenient for him — it was only a few minutes' ride, but the Brownvale depot was half a mile from the shop, and all around it was a bother. Yet Morris felt that he had no right to complain. Anything that amused Elsie and kept her good-humored was all right with him.

Charlie wondered where Elsie went on her afternoons of driving. She always gave an explanation — she had been to her mother's, or to Alviry's, to the store, or a Ladies' Aid meeting. She even claimed she had visited friends who had been too far away for frequent calling with just the old horse and team as conveyance. Charlie had no mind to inquire further, but there was a hint of furtiveness about it which was uncomfortable. If Elsie had been really telling the truth, she would have felt no need of explaining at all. At any rate, she was working Morris for all he was worth — the car, the plan for the larger house, in Brownvale, a new coat and hat — and all the while there was her housekeeping slipping back.

Morris came home one night, his face black with anger. He said nothing until after the children had gone to bed, and then the explosion came.

"Where was you yesterday, Elsie?" he demanded.

"I was over to Gladys'," she said.

"You was not. You went ridin' round with Fleta Carmel, and I know it."

"Well, what if I did?"

Morris stood up and took a step nearer Elsie, and she rose, too, so that they were facing each other — he, tall, furious, menacing, and she sulky and defiant in her dumb, stubborn way.

"So long as you wear the name of Ashburn," Morris said, "you'll keep clear o' that slut, do ye hear?"

Elsie did not flinch. She had a weapon in her hand now!

"I ain't wearin' the name of Ashburn for my own pleasure," she answered. "Besides, I got as good a right with Fleta Carmel as you have."

Morris gave back, flushing brick red, and shut up like a clam. Charlie felt a wave of nausea go over him. Great guns — more filthiness! Morris, too, caught in this tangle, besmirched, degraded — it had to stop, right now, and no more dilly-dallying about it.

But maybe Elsie was wrong; maybe there was no justice in her taunt; maybe the shamed silence on Morris' part was not that of guilt, but merely of frustration and disgust. Maybe he really had shut up because he saw nothing to be gained by further talk. Charlie shrank from knowing any more just now. Knowledge might hurt too much!

Elsie had said definitely that she was moving; there was that much hope and consolation. But it surely was taking her forever to get ready.

Autumn set the hills ablaze. It was a sight to see — scarlet and gold and purple, with the bright blue sky and great white clouds. Charlie remembered that once he had loved autumn, but now he came close to hating it as much as he loved it. Such a fruitful, promising time, one way you looked at it, and so dreary and flat and disappointing when you came to line up the beauty of everything outdoors with the general messiness of things inside — inside of life.

Marian Parks was married in October. The wedding day was perfect — a good send-off for the girl! The whole community had been invited to the wedding reception, and everyone but Charlie went. Even Morris, looking rather grim, had dressed himself up and taken Elsie. He had thought it best that they appear together, especially that day. But Charlie simply did not feel up to it. He knew he was being talked about and laughed at anyhow. He was beyond caring what anyone said about him and Marian; there was nothing damaging that anyone could say, with truth, and the lies wouldn't count.

He elected to spend that afternoon picking apples. He had to do something, and that was the work at hand. Besides, if anything could assuage the pain of such complete and final renunciation, it would be a few hours up above the ground, trying to recapture his old love of beauty and fruitfulness, of clear skies, and the scent of autumn.

It was warm, in the sun, and from the tall ladder, Charlie could look through the deadened foliage of the apple trees and off across the valley. He had thought to keep to the trees which would not let him see the Parks place, but he decided that he might as well see what he could. And that wasn't much. Cars and horses crowded around the house, and even down the steep roadway — the township had turned out well — but that was all.

He picked the apples carefully, handling each one by itself, and laying it in the basket almost tenderly. He did despise anyone that would handle good fruit like it was gravel. Why, a fair, nice apple was a beautiful thing, firm, smooth, bright in color, with that bloom on it that the slightest touch would blemish. Let it get just the least bit of rough handling, and before it was ready to eat there would be a hard, brownish withered spot under the skin to show for it. Apples were some like people's lives. Handle your life too rough, and there was the bruise; and around that bruise, if you didn't look out, rot would set in.

The thing of it was not to let yourself get a bruise. That had been his mistake — he had let things hurt him too much. There was a big difference between a difficulty and an injury. Loving Marian Parks was a difficulty. Nothing bad about it, nothing low-down or disgraceful. Just hard to stand, like the good summer sun on your back, maybe. Uncomfortable, hard to put up with, but you wouldn't want to do without the sun.

She was getting married today — little Marian! Getting married, going off with Witham, to stay with him as long as they both should live. Resolutely, Charlie kept on picking apples, grasping each one with a sure but gentle hold, stowing it away securely in the basket, so that it would not roll about. Would Witham hold her like that — gently, yet so that she would not get away, and run afoul of trouble and hurt herself? Did the big brute have any idea what he was getting?

Probably so — or Marian would never have loved him. She had too much good sense to be fooled. She had told him once that, though she had never been much of a student, she had gained something by her career as a co-ed — she had come to understand men pretty thoroughly.

The cars and teams across the valley began to stir. Charlie could see men coming out of the house. The wedding was over, and the people beginning to go. His ladder was well placed; he rested the basket with the hook in its handle over a ladder rung and leaned back against the tree trunk. He wondered how long it had been since he had cried. Way back in his childhood, of course; maybe he had not cried since his mother died. He had felt like it sometimes, but always it had been possible to keep a stiff upper lip and act like a grown man. Now, he realized that all day he had been fighting this desire to break down and cry. His throat ached; his eyes felt strained; his breathing seemed to shake him all over. He ought to get down off the ladder now, and go where he could not see the Parks place at all; but from high up this way he might get one last look at her — the air was so clear today, so bright and shiny for the wedding. Charlie was glad for that good omen.

There — the front door stood wide open at the Parks place, and one car had come close to it. The crowd ran out, and he could hear their shouts and laughter; then, sure enough, there was Marian, with Witham towering beside and above her, coming down the front steps, getting into the car.

And the car started, gathered speed and shot down the hill, turned into the main road, and then was gone, clean out of sight.

Charlie lifted the heavy basket and climbed down the ladder. Carefully he eased the fruit into a waiting box — softly, two by two, as if they were eggs. A big fuzzy caterpillar was clinging to the edge of the box, and he took it in the hollow of his hand and set it down in the grass. There was pain enough in the world without hurting innocent things.

Then, his work finished, Charlie tried to straighten up and go to the house; there were the chores to do, the family to face — things must go right ahead, of course. But he found he could not go in yet. He could not even straighten up. Of course, this was not going to bruise and injure him any more; it was not going to form the center of another rotten spot — love was a precious thing, and it could not really injure anyone, unless they allowed it to.

But now, Charlie slumped down, face forward in the dried and brittle orchard grass, and cried.

Elsie reported on the wedding reception, showing more animation than she had for weeks, though her voice was spiteful, as if she had been chewing a pickle.

"Marian looked fine," she said, "and awful happy. But I thought her dress was too plain. Just dark brown serge. But she had some roses and a swell looking hat. She asked me where you was, Charlie."

Charlie got up from his chair and stood back-to in the doorway. It was sunset, and the hills were a blurred flame in his eyes.

"Her mother told me they was goin' to Chicago," Elsie continued, spurred by her malicious purpose. "I wonder what kind of a trip they'll have. They're stoppin' overnight in Boston, Charlie."

"Aw, lay off him, Elsie," ordered Morris; and she went sullenly upstairs to take off her best dress.

For days after that, she nagged at Charlie about the honeymooners, though she was careful not to do it when Morris was there. Once she said, "Maybe they ain't as happy as they ought to be. Maybe she'd rather have had you, Charlie." And he thought he was doing well not to add murder to his other crime.

Those weeks showed an increasing change in Elsie. It was something almost intangible — a sort of slackness, a letting down, a carelessness. It puzzled Charlie. A sour milk strainer one morning; a smoky lantern chimney another; a soiled roller towel in the kitchen, dust on the dresser. She had always been neat as a pin and this shiftlessness was totally unlike her. Much as Charlie deplored it, perhaps it was a hopeful sign for him — perhaps she was really giving up and would really soon be gone out of his sight, out of his life forever.

He had come to bear her no ill will. She really could not be blamed if she was of tougher stock, if her morals were weak and her appetites demanding. She had not had the choosing of her place in the world. She had not asked to be born, any more than Charlie had.

Chapter Nineteen

November was bad that year, dark and stormy. It seemed as if the sun couldn't make out to shine, no matter how hard it tried. The brilliance of autumn was subdued and washed away, leaving the bare, dreary earth and the grimly courageous evergreens of the wood lots waiting as best they might for the soft white comfort of winter. Gray day followed gray day, and it was on one of the worst of these that Elsie announced that she was going to drive to North Brownvale. She would take Morris to the early train, and be back that night in time to meet him at the depot, and to get supper.

"What in time do ye want to drive through the mud on a day like this for?" Morris demanded.

"'Cause there's Pomona Grange meetin' over there," Elsie retorted, "and I been shut up in the house all the week. I got to have some fun, some time."

"All right, if ye call it fun to face a storm like this. Ye can take the kids to school first anyhow."

It looked good to Charlie — a long, dull day at home, with Elsie out of the road. Things would be peaceful. He wondered how much longer it was going to take her to make up her mind — if she had any! (He had never been any too sure about that.) She was a queer make-up. So stupid in some ways — simple, sort of — and so complex in others.

She was stepping lively now, more so than she had for weeks. She had on her best dress, too, instead of the second-best one she usually wore to daytime meetings. She was getting ready to take Morris to the depot.

"I'll be right back, Charlie," she said, "and put up the kids' lunches and git 'em off to school. You'll find your dinner in the butt'ry. Just keep up a good fire, so the house won't be damp."

"I'll git on all right," Charlie said.

"If it still rains, you might take the horse and go after the kids, round about half past three."

"All right. I'll go for 'em. No sign of it lettin' up today."

Elsie went out, and Charlie got into his wraps and went to the barn. He kept thinking about Elsie as he did the chores.

She had started out well enough. He remembered that first winter, when Morris had gone to the woods, and no one but keen-eyed Pop had suspected that Elsie was in a family way. She had been spunky about that — no complaints, no slackness about her work. Charlie had been fond of her then. Never in love with her, never seriously tempted by her, just fond of her, that was all.

Now, the old fondness, the easy familiarity, were things of a past long gone and never possibly to be recalled. That was the deuce of such an entanglement. It could never be wiped out of his mind, never be erased. He would carry the ugly scar of it beyond the grave, he supposed. That was what hell must be made of — the things no human forgetfulness or repentance could ever blot out.

He was crossing from the barn to the chicken runs when he saw Elsie come back to the house; he was still there, puttering about with the feed and water, when she came out again, and he heard the car rattling down the rocky lane. Elsie had no more idea how to handle that car than nothing at all, but she seemed to get along with it somehow. And if she got stuck today, there would be plenty of passing on the roads. Someone would haul her out and bring her home. Charlie didn't care much what might happen to her. Funny, how often these all-day meetings fell on stormy days, and how many people would get out and attend them anyhow — tired of being house-ridden, like Elsie had professed to be, most likely.

By the time he had finished the chores, the mail had come, and he sloshed down to the box at the end of the lane after it. He could still see the marks of Elsie's departure, but the torrents of mud and water were fast sluicing them away.

The mail was, as usual, uninteresting. The Portland paper, a circular from some insurance company or other, a magazine that Elsie took and never read that Charlie knew of. She did look at the crochet patterns, and let Little Elsie cut out the fashion pictures for paper dolls. The youngster would like to look it over after school, Charlie thought, as he laid the handful of mail on the dresser in the kitchen.

He went to the woodshed for an armful of stove wood, and paused to listen to the beat of the rain on the low roof. Back again in the kitchen, the fire crackled cheerfully in the stove; the teakettle sang a song; the cat rose up and stretched himself, yawned, and sank back again in a neat little heap on the rag rug by the hearth. Charlie took off his larrigans and set them to dry behind the stove, drew up a chair, and sat with his stocking feet in the oven. It was quiet and peaceful in the kitchen.

That old stove seemed to be the center of the house, somehow. It was used to cook the food, to heat the kitchen, which was the family living room as well, to heat water, dry out socks and mittens, boil the wash, try out the lard; it served as a supplementary refuse burner, and as an ash tray and cuspidor. Baby chicks were warmed and nursed within the radius of its heat, as well as cosset lambs and succeeding generations of kittens. At present, the tall, cylindrical milk cans were up-ended on the back shelf; Elsie had scalded them and put them there before she left. The dish towels and the milk strainer were on the bars overhead. There was no sunshine in the corner of the L for them today.

Charlie thought some of getting the paper to read, but he didn't move. Time enough — he would get warm and dry himself, along with the kitchen linens and tinware.

And he returned to wondering, as he drowsed there, just how everything had come about this way. Just when had Elsie set her mind on him, and how long had he known it without really knowing — just had that uneasy irritation all the time, without brains enough to deal with it squarely before it got strong enough to deal with him?

Maybe it had begun that very first winter. Maybe it had grown, little by little, through the years, without anyone — but Pop! — fully taking in the trend of things. Maybe it had grown on her something the way the drink or the drug habit will grow on a man, inch by inch, until it had had its way even with him.

Getting a different slant on it, now that it was over and done, Charlie could trace this growth, from the small beginning of a companionship which had not even included the deep love and loyalty such as Charlie felt for Gladys and Hilda. Charlie admitted to himself that he had sometimes thought of Elsie with a trace of desire — he had been lonely, she had been at hand and had represented to him the domesticity for which he was hungry. He had often, in his solitude, thought of her in her solitude, with Morris away so much, and he had played some with the notion that he, and not Morris, should have been the married man.

But that was all. Such mild imaginings were as nothing compared with his hunger for another girl, who was also another man's wife now.

He retraced it all. Elsie had been ruthless in her maneuvering, laying in wait for him — hard, tough, determined. Yet according to her lights, Elsie had loved him, and still did love him, of course. She was still hoping he would relent, would get Morris to agree to a divorce, would marry her.

Charlie shuddered at the thought. He guessed it just wasn't in him to play fast and loose with a woman. The only one he really wanted was out of his reach. The ones to be had for money or for the asking nauseated him. He got up and shook himself. His feet were dry now, so he took the newspaper to the corner by the window, where Pop's rocking chair still stood, and read awhile by the meager light of stormy noon.

According to the paper, the world was in the usual sort of mess. Three murders and a suicide on the front page; a short bit about affairs in Washington, which Charlie thought might be more important if only there was enough told about them to make sense. He gave a look at the weather forecast, then turned briefly to the market reports. The sports page had little to offer. If there happened to be anything about the state university,

Charlie usually read it out of respect for Alf and his interests, but there was nothing this time.

Charlie was getting hungry. He searched the butt'ry and found some cold meat and potatoes, so he made hash, and got himself a cup of tea. There was plenty of bread — Elsie made good yeast bread — and he fished a cucumber pickle out of a big glass jar of them. Elsie made good butter too. After she left, he would have to sell the cows. Elsie — drat her — she had fairly built herself into the place. Pity she couldn't have behaved herself. Why, that was just what she had gone and done — fitted herself into the Ashburn place so snug that there was no getting her out. By godfrey, throughout the years, she had done it deliberately, knowing all along just what she was up to! What had Pop said? "She goes it as if somethin' was drivin' her."

Charlie got up and poured his cup of tea down the sink. He had been about to forage for pie, but his appetite had left him suddenly. It was himself — Charles Ashburn — she had been after all along. She had tried herself to make him comfortable — all that fussing over him — that painstaking attention to little things—

But wait a minute! The recent slackness and indifference that had fretted him really were signs that she was giving up. After all she was slipping out of the place she had made for herself! Charlie poured another cup of tea and hunted out the apple pie. Things wouldn't be so bad after all. She really was giving up. She really would go.

Charlie stacked his dishes in the sink and sat down by the window again. Sitting there made him think, as usual, of Pop, and that led to memories of his mother, and of her ambitions. He thought of her neatly written little book which he still kept in his room and looked over sometimes. She surely had been set on education.

Well, education was a wonderful thing. It could make all the difference between a satisfied life and a frustrated one. Suppose he, Charlie, had had Alf's opportunities, had been a younger son instead of an older one. Then he might have gone to school and college, and might have had a chance with Marian even if he was so homely his face ached. Marion had always liked him. If he had seemed to her so hard to look at she would never have been happy spending so much time with him.

She had said she would never fit into his life, nor he into hers. It was education on the one side and lack of it on the other that put the distance between them. Maybe education would bring Graham and Hilda together. It would be a good chance for Hilda; she surely ought to have every advantage. If Charlie couldn't be happy himself, he could at least do his utmost to see that the rest of the family got along.

All they had spent on Alf had been a good investment, and they would always be glad they had done it. Herb needed nothing more than he was getting for himself. He was satisfied, working on the railroad, saving his money, buying a parcel of land now and then, dickering over a few head of cattle, seldom coming out at the small end of a trade. Herb was shrewd. Gladys was contentedly settled, too. Only Morris and Charlie, on whom the brunt of family responsibility had fallen, had seemed to be short-changed.

Charlie wondered what might have been the outcome if he had never seen Marian. He couldn't imagine seeing her without falling in love with her, though probably comparatively few of the men of her acquaintance were as hard hit as himself, and Morris, and Witham. Even Morris claimed he had got over it, but Charlie had his

, doubts.

Morris was a problem. He had been drinking for some time, but it seemed to have little effect on him. He was never drunk. It was Elsie's sharp reference to Fleta Carmel that was disquieting. If Morris was carrying on with that woman, what was the use to break their necks to avoid scandal in another quarter?

But probably there was nothing in it but some gossip, and Elsie's spite. Poor old Morris! Whenever Charlie thought of Morris, there was a feeling of warmth around his heart that he would never have dreamed of communicating to anyone. There was in Morris something of the lightness and gaiety which Charlie lacked, something of the delicate fire of imagination for which Charlie had great sympathy but scant understanding.

Charlie, for example, never read much of anything. His one excursion into literature had been the memorizing of that verse from Longfellow — about the house where gods might dwell, beautiful, entire, and clean. Lately, in his long battles with passion, repression, and shame, he had almost forgotten his dream and his ideal!

But Morris was different. Charlie had been to his room in Brownvale and always there were books around. Morris said he had been reading the Brownvale public library clean through. That looked to Charlie to be quite a chore, but Morris had said he was getting along pretty good with it. He had been taking the books as they came along the shelves, reading two or three every week, and he'd been at it — how long was it now? Three or four years, most likely. There must be a thousand books over there, in that room above Weeks' hardware store.

If Morris did all that reading, and tended to his job,

he really couldn't have much time left over for foolishness with Fleta Carmel's kind. Not that such affairs took much time — it was peace of mind and energy that they consumed! Still, it was queer that Morris should get tangled up with such scum — if indeed he had done so. Probably it was just talk, yet even so it might be just as well to find out more about it.

Sort of a mean trick of fate that Morris, with his liking for fineness and beauty, should have married a woman as tough as Elsie. And it was downright heroic of him to be even reluctantly ready to take his wife back, and to take her more fully than he had ever done, to live with him and make a home for him. Of course, in time their married life would be resumed. Maybe if Elsie had more children it would keep her out of mischief. Yes, maybe Morris stood some chance of having a real home, and real contentment of a sort. Charlie hoped so. Both brothers had been hard hit by Marian Parks — by her intelligence, her spirit, her fine-grained gentility, as well as by her girlish appeal to their manhood.

The old-fashioned mahogany clock over the kitchen sink struck three, and Charlie roused himself. It was time to go for the children. The rain on the woodshed roof was quieter, hardly audible now. He brought in the wood and crammed the fire box full, and closed the drafts. He got into his larrigans and coat and cap, and took his canvas gloves, warm and dry, from the stove shelf. Outside, the rain really had stopped, and a clear wind was blowing. Loose shreds of gray cloud were breaking away from the mass above and scudding toward the east. Tomorrow would be brighter. Maybe this storm would mark the end of the bad season, and usher in the fresh, dry cold of winter. Clean — white—

Charlie was glad to get out, glad to see the children,

after his quiet, lazy day. He brought the young ones home and got them settled in the kitchen, filled the teakettle and opened the drafts of the stove, before he went about his evening chores. By the time he had finished these, night was closing in, and there was a crimson slit in the sky next the horizon. He stood still and watched it. That was a sightly thing — the soft, deep, passionate color. It pulled at his heart, made him long to go toward it, to go on and on, never stopping until he had waded deep into that ruddy sea, had drowned all his individual being in it, had merged his very self with that grandeur and beauty. Till he had forgotten pain, and remorse and loneliness — till he was sunk forever into that rose-red glow—

Charlie picked up his milk pails and went into the house. He thought he must be going daffy, sap-headed, dreaming about a miserable little strip of sunset!

The children were hungry. Elsie had said she would be back in time to get supper, and it was after six already. Probably she had got stuck. Charlie strained the milk and then began looking for something for supper. He had pretty well cleaned things up at noon, but there was still a kettle of apple sauce, and some bread, and the milk. They would make out. Young Morris helped set out the food and the cups and spoons, but Little Elsie sat, quiet and subdued, in Pop's old chair. She was solemn, even.

"What's the matter, Baby?" Charlie asked her. But she didn't answer. She was missing her mother, most likely. She looked so small that Charlie took her on his lap and broke her bread into her cup of milk for her.

"What do you spose makes Mama so late?" asked Morris.

"Oh, do'know — stuck in the mud, I guess. Mud's awful between here and North Brownvale."

"Who'll pull her out, Uncle Charlie?"

"Oh, somebody. Your Pa'll be here pretty quick. He can take the old hoss and go hunt her up."

Elsie began to sob — not to cry aloud, child fashion, but to sob deeply, slowly, like a woman in patient grief. It was uncanny, and suddenly Charlie felt a chill of dread. Something was badly wrong, somewhere. His own head, he now realized, had been aching dully for some time. The room seemed strange, the two childish faces distant and unfamiliar. He wondered if he were coming down with a spell of something, and Little Elsie too. He had never felt like this before.

Elsie was altogether too late. She was bound to miss Morris at the depot. It was too bad for him to have to walk through the mud, but it wouldn't do for Charlie to leave the children here alone, nor to take them out again either.

He drew Pop's chair up to the stove and sat there rocking the little girl, while the boy Morris sat, still and wide-eyed, close beside him. He spoke to them occasionally; Elsie's sobs did not stop until she fell asleep from sheer fatigue.

The teakettle and the clock kept up their homely duet. The time dragged along. This was a hell of a note — that he should be sitting here waiting for a woman he despised, who was worse than nothing to him. Why should he have to worry about her? What was it to him anyhow? He laid Elsie down on the sofa and covered her with a shawl.

"Lie here at the other end," he told Young Morris. "Your mama will soon be back." But Morris did not close his eyes.

The wind still howled; the teakettle kept up its song; the clock ticked away the minutes.

Even allowing for delays, the night train must have

come in long ago; Morris had had time to walk home. Where was he? Where was Elsie? Charlie got up and paced the floor. Where the devil had this headache and fret and worry come from anyhow? He felt sick, and it was a relief when Young Morris stopped following him with his strange, clear-seeing eyes, and went to sleep. Lucky kid — that he could sleep—

It maybe was not so very long, but to Charlie it seemed hours before he heard the blare of an automobile horn in the lane, and went to the door. Two round yellow eyes of light were wavering through the darkness. Would Elsie be able to make it up that steep grade? In all that mud? But of course Morris was driving — she would have picked him up somewhere along the way. Maybe the two of them had stopped at the store, never thinking that he might be worried. In his relief, Charlie was about to drop all his annoyance and anxiety, when the horn sounded again. It was not Morris' horn; those lights were larger, lower down, wider spaced, than Morris' lights.

It was not Morris' car, but Morris was in it. Pale, wild-eyed, disheveled, he stumbled into the kitchen, and Ben Sparks followed him.

"Git him a drink, Charlie," said Ben. "He's had about all he can stand. A swig o' cider'll brace him up."

"Ain't he had too much already?" asked Charlie.

"Hell, no. 'Tain't that. They met him at the train and told him — they'll be here pretty quick — the undertaker — and what's left — of Elsie—"

Something clicked inside Charlie's head and stopped the aching. He got Morris a drink from the cellar. Then he took Little Elsie tenderly up in his arms, and roused the sleeping boy.

"Come on, youngster," he said gently, "come along — Uncle Charlie's goin' to put ye to bed tonight."

Chapter Twenty

When Charlie came down from putting the children to bed, he found Morris still huddled in Pop's chair, tense and silent, while Ben Sparks stood back to the stove, his hands held behind him toward the warmth. Charlie crossed over and stood, there, too, but he sagged wearily against the stove shelf, stunned and awed by what was taking place.

Ben had been waiting for Charlie to come to tell what had happened.

"I'd ben to East Parkston," he began. "I'd ben over there to see a feller on business. Day like this is a good one to find folks at home, an' ready to talk. I'd finished up with him and was drivin' back home. I was takin' it slow. I don't see no sense in takin' chances with a car nohow. I ain't aimin' to ruin mine, now I got it—"

"No, no. I'll warrant ye ain't," muttered Charlie, vaguely thinking to get Ben back to the subject.

"Well, that car cost me good money — but, as I was sayin', I was takin' my time, and just where the North Brownvale ro'd meets the main ro'd, this car come out ahead o' me. They was goin' at a pretty good clip, with their curtains buttoned down tight. I didn't know who 'twas. But I kept behind 'em, and they was gainin' on me some. Still, I had 'em in sight — I couldn't help wonderin' who 'twas — when we come to that turn — by God they ought to do somethin' about that crossin'. Comin' like it does, turn in the ro'd, curve in the railro'd, big slice o' ledge juttin' out so's ye can't see any more'n fifteen foot either way. Seems-so they's ben folks enough killed there already — if they'd blast out that ledge it'd help some, and they ought to put a gate there too."

"Yes, they sure ought to—" Charlie wished the man would either tell what he was going to or shut up.

"Well, I heard the train whistle. Ye see, I didn't have my curtains buttoned — rain had stopped a spell before that — and even then I didn't hear it real plain. Still, I sort o' knew a train was comin', and I tooted my horn, but they didn't pay no attention — couldn't hear a thing, I spose. And then — oh, by golly, I saw the whole thing—"

Ben's voice broke sharply, and Morris and Charlie had to wait before he could go on.

"I saw — and I couldn't do a single damned thing about it. Train come around that bend just as they was speedin' up the grade to the crossin' — they couldn't stop quick enough — engine hit 'em jest hard enough to spin 'em around — kersmash! By the lord harry, I'll see that sight till my dyin' day!"

Morris shivered; Charlie rubbed his rough, thick, shaking hands over his face and clenched them in his scanty hair.

"You must-a been about the first to git there?" he suggested.

"Yep — but say, where does a crowd come from

when a thing like that happens? 'Twan't no time at all before the whole township was there, standin' around, jabberin'; lord knows who sent for the doctor, and the undertaker. Course, there wa'n't no use for the doctor, though. Then some feller from down this way — it was that gormin' kid that hangs around the depot so much — he said he'd seen Morris go to work on the train this mornin', so a wagon-load of 'em went to meet the night train, an' tell him. They brought Morris back there."

"Spose I'd taken the car, 'stead o' the train, today," muttered Morris.

"No use sposin' things," replied Charlie.

"No, no use thinkin' like that," Ben Sparks agreed. "'Bout time that hearse got here," he continued. "Course, it takes longer, with horses; still they ought to be gittin' here."

There was a thick, tense silence for a while; then Ben Sparks spoke what was uppermost in his mind.

"The other woman — the one with Elsie—"

Charlie started up, astonished.

"Who was with her?" he asked quickly.

"It was Fleta Carmel. I didn't know they was acquainted." Tragedy could not down the curiosity in Ben Sparks.

"She was with Elsie?" asked Charlie incredulously.

"Yep — dead, now. Dead — both of 'em."

"They wasn't acquainted — much," said Morris dully. "Leastways, not that I know of."

"Well, anyhow, I guess they've parted comp'ny now. Poor Fleta wasn't so much—" Even Ben hesitated before defaming the dead.

Charlie felt sick. Elsie's words came back to him. "I've got as good a right to be with Fleta Carmel as you have," and the answering flood of color in Morris' dark face, as she said it.

But Fleta was dead. They surely wouldn't talk about her right now. The three men waited there, and at last the hearse came, and neighbors, and Elsie's parents. It was fuss and flurry and excitement, that night, and the next day, and the next.

Funerals, Charlie had always thought, were an awful hullabaloo. He had never been able to enjoy one, as many folks seemed to do, standing around, forever talking in hushed tones, eating and drinking, crying and sometimes laughing too. And at this particular funeral there was an unbearable amount of subdued but agitated chatter. The coffin was sealed, necessarily, and Charlie was sure some of them would have liked to pry it open and look. He wouldn't. He had been glad he had not been able to see. Glad that the children were safe with Hilda at the Freemans'. The Ashburns were of a different stripe than some. They had no appetite for horror; they did not gloat over suffering. They seldom wept.

"Hard as nails, ain't they," was the comment of one of the women who had come in, ostensibly to help.

"They seem so, until ye know 'em," Alviry Simms had answered.

All these women, so eager to help, had found things in rather bad shape, and they had been astonished. Elsie Ashburn had been known as a neat housekeeper, yet here was dust and dirt and litter all over the place. It was beyond them — they couldn't figure it out. Elsie had been in good health; nothing could account for it.

Charlie, hungry yet unable to eat with the rest, unable to think of anything he wanted to eat, had started for the butt'ry, but stopped just short of the doorway when he heard Alviry puttering around there, muttering to herself.

"Soul and body," she was saying, in a sibilant undertone, "this place ain't been cleaned out for weeks, I bet. Never in all my born days did I think to find, in this house, such an ungodly mess. Look-a that! Paper all tore up and smutty on the shelves — grease spilled — mouse tracks—"

Charlie was suddenly not hungry. He tiptoed away. Alviry, loyal to the Ashburns, wouldn't talk much to the others, he was sure, but it was bad to have even her know that his house was not clean. And naturally the other neighbors would find out plenty, and talk without let or hindrance.

He wondered if Elsie would have put the house in order first if she had felt her time was near. He thought not. She had been done, finished, her interest gone. The tragedy at the crossing had been merely a climax, and, except for the horror of the circumstances, Charlie could not make himself regret it.

The funeral was set for the afternoon of the second day. Fleta's had been held at the undertaker's that forenoon, with no one there but her aged mother, too feeble in mind and body to understand what had happened, and a few whose curiosity was ahead of their fear of public opinion.

Elsie's funeral was different. Daughter of the stolid yet respectable Dennises, wife of the eldest of the Ashburns, mistress of a prosperous and respected household, active and reliable member of the Grange, and of the Ladies' Aid, Elsie had been somebody in the community, and people came from three townships to pay their respects. The yard was crowded with teams and cars; the chill, gloomy parlor was banked with asters and roses and carnations. The preacher had come, had tried to speak a word of comfort to the silent Ashburns, but had turned away, rebuffed.

After all, what did this preacher know of them, of their lives, their dreams, their difficulties, their sins? His job was to speak and to read the proper things, to maintain the conventional atmosphere, to set the seal of order and respectability on the occasion. No preacher could get under the Ashburn skin!

The family — gathered in the big upstairs bedroom, which had been Morris' and Charlie's, then Morris' and Elsie's, then Elsie's alone — could but dimly hear the service that was spoken in the parlor. The downstairs was jammed with people. The doors were open so that those who could not get in could hear. Pop had been even more widely known, more generally beloved, than Elsie, yet his passing had caused no such furor as this.

Finally the signal was given for the family to come down; there would be no last formality of "viewing the remains." Morris and the children, Gladys and John, Hilda and Alf, Herb and Charlie, they filed down the stairs, through the narrow hall, out to the waiting cars.

And as they passed through the hall, one thing happened which arrested Charlie's attention, a thing so odd and subtle that he tucked it away in his mind for future consideration. He was the last one down the stairs; the others were ahead. Near the door, crowded back against the wall, quiet, soberly dressed, stood Maud Ripley. She was watching, gazing, not at himself, but at Morris. He forgot for a moment the decorous indifference to surroundings which is the correct thing in a bereaved relative. What was the meaning of that look in Maud's eyes? Where had he seen the like before? She surely would know Morris the next time she saw him!

And then, in the gloomy farce which was the funeral procession, Maud was forgotten.

What a performance, Charlie thought! Cars and buggies and two-seated wagons, all strung along the road, the cars churning and bucking in their effort to hold to the slow pace of the horses; people of all kinds riding to the cemetery, some out of curiosity, some out of love and respect, some just because it seemed to be the proper thing to do. And what did it all matter to Elsie?

Well, had she had the planning of it, she would have wanted a good, stylish, showy funeral, and she was getting it. The Ashburns gave scant thought to appearances, to be sure; but it was fitting, in their mind, to have the best they could possibly afford, and the dramatic circumstances of Elsie's death had surely brought out a crowd.

At last, it was over. Gladys and Hilda took the children back with them to stay a few days more; Herb and Alf returned to their jobs, and Morris and Charlie to an empty house. Night was closing in; Ben Sparks had done the chores for them, but Charlie made the rounds to see if all was in order, while Morris brought the cans from the cream-safe and strained the milk. He had done it before, and had seen it done all his life, but this lonely performance of a woman's task gave him a pang of desolation. Charlie came in, silently, and took off the sweater and overalls which he had put on over his good suit before his tour of the barns.

"Want to eat?" he invited.

Morris gave a shuddering sort of sigh. "No, I guess not," he answered vaguely.

"You will, by-'n-by. Seems good to be quiet, don't it!"

"Yeah — oh, I donno — too durn quiet, ain't it?" Morris lighted his pipe for comfort. "I most wish the kids was here."

"I don't. It's no place for 'em. Not till we get squared round some."

"Oh, o' course. Say, Charlie — this whole thing has been queer. Elsie never did go near that Pomona Grange meetin'. Her mother told me. Gosh, how the women have been talkin'!"

"I ain't blind. Nor deaf. What was Elsie doin' with Fleta Carmel?"

"You tell me." Morris shrugged his tired shoulders. He was pathetic, hunched over in his chair sucking his pipe; somehow it would have been easier to stand if Morris had been really grieved, as a man ought to be that has lost his wife.

"They'd been up to somethin'!"

"Well, I'll say this much. If they'd been off on a junket o' some kind, it's a damn good thing they was alone when they got hit." Morris sighed again, and shook himself as he got up for more tobacco from his can on the shelf over the sink. Charlie was watching him, and thinking. He had seldom, in all his years as head of the household (subject only to the acquiescent Pop), felt called upon to assert his authority. But he thought it best to do so now.

"Morris," he said, "I want to ask ye one thing, and then I want ye to tell me the truth. After that, I hope to God we can put the whole damned mess out o' mind."

"Well, speak your mind," replied Morris.

"I want to know — what was goin' on between you and Fleta Carmel?"

"Want to know that, do ye!" Morris was unsurprised.

"Yep."

"Oh, gosh, it's nothin' much to tell. Not that I'm proud of it. You remember how she started out, don't ye? Oh, it was years ago, seems-so. She must be older'n we are. Pretty, she was. High stepper."

"It was hard on her," Charlie admitted, "after she married that drummer, and he turned out to be married already, seems-so the whole township just put the blame all on her. And on her folks, for lettin' her run wild the way she'd been."

"Most likely her folks didn't have much say about what she did. She was always headstrong, and her folks was old. Didn't have enough spunk to handle her." Morris had evidently given the subject thought before this. "Anyhow," he continued, "after the drummer left her, there wa'n't anything for her but to go to the bad. No matter how careful she might-a been, folks would never have thought her a decent girl any more. That wasn't fair."

"No, don't spose 'twas," said Charlie.

"I used to see her often there in Brownvale. Had a job at the hotel. Always wore brown — dark or light — some shade o' brown. School teacher called her the 'Symphony in Brown,' whatever that means. She sure is handsome — or was."

"Tough-lookin'," was Charlie's opinion.

"Well, maybe so. But handsome. Say, Charlie, do ye remember that affair she had with the Burnham boy? Roy Burnham?"

"Why, yes. There was lots o' talk. Old Man Burnham bought her off, didn't he?"

"Yeah. And sent Roy off to school. He was just a kid, but she had him wild for a while — oh, for the better part of a year. But he got over it. Came back to Brownvale often and never went near her. Couple of years ago he brought his wife back, and stayed. Cute little girl, his wife. Their kid's about six months old now."

Charlie waited. He was wondering what all this had

to do with Morris and Elsie and Fleta, but he knew Morris would get it told after a while.

"It was while Roy's wife was still laid up with the baby," said Morris, "that I was in the post office one day and I saw Fleta standin' there just loafin', I guess. Pretty, she was. Brown fur around her neck, her cheeks red. In comes Roy Burnham, and Fleta watches him gettin' his mail out of his box. She moves so he can't help stoppin' to speak to her. I keeps my eye peeled, wonderin' what deviltry she was up to. Roy looks up and sees her — and if she don't give him the meanest, dirtiest look—"

"Mad at him?"

"Gosh, no. That look was a come-hither. Roy, he was pretty much fussed up, and I could see he was sort o' tempted. It made me boil — gettin' after that boy just when he was settlin' down and bein' somebody; just when his wife was laid up. It was dirt mean. So I just steps in and says 'How are ye' to Fleta. That's all. Roy got away, but she hooked onto me, and it struck me nobody would give a whoop in hell what I did. I was wrong, of course. I ought to have had sense enough to keep clear o' such filth. But I acted the fool. Then Pop died, and after a while all this came up about Elsie, and I got sick o' the whole business and told Fleta so. She didn't mind. It was all in the day's work for her."

"Humph. Queer world, ain't it!" remarked Charlie. "Well, I spose there was talk, and Elsie heard some of it."

"Oh, yes. Ye can't keep a thing like that dark in a place like Brownvale. I saw Fleta — why it must-a been last week sometime. She told me Elsie was sort o' tryin' to make friends with her. Tryin' to find out sure enough, Fleta thought. Tryin' to git the goods on me so she could sue. But Fleta never would talk, ye know."

"No, I don't know. How should I?"

"Well, she was a master hand for keepin' her mouth shut — I'll hand her that. Say, Charlie, I've been thinkin'. I bet I know where they'd been."

"Where?"

"To Wally Rice's camp, on Sebago Lake. They was on the way home from there. Wally gits a houseful together, out there forty miles from nowhere, and they have themselves a time. City fellers, liquor, fishin' and huntin', women — the whole works. You know."

"I've heard," said Charlie.

"Charlie, you'd think I'd be sore, wouldn't ye! You'd think I'd want to wade in and git even with somebody for this. But I don't. I don't grieve. My God, Charlie, where was Elsie headed? It's awful to say it, but maybe it's best—"

"Sh — sh — don't talk like that, Morris. She's paid up. She don't owe us a thing. It's done with."

Morris leaned forward and covered his face with his hands. Charlie touched his shoulder experimentally, but Morris shoved him off. That was all right. They understood each other.

Just to be moving and doing something, Charlie went to the parlor, and turned the light on there. Anything would be better than to go soft and fuss over poor old Morris!

The fire in the parlor stove had died down, and the room was cold; the chill of death and the sickening smell of flowers fairly hit him in the face. Here was disorder and desolation; he would put things to rights.

He opened a window and let in the clean night air, clear, dry, and frosty — bracing. It came with a free, cleansing rush. Charlie moved some of the chairs back to their accustomed places, picked up a few broken flower stems and put them in the stove, straightened a picture that had been brushed awry. Then he moved the marble-topped table back to the center of the room, where it belonged, and as he did so, his hand encountered the modest pile of books that constituted the Ashburn library.

He recalled seeing Nell Simons dust that table, the day before; he realized that he had been unduly watchful and sensitive about the women dusting around. The untidy house, he thought, could well have been a dead giveaway, telling the township that there was nastiness in the family as well. An ugly house, empty and unclean!

Charlie's memory stirred. He bent over the table, picked out the old Longfellow, and opened it. Yes, the cigar band was still there, right where he had seen it, off and on, throughout the years since he had first located that verse. It was a long time since he had stopped and really read the lines. He might as well do it now. He read, taking his time, pondering, remembering, regretting—

"Make a house where gods may dwell,
Beautiful, entire, and clean."

He closed the book. Good God—

That fresh, dry wind blew in, scouring out the heavy scents of the funeral, the humid memories of shame and passion, the clouds of deceit and suspicion and frustration. This air must sweep through the house, make it pure again. Joy for him and Morris there might never be, perhaps, but at lease they could have peace, and satisfaction of work well done, and decency—

He threw open the door and left it open as he went back to the kitchen. Morris looked up.

"Think it best to air out some?" he asked.

"Yep," said Charlie.

Chapter Twenty One

I f holidays, as Charlie once had said, were meant for happy people, then it was not unfitting that the holiday season that year should pass the Ashburns by.

The children remained with Gladys and John and Hilda for several weeks, while Morris and Charlie, like two old hermits, (in the place of the one, so long ago, who had been Pop), puttered about the place, doing barely enough chores to get by with. Business was slack at the shop, so Morris took a vacation, doing the cooking and cleaning in the house while Charlie worked outside. They had settled on this temporary arrangement, hoping for some better plan to present itself.

Hilda had protested hotly. She would come home, and keep house, and take care of young Morris and Elsie; would do her duty by them all. Charlie liked her spunk, but he would not consent to her plan. He had seen enough of that when Gladys was young; though Hilda was older now than Gladys had been, still she was too young to take over the responsibility, aside from the fact that her voice must have a chance. Hilda must not be tied to the farm.

On the other hand, the children could not stay on

indefinitely with Gladys. It was not fair. She had two of her own and would probably have more before she was done; Freeman was generous and, for that very reason, his open-heartedness must not be imposed upon. The Ashburns would find a way to care for their own.

Of course, Elsie's parents wanted the children, but that was out of the question. They were alien; Ashburn tradition was nothing to the Dennises.

The matter of hiring a housekeeper was discussed thoroughly, and several prospects were interviewed. There was nothing to it. The only one whose terms were within their means was not neat enough in her own person — you would know just to look at her that she would leave dirt in the corners and let the dish towels turn gray. Of course, Alviry would have come; but Alviry was getting old, and she still had with her her daughter Nell, single and yearning; with two marriageable men in the house, that was unthinkable.

"It's not a bit o' use, Charlie," Morris stated; "we don't want no more women around here anyhow. Let me keep on, and the kids can come back with us."

"But how about your job?"

"It's about petered out anyhow. All the old houses that needed wirin' are done. The shop don't bring in enough for two men any longer. Why don't I come back home for good? Farmin' looks better to me than it used to. Herb will let us use that last parcel o' land he took over for taxes. You're always wanting more acreage."

"Think we can do right by the kids?"

"We can if we put our minds to it."

So with the new year, the new regime was begun. Gladys helped, coming over on alternate Fridays and working with Alviry. Hilda came each week-end, and, though it made a busy time for her, she did well, cooking, cleaning, changing the beds, and so on. She was a capable little thing.

The cows had to be sold, as there was no one to care for the cream and stake the butter. For the first time in their memory, the Ashburns bought milk and sent their washing out. This cost money and, with Morris not earning, it was a tight fit; but anything was better, as Charlie said, than havin' a naggin', chatterin' housekeeper around.

Herb was glad to have his land in use. They planned to put it in sweet corn in the spring, and sell to the Brownvale canning house. That would be another cash crop.

As the winter wore on, they gradually settled down and the strangeness of things gave way to a deep sort of contentment. Somewhat of Morris' natural buoyancy of spirit returned to him, and again there came a glint of fun in Charlie's swift, sidewise glance.

The children improved, too. After Pop's death, and with the gradual disintegration of the family peace, they had shown a certain dullness of color, a listlessness and a guarded silence, as children always do who live under a shadow. Charlie had wondered if after all the Dennis stolidity could be stronger in them than the Ashburn wit and sensitiveness. For one winter night, as they sat by the kitchen stove in their long outing-flannel nightgowns, warming themselves before going to bed, he noticed that their cheeks were redder than usual.

They were sitting close to Morris, one on either side, and he was talking with them off-handedly, casually, but with occasional quick laughter. It occurred to him that this was getting to be a nightly ceremony and that the three of them were happy — happier than they had ever been before in each other's company.

Elsie had been a good enough mother. She had been careful, capable, and for the most part kindly. But she had never been joyous and companionable. Morris had always been their joy, but he had not been at home! Now, he was right there all the time. And as the days went by, Charlie watched the change in them with satisfaction.

Young Morris particularly began to do better school work, and the teacher spoke to Morris about it. She found reason to speak to Morris frequently, and of course tongues began to wag. She was a brisk and business-like girl from Sebago township, and her family, her reputation, and her character were well known. She was a steady sort, brought up to be a good housekeeper as well as a schoolma'am. The neighbors were much interested. But Morris seemed woman-shy. Well, he would get over that. Charlie knew him — he would soon be an easy mark for someone.

Of course, their present womanless household was far from ideal. There were rough edges everywhere, and in spite of the combined efforts of Hilda, Gladys, and Alviry, the dish towels were not quite so white, and the dust would accumulate. Morris made mistakes with the cooking, and Hilda found considerable to take him to task about when she came home. It was inevitable that either he or Charlie — or both! — should marry.

Logically enough, Charlie began thinking again of Maud Ripley. He was pretty sure that so long as Marian stayed with Witham in the middle west, he himself could hold onto his good sense, and make Maud contented here on the place. It would never be any use to lie to Maud; he would have to wait until he was sure of himself, wait until he could look off across the valley without a pang of loneliness, could go to sleep at night without a thought of bitterness or jealousy, could think back over the past without a sense of grief or frustration.

He was gaining on it all the time. With the house in running order, cleansed now of the ugliness that had flayed his spirit, he began to have hope, to think that he might after all see his ideal, a house where gods night dwell, beautiful, entire, and clean. It might indeed be better than he could have hoped, for he would have worked and suffered to gain it.

It was late in March that Morris sprang something new, thereby bringing back to Charlie a slight but not totally forgotten incident.

Morris had been to the store, getting his groceries and an earful of local news. The going was heavy, with the mud axle-deep or worse in spots, but the thrill of spring far overbalanced the annoyance of bad roads, and of spattering slush and flying horse hair. The sun was warm, and a fresh wind from the southwest seemed to suck up the melting snow from the fields; to draw forth the swelling pussy-willow buds by the river. The ice was out, and Morris had seen a robin. He came home replete with spring.

"Say, Charlie," he remarked, as he put up the team, "Maud Ripley's sort of a nice woman, ain't she!"

"Yeah. Did ye see her at the store?"

"Uh-huh. She's good-lookin'."

"Well, fairish."

"Maud looks better'n most," Morris insisted. She looks clean, sensible, good-humored."

"She's all o' that, Morris." Charlie felt a glow of satisfaction. He had not really had a talk with Maud, nor taken her anywhere, for about a year. Probably it was time for him to renew the affair; if so, it was good to have Morris pleased. If they must have a woman in the house — and every house needed a woman — it was well to have both of them content with her, instead of neither one, as in the case of poor Elsie.

"Charlie," Morris had stabled the horse, and now he stood, his arms full of packages from the wagon, a fatuous, boyish grin on his face, "Charlie, do ye remember one night, when we was just young-ones — it was before I got to goin' with Elsie — there was a party over to Jim Sanford's? You and I went. Maud was there — all that crowd. By gorry, I kissed Maud, and how she did fight me! Let me tell ye, that girl was an armful!"

Charlie glanced at him sidewise. "What makes ye remember that?" he asked sharply.

"Oh, I donno. Spring in the air, I guess." Morris chuckled as he went into the house with his packages.

Morris had undoubtedly kissed enough girls, in those far-off days, to make it rather queer that he should remember one so well. Why had Maud fought him? A casual kiss was nothing to worry a girl like Maud, big, vigorous, well used to back-woods gallantry. Maud — Maud's eyes, the day of Elsie's funeral — what was it that Charlie had seen and tucked away in his mind for future reference?

That expression in Maud's eyes — it was something he had seen often enough, in all conscience! It was desire, adoration, the tenderness of understanding, all mixed up with a flash of naked passion. He had seen it directed toward himself in eyes now dead; he had seen it sometimes when Gladys and John Freeman were together; he had seen a faint trace of it at times when Marian had talked with him of Ham Witham. But never had Maud Ripley looked at Charles Ashburn that way! It was Morris—

Just about a year ago, Maud had said, "I'd have married — a certain man — if he'd asked me. He didn't.

I got over it."

That man was Morris, and Maud had never really got over it. She had no need to get over it now. If Morris tried to kiss her again, she would not put up a bluff; she would not fight him off the next time.

He stood, for a moment looking off across the hills, his mind recording nothing of what was before his eyes. He was increasingly conscious, rather, of the feeling of relief, gradually deepening.

Then, he realized that it was spring; a warm, soft, intoxicating day in spring. Sights and sounds and fragrances began to creep into his consciousness and demanded attention, and almost automatically he replied to the demand — he went around and sat down on the south side of the barn, where Pop had loved to sun himself, and leaned his back against the warm, satiny shingles.

How long, be wondered, had this been the favorite thinking-place for men of the Ashburn tribe? Whoever had first put this slab of field stone here, where it was always one of the first spots to be warmed by the sun, affording a dry and comfortable rest for anyone that felt like settin' a spell? That stone was worn pretty smooth, and no mistake.

From the chicken runs not far away came the racket of the poultry — the crooning cluck of drowsy contentment — the triumphant excitement of a laying hen — and the rowdy crowing of a cock. Did they change their tones with the seasons? Of course they didn't; yet there was spring in their chorus today. Not a change of tone — but a change of feeling. That was it. A change of feeling everywhere. The old blind horse, whose stall was back of the wall against which Charlie leaned, was moving about restlessly. He wanted to stay outside. He knew it was spring. Charlie would turn him out to pasture tomorrow for a little while. Again there were cows in the barnyard right now, chewing slowly with lolling tongues and drowsy eyes. They had a way of stretching their necks and rubbing their heads up and down as if caressing the atmosphere — loving its softness. A robin sang in an apple tree, and then, after thinking it over a while, came down and scratched around in the barnyard along with the sparrows that were always there. Why was a robin any prettier than a sparrow? Just because of his brick-red breast? No, it was more than that. It was because of his courage and promise. But didn't it take more courage for the sparrows to stay all winter than for the robin just to come back with the spring? Charlie felt a rush of love and sympathy for the sparrows — the gray-brown, prosaic little fellows that everybody took for granted, or sometimes even despised.

Charlie was a sparrow; Morris, a robin. What was Hammond Witham? A blue jay, handsome, brilliant, conquering? Well, not handsome, perhaps, but sleek and sure of himself — successful. Blue jays always had a well-dressed look, like city fellows. Charlie himself might look like a sparrow to others, but he felt more like the big, rough, red-crested king o' the woods that Marion had always admired. Angular, awkward, powerful, sweeping through the tree tops on widespread wings that flapped downward with a creaking sound — that was what Charlie felt like, and wished he might be. A bird like that would never have to let himself be set aside by a blue jay—

Maud Ripley was a nice, full-feathered Plymouth Rock hen. But a hen would never mate with a sparrow, so Charlie pulled himself back to reality. He never did go off on a tangent like that, and imagine all sorts of things, without getting pretty well gummed up.

Morris was a man in need of a wife, and Maud was a woman who loved him. That was plain and simple. Charlie had no least feeling of jealousy or disappointment. He had never been in love with Maud, and now, this pervading sense of relief was because he need never try to love her. Never again.

Relief — yes, sir, that was it. That was the deep peace and contentment that was soaking into him with the spring sunshine. A nagging restlessness, like the knowledge of a neglected chore, had been removed forever. He need not marry Maud, nor anybody else if he didn't want to. Morris would do the marrying for the household, and be the happier for it. Morris would provide a real home for the children, give them another and a better mother; probably there would be other children too, for Maud was young and strong. Not a mere girl, but a vigorous, warm-natured woman. Something like their mother, maybe — yet Charlie could not imagine Maud writing a diary. She was less a fine lady than their mother would have been if she'd had a chance, but she was not less a woman. Morris would be doing well.

Maybe Alf would marry a real lady, educated, refined, like Marian Parks. Alf could. Herb had said nothing, but he had looked rather knowing when Charlie had suggested that there might be a girl on Alf's mind. Their mother would like it if one of them really stepped up in the world and married accordingly.

Funny about the seasons. You would have thought that in this sunny spot the frost would have melted and dried out by now; but, sitting there so still, Charlie could hear the trickle of water down inside the soil, a sound that scarcely came to the ear — that was felt rather than heard. Down inside the soil — little roots waking up and sucking in the moisture and the richness, little sprouts creeping up toward the light on the surface, little animal-creatures stirring around with no need other than to eat and work and propagate — no tearing their shirts over things they couldn't help!

That was a good idea, maybe. Just to accept, without raising a fuss even in your own mind. Just to accept loneliness, not fight against it. Just to take things as they were handed out and make the most of it and not complain or rebel. Weak, maybe, if what you wanted happened to be possible to obtain; merely common sense when you wanted what you never in the world could have.

Suppose he had never even seen Marian Parks — what then? He would probably have loved some other girl and married her and had children and a home. He would never have known what he had missed.

What he had missed! Great scot, he would have missed all this suffering, sure enough, but what else?

Charlie sat up suddenly, threw his head back against the south side of the barn, and breathed deep and long. If he had never seen Marian Parks, he would have missed the best and biggest and most beautiful thing in his life. Missed the glory of a love that was beyond all reckoning. Why, it was happiness just to let himself be miserable, happiness to give up all struggle and hug to himself every memory of Marian Parks, to shut his mind against the present and the future and drift back to summer days by-gone. He heard again the beat of waltz time, heard Marian singing softly as she danced,

"Meet me tonight in Dreamland,
Under the silv'ry moon!"

He could feel again the lithe body in his arms, the soft hair brushing against his chin, could see again the shine of her eyes. He had not forgotten her in the least, and he never would forget. She was the best part of him. This love was strong, and good, and beautiful, even if it did hurt unbearably sometimes; it was his own, and he wouldn't forget it for anything or anybody!

Charlie threw his powerful arms wide and spread his hands on the warm shingles behind him. The sun beat down on him, and he let it come, of course. Let love come too, and take him completely. It would burn too hot sometimes, but what would life be without it? Would anyone fight against the sun, and rebel, and wish never to have it, just because sometimes it blistered men and crops and baked the earth too dry for fruitfulness? No, of course not. The next season, the next month, even the next day, perhaps, that same sun would be all blessing and comfort.

"Don't tear your shirt" — That made a pretty good motto, maybe.

So, sitting there holding up the south side of the barn as Pop had always done, chewing methodically on a toothpick, his eyes half shut against the brilliance of spring, his battered felt hat pushed back on a head already bald, his thick red hands fiddling with a jackknife and a sliver of wood, which after his flight of exaltation he had picked up — sitting there on the smooth old slab of field stone, Charles Ashburn was not a romantic figure.

Yet right then he was shutting away in his inmost soul a thing of poignant beauty, closing the door on it forever with the peace of resignation. The years would be long, and he would always be lonely. But he would take it easy, live it a day at a time, and not raise a fuss, even in his own mind. It was the best he could do.

JUNE WAS NEARLY GONE before Morris began to talk matrimony. He had been fooling with the idea all the spring, and the school-teacher had been putting in the licks too. Morris had even taken the teacher home from school a few times when he happened to meet her on the road. Some folks wondered that the girl should have set her mind on Morris instead of Charlie; others said any girl would prefer Morris, since Charlie was gittin' to be a regular old grouch.

But take it by and large, Morris preferred Maud Ripley to the teacher. Charlie figured out most likely why. It was because Maud was a comfortable woman. The teacher was little and spry and would dry up and grow acid with the years; pretty enough now, but too thin, too sharp. Maud — well, Maud was just comfortable. Morris wanted peace and comfort.

Old Mrs. Dennis renewed her plea for the children. She said plainly that neither of the boys need marry just to get a housekeeper, since she herself really wanted her grandchildren. But Morris was firm. Ashburns must remain Ashburns; those children were not to go into the home that had bred Elsie, with her warm, desiring eyes and her thick-skinned stubbornness.

"You're right," Charlie agreed. "We'll keep 'em. Go on and git joined, Morris. I'll move out any day you say, if that'll help any."

"Why not git joined yourself?" Morris asked curiously. He knew the answer, but wondered what Charlie would say.

"I don't want to, I guess. I did think some of Maud, but she'd rather have you. That lets me out."

"Ain't it hell," said Morris mildly. "Me and you go and pick out the same woman every time."

"I've never done any pickin'," objected Charlie. "Seems-so it's just been handed to me, and I could like it or lump it. I'd never have chosen—"

He shut up abruptly. That beautiful thing that had been handed out was his to keep; the ugliness of the other was best forgotten. As for Maud, there had never been anything to that affair. Morris was more than welcome to her.

So Maud and Morris got published the last week in June, and on July first they drove around to the preacher's and were married. The talk at Gag Corner and elsewhere was lively but not unfriendly. It was rather too soon after the tragedy at the railroad crossing, to be sure, but meantime there were young Morris and Elsie needing a mother's care; and, of all the single women thereabouts, Maud Ripley was the best one to give it to them. Morris had done himself proud.

Of course, it would better have been Charlie, but he hadn't been the same since Marian Parks turned him down. He might get over it some day. There was still the school-teacher; even Nell Simms might hope—

Charlie talked of building himself a small house, or of finishing off a room over the carriage house, now used to store grain. But Maud and Morris insisted that he stay where he was.

"Should think you'd fight shy of that arrangement," he said privately to Morris.

"Gosh, no. Maud's a boss of another color. No nonsense about her. And besides, I'm staying right here myself. Me and you, we'll pull together from now out. I'm done with leavin' the brunt of it to you."

Charlie understood. Somewhere he had heard the words — most likely they were from the Bible—"Greater love hath no man than this—"

Postlude

Years had passed. Charles Ashburn, lying under the apple tree by the stone wall, his back in the tender grasses, had lived it over again.

He did that every time she came back. It was a fool performance. Always, as now, he was obliged to fight down once more the old bitterness and rebellion, had to regain painfully the peace and quietude of resignation. But after all, perhaps this mental journey into the past and the aching struggle of return to the present kept him balanced, sort of — kept him from being absolutely the crabbed old bachelor people thought him. It kept him sensitive, softened him maybe, as nothing else would have done.

For, grouchy as he seemed outside the family, he was beloved within the circle, and he knew it. Nieces told him their love affairs; nephews came to him for sympathy; small children climbed all over him and pulled the fringe of hair at the back of his neck.

There had been changes. Herb was dead. He had gone to France with the famous Yankee Division, and had not come back. Alf had married his co-ed and had a family in New Jersey; sometimes they came home. Hilda and Graham came oftener; and Gladys and her brood.

Charlie had nothing much of his own, to be sure; but still, life had not used him so badly. Tomorrow, Marian would come to see him. She always did. They would sit on the stone wall and talk; Marian would tell what she had been doing; tell funny little yarns about her girls, about Ham's business, about happenings in the world outside. He would tell her the Gag Corner news; show her the new chicken runs; tell her a couple jokes he had saved up. They would go into the house, and Maud would give them some of her good fresh doughnuts, or wedges of rhubarb pie, with glasses of milk. The whole family enjoyed a call from Marian.

Marian had gained a little weight, but she was still trim and small, still full of energy, clean-cut and honest. Her hair was now cut close to her shapely head, and it was as much gray as brown. There were fine lines around her eyes and mouth; her hands, her neck, showed plainly that she was all of forty. She didn't care. She'd taken to using a little rouge, but she made no effort to seem young.

To Charlie, she was always just the same. And he was still her good friend, Charles Ashburn.

What matter if his heart did turn over at the sight of her? He knew he was alive, anyhow.

Charlie rose slowly to his feet, settled his hat over his eyes, took up his tool and went back to hoeing corn.

About
Margaret Flint Jacobs

by Sara Mitchell Barnacle

Margaret "Peg" Flint was born at Orono, Maine, in 1891 to Hannah Ellis Leavitt and Walter Flint. Both parents were graduates of the University of Maine at Orono, and her father had become a professor of civil engineering there. Margaret spent her childhood in Orono, but her family moved to Port Deposit, Maryland, when she was ten. She attended high school at the Jacob Tome School where her father taught. Her strength of character and social skill showed early on, as she was elected class president all four years.

Of the family's subsequent move to her father's ancestral home in West Baldwin, Maine, after seven years in Maryland, she wrote: "I felt when the family moved to the farm . . . as if we had come home. There was welcome on the face of the old house under the elm trees – a house which originated as a log cabin back in 1790."

Margaret attended the University of Maine at Orono and, briefly, Simmons College, majoring first in biology, then philosophy. She did not enroll for her senior year at UMO, but although she did not earn a degree she had gained a passion for writing. She soon married fellow student Lester Warner Jacobs, who had graduated with a degree in civil engineering.

Lester Jacobs' civil engineering work in the coal industry and later for the Army Corps of Engineers relocated the family several times—to Norfolk, Virginia; Slidell, Louisiana; and Bay St. Louis, Mississippi. It was in Norfolk that Margaret obtained the roll-top desk that served as her writing center for many years. She and Lester had six children, three "ante-bellums" born before World War I, three "post-bellums" born after. During the war years, during which her husband served in the US Army, Margaret lived in her beloved Maine, in a small, white, New England house in the village of Cornish. Upon Dad's return from the war, the family moved to Louisiana and later Mississippi, following Lester's employment.

For 30 years, she stayed up nights to write short stories, but collected a steady stream of rejection notices. Some inspiration turned her attention to writing in a longer format.

Margaret's first novel, *The Old Ashburn Place*, proved to be a winner. It was published under her maiden name of Margaret Flint and earned a $10,000 national prize for best first-novel-of-the-year in 1935. A phone call from the publisher, Dodd, Mead & Co., had told her she was a finalist. But the follow-up news of her win came over the airwaves, announced by Walter Winchell during one of his radio newscasts. The prize was reported in major papers nationwide, such as the *Los Angeles Times*, *The New York Times*, *The Christian Science Monitor,* and the *Chicago Tribune.*

The change in her life from obscure housewife to famous author was as dramatic as it was instantaneous, but her success was severely offset by the loss of her husband in 1936 to the after-effects of WWI mustard gassing. The cash prize, however, enabled her to move the family back to Maine. Margaret had not learned to drive, but she had a car and the drive to Maine was accomplished by her son Dana, a young teenager but the oldest son still at home. Margaret never did drive.

She renovated the former Pequawket Inn in West

Baldwin, which lies within the large acreage land-granted to her father's family after the French and Indian War. The home soon became – and remained for decades -- the beloved family center, a place of return and refuge.

Eight more novels and a flood of newspaper and magazine articles followed her first success, but she never achieved her goal of self-sufficiency as a writer. Homemaking was a more immediately successful passion. People of all ages and backgrounds were attracted to her quiet hospitality. Guests often enjoyed an afternoon tea before the fire, featuring good conversation and her soft molasses cookies or fudge, or a bean supper on the porch, featuring the baked beans and brown bread for which she was locally famous.

As a novelist, her forte was psychological insights into family and neighborhood relationships. The frankness and grittiness of her depictions sometimes shocked her neighbors, especially those who thought they saw themselves in her novels. It is commonly accepted that she saw herself as the educated city girl Marian in *The Old Ashburn Place,* her cousin John Flint was the model for Ephraim in *Deacon's Road*, the sequel to *The Old Ashburn Place.* In the newer book, the action has shifted forward half a generation. Morris has remarried, and he and Uncle Charlie are now the older generation. The scene has shifted, too, to a farm modeled after the one owned by the real Henry Black.

Margaret Flint was also noted for her uncanny ability to convey the speech patterns of the small region between Sebago Lake and the New Hampshire border, the setting for most of her stories.

Her essays on family life, on the character of Maine, and on national events as they impacted local life appeared regularly in several Maine newspapers and in *The Christian Science Monitor*. A life-long member of the Christian Science church, she also published inspirational articles in the church's periodicals.

Her books include:

- *The Old Ashburn Place* (1936): Novel of bucolic Maine life
- *Valley of Decision* (1937)
- *Deacon's Road* (1938)
- *Breakneck Brook* (1939)
- *Back O' the Mountain* (1940)
- *Down the Road A Piece* (1941)
- *October Fires* (1941)
- *Enduring Riches* (1942)
- *Dress Right, Dress: The Autobiography of a WAC* (1943)

Sara Mitchell Barnacle, along with Matthew Sternberg (president of Istoria Books) and Leslie Lebl, contributed to the digital conversion and reprinting of *The Old Ashburn Place*. They are all grandchildren of the author.

THE COVER IMAGE:
"And Everything Nice" by Bryce Cameron Liston
Used by permission of the artist

Bryce Cameron Liston believes that the highest form of art is the representation of the human figure. As a traditional painter and sculptor, he considers sound draftsmanship and a solid knowledge of human anatomy essential for the successful execution of his work. Collectors around the world are very familiar with his knowledge and talent. When viewing Liston's work in person you can't help but to be drawn into the evocative scenes. His paintings scintillate and vibrate with the poetry of light and subtle color variations.

But Liston's paintings of timeless beauty embody so much more than sound draftsmanship. He believes that an accomplished artist has the power to convey emotion and even passion through his work by virtue of imagination, talent and experience. The artist's sensibilities, along with his practical knowledge allow him to merge together the technical with the aesthetic, the physical with the spiritual.

Liston's artistic inspiration comes largely from the late-19th century; he lists John William Waterhouse, John Singer Sargent, Joaquin Sorolla, Anders Zorn and William Bouguereau among his strongest influences. "As an artist my career is dedicated to the integrity and quality of representational fine art.", says Liston. "My goal is to regain the traditions of the past along with the standards of craftsmanship and training. By studying the great artists of the past, we artists of today can once again regain a full command of proficiency to create great works of art…art about life."

About Istoria Books

Istoria Books is a boutique publisher handling only fiction, selecting books we consider to be "good stories, well told."

All our books are very competitively priced, and we run many discount specials.

Visit the Istoria Books website (www.IstoriaBooks.com) and sign up for the mailing list to learn of special discounts and deals.

Literary, Mystery, Romance, Women's Fiction, Short Stories, Historical and more…

Istoria Books
www.IstoriaBooks.com

29391881R00171

Made in the USA
Middletown, DE
17 February 2016